EMMA'S SE

'How dare you question my orders?' she said. Then she paused. 'Very well then, if you're not prepared to do as you're told for my friend Francesca, then you'll just have to learn what happens to girls who dare to disobey me!' She turned to Sabhu. 'Take this disobedient little slut next door and thrash her,' she ordered.

'No, no, please,' Emma sobbed, as she knelt contritely before Ursula; but then she felt Sabhu's hands grip her and pull her up on to her feet. She lowered her eyes.

'Twelve strokes!' she heard Ursula order in a clear harsh voice.

'No! No!' she pleaded.

'And leave the door ajar.' Ursula reached for the house phone and dialled a number. 'I'll invite Francesca down so that she can hear the slut getting her come-uppance whilst we have breakfast together.'

By the same author:

EMMA'S SECRET WORLD
EMMA ENSLAVED
EMMA'S SECRET DIARIES
EMMA'S SUBMISSION
EMMA'S HUMILIATION

A NEXUS CLASSIC

EMMA'S SECRET DOMINATION

Hilary James

This book is a work of fiction.
In real life, make sure you practise safe, sane
and consensual sex.

This Nexus Classic edition published in 2005

First published in 1998 by
Nexus
Thames Wharf Studios
Rainville Road
London W6 9HA

Copyright © Hilary James 1998

The right of Hilary James to be identified as the Author of
this Work has been asserted by her in accordance with the
Copyright, Designs and Patents Act 1988.

www.nexus-books.co.uk

Typeset by TW Typesetting, Plymouth, Devon

Printed and bound by Clays Ltd, St Ives PLC

ISBN 0 352 34000 2

All characters in this publication are fictitious and any
resemblance to real persons, living or dead, is purely
coincidental.

This book is sold subject to the condition that it shall not,
by way of trade or otherwise, be lent, resold, hired out or
otherwise circulated without the publisher's prior written
consent in any form of binding or cover other than that in
which it is published and without a similar condition
including this condition being imposed on the subsequent
purchaser.

Contents

	Prologue	1
1	Emma's Homecoming	7
2	The Governess	15
3	Ursula Takes her Pleasures	27
4	Startling Developments and Pleasures	35
5	Ursula Seduces Another Woman	45
6	Three Schoolgirls	58
7	Emma Overhears a Strange Conversation	67
8	The Prince Returns	73
9	The Stallion	83
10	Covered!	91
11	Stabled!	97
12	A Veterinary Inspection – and the Prince Explains	104
13	In Training	115
14	Used!	122
15	The Race	128
16	The Missing Girl	132
17	The Prince Shows Off his Piety to the Mullahs	139
18	Henry!	144
19	A Fond Farewell – and the Key Disappears!	147
20	Masseuse!	151
21	Henrietta Discovers Some New Delights	155
22	Ursula's Little Present	161

23	The Belt	169
24	Emma Meets her Little Companions	178
25	Strange Preparations – But For What?	183
26	Shorn and Cleaned Out	192
27	'Oh, What Pretty Little Bitches!'	201
28	The Kennels	209
29	Entertaining the Houseparty	218
30	A Gala Performance and a Gala Dinner	223
31	Goodbye to the Kennels	233
32	An Offer has been Made for Emma	236
33	Emma has to Decide	243
34	Cash On Delivery	247
35	Found!	252
36	Francesca's Baby Girls	258
	Epilogue	264

This, the sixth book in the Emma series, concludes the erotic adventures of a young married woman in the world of lesbianism and of domination. This time not only does she have to do the bidding of her cruel Mistress, but also that of her ruthless Master, an Arab Prince.

Prologue

(Taken from the end of *Emma's Humiliation*)

'Now listen,' he said. 'You're going to be my mistress back in England – waiting to be summoned to give me pleasure. Do you understand?'

'Oh, yes, Master,' came a little voice. 'Oh yes, please!'

With a little grunt of pleasure at having so decisively won her over, the Prince rose up a little higher on his knees.

'Then take this as a sign of your acceptance and submission.' He thrust his manhood into her mouth. 'Suck it and lick it,' he ordered. 'Worship it humbly and dutifully.'

He thrilled to the sensation of her little tongue running over the tip of his manhood. He thrust past it and exploded. 'Take it!' he breathed. 'Take it all! Swallow your Master's seed, like the obedient little slave girl that you are, that you enjoy being. Take it ... take it all ... as a sign of your new servitude.'

Moments later the pageboys unchained Emma and slid the large bolster out from beneath her hips. The Prince lifted her up and held her to him. She was crying with helpless delight. 'Master, Master. I just want to be your helpless slave – for ever.'

'And so you shall be, my dear,' he laughed. 'But I think that you being the hot little number you are I shall have to take precautions so that you do not go offering yourself all over London to other men – or women.'

'You mean you're going to keep me locked into a chastity belt when you're away?' murmured Emma excitedly.

Well, she's certainly accepted her new role, thought the Prince. It was time to take certain steps. 'Not quite,' he laughed. 'But you'll soon see!'

'Oh, anything,' breathed Emma. 'Whatever it takes.'

At this, one of the pageboys handed her a glass of something cool and refreshing. Eagerly she drank it and within seconds she was fast asleep.

Light was streaming through the windows when Emma awoke. Quickly she pulled the bedclothes over herself. Memories, wonderful memories, slowly came back to her. Oh, the Prince! What a man he was. Oh the excitement he had caused her. She blushed with shame as she remembered how he had used his pageboys to arouse her, and how they had guided his manhood up inside her. Oh, how could she ever look these boys in the face again?

The fact that she herself had not had any relief did not seem to matter. Her satisfaction had been derived from pleasing him. She remembered his decision to keep her available as his lover in England. Oh, how exciting! Would she be rich and famous? She remembered that he had earlier said that he sometimes took his pageboys with him to Europe. Would he always have them with him in his bedroom when he took her? Oh how awful – but how expert they were!

Was she still in the Prince's bed? Or was she locked up in the harem dormitory? She raised her head above the bedclothes and looked around. To her astonishment, she found that she was back in her room in the guest house.

She glanced at the clock. She must have been asleep for a whole day. She remembered the strange drink. Had she been drugged and brought back here? But why? She saw that she was now wearing her nightdress again – the one with the Prince's crest embroidered over the right breast.

She looked up longingly at the portrait of the Prince on the wall. With a laugh, she remembered the similar one in the harem – and the red flashing light. Jealously, she wondered whether the Prince had enjoyed other women whilst she had been lying fast asleep. His concubines were all so beautiful, so irresistible.

But, she laughed, she was now going to be Number One when the Prince came to England!

Then she noticed a strange feeling in between her legs. She put her hand down – and felt a line of little rings. And there was something else! With a cry of surprise, she pushed back the bedclothes, jumped out of bed and stood in front of the long mirror. Immediately she noticed that the gleaming metal collar had gone. Instead, around her neck were three strands of pearls with a lozenge-shaped diamond clasp. It had two large yellow stones in the centre and she thought that she had never seen anything so beautiful.

Then again came that strange feeling between her legs. She lifted up her nightdress. Yes, gleaming against her hairless beauty lips, and half-hidden by them, were two lines of little golden rings. But that was not all, for threaded through them, and kept in place by a tiny padlock that hung between her legs, was a little curved golden bar that was also half hidden by the lips themselves.

Astonished and now slightly appalled, she looked down and examined them. Ten tiny rings had been threaded through each of her beauty lips, between the front of them, near her mound, and the back. And the long thin curved golden bar had in turn been carefully threaded through each of them, keeping the lips tightly closed. No strange manhood, she realised, could penetrate her now. Nor, she found, could she herself properly reach her little beauty bud.

Panicking, she tried to pull out the little golden bar. But the padlock at the bottom was just too big to pass through the rings. The bar could not be removed. She tried instead to pull it down through the rings, but a wide flat flange at the top of the bar stopped her from doing so. It was also too large to pass through the little rings. The flat flange too she saw, was raised so that it covered her beauty bud. It was this that made it almost impossible for her to play with herself.

She tried walking up and down. She hardly felt the rings, provided she took only small, ladylike steps. The pull on her beauty lips, however, made it uncomfortable if she tried to part her legs wide. Yet, she realised, it would not prevent her from spending a penny.

She could not help admiring the ingenuity and unobtrusiveness of it. Was it the Prince's idea – or that clever Ali Efendi's? Or was it just an age-old harem trick?

She saw a note by her bedside. It was from the Prince.

Your plane leaves shortly, she read. Goodness, was the week really up already? Oh, how sad. She still hadn't seen anything of the country. Was this the Prince's deliberate plan? To keep her hidden away in his palace compound and then discreetly to fly her out back to England?

> *My car will take you to the airport*, she read on. *I shall be coming to London in a week's time and my secretary will contact you with instructions as to where to meet me. You are to keep yourself entirely free for me for ten days. He will also give you an advance on the substantial allowance you will now be receiving. I enclose the address and telephone number of a leading Arab doctor in London. He is a friend of mine and has one key to the padlock hanging between your legs. I have another. You may ask him to remove it at any time you wish, but in that case I do not promise to go on paying your allowance. Whilst the padlock is in place, you are my paid servant – a very well paid servant, but with the rights only of a slave . . . I look forward to continuing our little bedroom scene in a week's time.*

Emma's head was reeling. To be the pampered mistress of one of the richest men in the world! Oh, how exciting! And how equally exciting to have her sensuality locked up behind those rings and that gold bar. She put her hand up to touch the pearls around her neck. Would they be the first of many such gifts? Goodness!

Again, she read on.

But remember, too, that Ali Efendi also has a copy of the key and that, if necessary, I shall have no hesitation in flying you back here for a little refresher training in obedience.

So that was why the Prince had shown her his harem and had had her beaten by his chief black eunuch. To impress upon her his power and authority, so that she would behave properly, even when she was back in England. Well, he had certainly succeeded in that – her bottom was still sore from her thrashing.

Oh, yes, by bringing her out here, he had now cleverly subjected her to his power and authority, all right. And that was not all. She also remembered what he had said about Arabs having a long arm and that anyone who opened their mouth about his harem would be sure to regret it. She gave a little shudder of fear. She would certainly never dare mention it to anyone. She was indeed in his power now. How terrifying, but also how exciting. Thank heavens she did not know the identity of any of the women she had seen.

But what should she say to Ursula when she came back to London again? She would explode with rage if she were to learn the truth – or if she ever saw the rings and the bar. And what about Henry? He had been very broad-minded in the past, but what will he say about the Prince? And how was she going to fend off Paddy, now that they were both working for the Prince? Of course, were she to ask the Arab doctor to remove the bar, then she would lose the Prince altogether – and he was so wonderfully dominating, madly exciting in bed, and very rich.

And then there was the problem of John. He was not due back for several months, but after his return she would have to go back to his bed at some time. Would he accept being fobbed off again?

Oh dear, what shall I do? she wondered, as, hastily, she packed.

The same thoughts weighed heavily on her mind as the car taking her to the airport slowly drove past the high walls of the harem. Who would ever have guessed what went on behind those walls?

Then the car turned and passed the front of the palace itself. There standing on the steps was the Prince! Her heart was in her mouth as she saw him smile. Oh, how she longed to fling herself into his arms. She hammered at the darkened window separating her from the chauffeur, to tell him to stop the car. She must say goodbye – or, at least, *au revoir*. But it was all to no avail. The chauffeur paid no attention and the car drove slowly on, with Emma desperately looking back at the Prince out of the rear window. How sad! But Moslem men, she remembered, do not embrace, or even acknowledge, women in public.

Then suddenly the car passed Ali Efendi, his dreaded cane in his hand. Was that terrifying sight, she wondered, intended to be her last memory of the Prince's palace?

On the way back to the airport, and indeed throughout the entire journey back to London, she could feel those little rings. She could think of nothing but the Prince, her new Master, of the key, and of when she going to meet him again.

Oh, how exciting life was, she thought. But also how complicated!

1

Emma's Homecoming

Prince Faisal's racing trainer, Paddy, Emma's great childhood friend in Ireland, was waiting for her at the airport.

'And how's His Highness's favourite girl groom?' he laughed, for Emma had officially gone out to the Prince's oil-rich sheikdom in charge of some racehorses he was sending out to Arabia for the winter.

'Girl groom?' laughed Emma. 'More likely one of his fillies!'

'One of them? You mean he has a whole harem of girls like you?'

Emma bit her lip, remembering that she had been warned of the dire punishment which awaited her if she opened her mouth about the Prince's harem of European women – quite apart from losing the very generous allowance that the Prince was going to pay her.

'Oh, I don't know anything about that,' she said with a smile. 'I just stayed near the stables and looked after the horses whilst they settled down in their new environment.'

'Oh yes?' said Paddy, then laughed in obvious disbelief. But it was clearly a taboo subject, and as his livelihood depended on the Prince, he did not press her. But, regardless of what had happened out in Arabia, she was obviously happy to see him again and to be back in England.

In the car driving back to town, she told Paddy that she had accepted the job of being the Prince's hostess and companion, officially his social secretary, during his visits to England.

'You mean his mistress?' gasped Paddy. 'Goodness, girl, you've done very well for yourself.'

Emma nodded.

'I shall have to be very careful in how I treat you, now. I don't want to be losing my job for rogering the boss' Mistress, do I?'

Emma did not know what to say. She was thinking of the little gold bar nestling down between her legs and threaded between the two lines of little gold rings which were now embedded along each of her beauty lips. Even now she could feel it holding the lips tightly closed and barring any access. That bar and the tiny padlock that stopped it being removed, ensured her faithfulness to the Prince, her Master. It even made it almost impossible for her to play with herself, for it also kept her precious beauty bud hidden.

But with the bar locked in place, surely there would be no harm in her going out with Paddy? He was such an old friend and, after all that she had been through in the Prince's palace, she needed a little company – preferably male company.

After all, she told herself, if it hadn't been for Paddy she would never have met the Prince. She owed him a little kindness.

Paddy took her back to the pretty little mews house he used when he was in London – just as he had done after the dinner at which he had introduced her to the Prince.

Emma remembered how he had made her go backward up the stairs with her dress hitched up, and licked her honeypot, as he called it, all the way up to the landing. Oh, how exciting that had been! But now?

'It's backward up the stairs again for you, my girl,' he ordered. 'And let's have your panties down and your dress up.'

Before Emma could protest or explain, he had her in position on the stairs. Looking down she saw him lean forward and then jump back.

'Holy Mother of Christ! What the hell has he done to you?'

Emma did not say a word as she felt his finger run slowly down along the slender curved gold bar to the little padlock and then back up again, touching each of the little gold rings in turn.

'Well, His Highness has certainly made sure of you, my girl,' he said sadly, pulling Emma's skirt back down again. 'Perhaps it's just as well, for I find you such a pretty young woman that, job or no job, I'd find it difficult not to have you.'

'I think you still can,' said Emma, with a smile.

Later that night an excited Emma was kneeling on the bed with her buttocks thrust back, whilst Paddy took her – this time in her rear orifice. She was longing to feel his hand on her hidden beauty bud, and although she was wildly excited she knew that she could not reach a climax. She was, she realised, being made to be faithful to the Prince – in her fashion!

Two days later, when Emma was back at her house in the country, the telephone rang. She was still feeling the effects of her fun and games with Paddy, and was walking as if still a little sore from having her secret opening stretched in such an ungentlemanly way.

Was this Paddy ringing to thank her for letting him use her for his pleasure? Even though it had not been in the way that he had envisaged? Yes, it had been rather fun – dangerous fun, though. She could imagine the Prince's fury should he ever suspect what had happened. Perhaps she should put an end to it, here and now.

She picked up the phone. It was the Prince! Ringing from Arabia. Was he checking up on her? she wondered anxiously. Had he heard in some way about her evening with Paddy? No, he seemed quite calm as he enquired about her journey back. Then his voice became serious.

'Listen carefully,' he said. 'Something unexpected has happened. We've just had some bad news. Our Crown Prince has been killed in a car crash, and we must choose a successor from amongst the royal family. But that is not all, for his papers have revealed that he had acquired a beautiful Eastern European girl, called Renata, in London, apparently from a rich lesbian woman.'

A rich lesbian woman in London! Emma's eyes opened wide as she listened to the Prince. And apparently one with an Eastern European girl whom she had been willing to sell to this rich Arab Prince! That was a description that would have fitted almost any of Ursula's friends – or even Ursula herself.

'It seems, however,' went on the Prince, 'that he tired of her and sold her back to her former Mistress. One version is that he was boasting that he would get a better price than that which he had paid for her – as she was now in the family way.'

'We are worried,' continued the Prince, 'that this girl could cause a great scandal for the royal family, even if she is not pregnant, and if she is, then the situation could be even more serious – possibly even a threat to the succession. It would be best if she just disappeared. So we are anxious to find the girl – and the woman who now owns her again.'

Emma's heart was pounding as she listened to the Prince. Disappeared? Did he mean disappear into a harem? His harem?

'I think you probably know a few people on the lesbian scene, so keep your ears open!'

But Emma was already feeling jealous. Why should she help stock the Prince's harem?

'We'd give a handsome reward to anyone locating this girl,' added the Prince.

A handsome reward! Ah, well, that was different. But how could she contact Ursula again without arousing her suspicions? If there was one thing that Ursula could not stand in one of her girls, it was inquisitiveness. Her Mistress had, on countless occasions, had her thrashed for being too curious and not minding her own business. Indeed, that was why Emma knew so little about Ursula and her friends.

'What does she look like?' asked Emma.

'Tall, slim and blonde,' said the Prince.

That's not much to go on, thought Emma. Finding this girl was obviously not going to be easy.

'Oh, and apparently the Crown Prince had his crest, a green hawk, tattooed on to the girl's inner thigh, so she should be easy enough to recognise!'

Well, thought Emma, but only in bed or in the bath! Did the Prince expect her to go around stopping pretty blonde girls in the street, or at cocktail parties, and ask them to pull up their skirts and pull down their panties?

'But enough of all that,' said the Prince. 'Now, tell your Master if you are missing him. Are you?'

'Oh, yes, Master, oh yes,' replied Emma fervently.

'And are you being faithful to him?'

'Oh, yes, Master,' whispered Emma, thinking of the bar and the padlock – and of Paddy.

'Good! Well the death of the Crown Prince will defer my return to England for a number of weeks, but make sure you don't get up to any tricks in my absence.'

'Oh no, Master, of course not,' replied Emma innocently. But anyway, how could she with that wretched bar locked in place?

'Good!' said the Prince, putting down the phone.

Emma was still thinking about the missing girl, about the reward, and whether she could pluck up sufficient courage to try to contact Ursula again, when the phone rang.

She put on a casual voice. 'Hello?'

'Well, little girl,' came a voice, 'and how's my little Emma?'

Emma jumped as if she had had an electric shock. It was the cool, slightly foreign-sounding voice that she knew so well – the hypnotic voice to which she never failed to respond. It was Ursula. Ursula! Back after all this time away. Emma could not help but feel a sudden charge of excitement surge through her.

'And has my little Emma been missing her Mistress?' came the hypnotic voice.

Trembling, Emma half-wanted to put down the phone. Instead, she heard her own eager little voice. 'Yes!'

'Yes what?'

'Yes, Madam,' Emma whispered.

'That's better. And has my little Emma been behaving herself?'

'Yes, Madam,' Emma heard herself murmuring.

'Good. Well, you must tell me all that you have been up to, little Emma.'

Tell Ursula about the Prince, about his harem? thought Emma. Oh no! Nor about Paddy! But the hypnotic voice went on.

'I thought you might like to come and stay for a week or so in my new house in Ireland – I know you'd love it.'

Ireland! Her own country! And Ursula had bought a house there! And she was inviting her to stay! How wonderful! And perhaps she would have the opportunity to learn something about the missing girl. She thought of the reward.

'Oh, it sounds lovely, Madam,' she said.

'Yes, I thought you might like to come. You can help me with a special, if rather tricky little project I'm planning to carry out. I think you'd be very useful!'

Ursula wanted her help! Ursula was actually asking her to help – not ordering her, but asking her, inviting her to stay. Surely the Prince would not mind her accepting an invitation from a female friend in Ireland? It would sound so innocuous! In any case, he wasn't coming back to Britain for another month or so. But just what was this special project? Could she really trust Ursula?

'So, what is this project?' she asked suspiciously.

'Ah!' said Ursula, with a knowing laugh. They both knew that Emma never could resist a mystery. 'You'll have to wait and see, but you'll find it very exciting.'

'Oh!' cried Emma. 'How intriguing!'

Ursula laughed again. The prey was taking the bait! 'Well, meet me at Heathrow on Saturday and we can fly back together – first class of course – and then you can spend a week or so with me.'

A week or so together! With Ursula, her wonderful and fascinating former Mistress! And flying together first class!

In the past Ursula had insisted on treating Emma as a mere servant girl and had put her in the back in economy class, whilst she herself enjoyed champagne in the front. Oh, how exciting! And what could this special project be? And could she learn anything of the missing girl and so earn the reward? Oh, how thrilling!

But, oh my God, she suddenly thought, what about the golden bar – and the rings? Ursula would have a fit when she saw them! How on earth could she explain them away to her? What could she say? And, more to the point, what would Ursula say? Oh dear, how complicated life was!

'Very well, then, I'll get your ticket and I'll see you at twelve o'clock at the Aer Lingus desk on Saturday.'

Before Emma could say anything more, the phone had been put down.

What was she to do? She did not know Ursula's current telephone number or even from where she had rung. Desperately, Emma dialled a number.

'Paddy? Oh, thank God you're in. I need your help quickly . . . Yes, you've guessed it right . . . Yes, it's about the gold rings and the bar. I've got to explain them away to someone. What can I say? What shall I do? Can you think of a story?'

'Oh, don't fret, my love. You can always say that you had it done by one these clever body piercers that are all the rage these days. Tell your friend you had it done for him – or is it a her?'

'A her,' whispered an embarrassed Emma. 'But what about the padlock? What shall I say about the key?'

'Just tell her you've lost it, darling. You're always losing things.'

'She'll smell a rat,' said Emma.

'Not if I get you a receipt from a body piercer friend of mine. You can show her that – and it'll be in your name.'

'Oh, Paddy, you are wonderful!'

'Aren't I always? And you can come and collect the receipt tomorrow. There'll be a price – the same thing as I got last time. Bar or no bar, I enjoyed it all very much –

and so, I daresay, will your girlfriend, provided she's got herself the right kind of dildo!'

Emma's heart jumped as she saw the tall elegant figure of Ursula approaching the Aer Lingus desk. Thrilled by the anticipation of seeing her former Mistress again, she had got there half an hour early. And now here Ursula was, looking as excitingly dominant as ever! All Emma's doubts evaporated.

'Well, little Emma,' Ursula said. 'Are you pleased to see your Mistress again?'

'Oh yes, Madam, oh yes,' cried Emma fervently, as she flung herself happily into Ursula's arms.

'And aren't we going to have fun together again! I shall have you all to myself!'

'Oh Madam!' cried an ecstatic Emma.

2

The Governess

It was now a few hours since they had left the airport in Ireland and it was beginning to get dark.

Emma had been thrilled to be taken by Ursula to the VIP lounge at the airport in London and then, during the flight, to be allowed to sit alongside her in the first class compartment, to laugh and to chat with her as they sipped their champagne.

To the outside world, it may have been quite normal behaviour by two women travelling together. But Emma knew only too well that being treated like this by Ursula, as an equal, was extraordinary. And now she was being allowed to sit alongside her in the front of the handsome Mercedes car that Ursula was driving.

All the time, Emma had been thinking partly about the missing girl and the reward, and partly about the rings and the little curved bar and padlock down between her legs. When should she tell Ursula about them? What would her Mistress' reaction be? She had expected Ursula to interrogate her about all that had happened to her since they had last met some months before. What should she say, she kept wondering, about the Prince and about her trip to Arabia? Would the truth about the rings and the bar then come out? Oh, how difficult it all was!

But, as usual, Ursula had shown hardly any interest in what had been happening to Emma. To Emma's great relief she had asked no searching questions about what she had been doing. Instead, as usual, she was only interested in herself, in her pictures, and in her plans for future exhibitions. As usual she simply could not be bothered to get involved in Emma's affairs – just as, Emma remembered, she had not been interested in the private lives and worries of her other girls. They had just been there to do what they were told – or be punished!

Emma had been too preoccupied with the rings and the bar to try to make out, in the gathering gloom, just where they were, as Ursula drove the Mercedes down a confusing maze of small roads and country lanes.

'Do tell me where we're going,' Emma had asked earlier, for Ursula had been strangely reticent about her new house in Ireland.

'None of your business, Emma,' came the reply.

Nor did she have any more luck in finding out about the special project that Ursula had talked about on the phone. 'Emma, you know very well I can't abide inquisitiveness in a girl. Another question from you and I'll take you straight back to the airport,' Ursula had snapped when she had tried to bring up the subject.

Oh dear, thought Emma, I'm certainly going to have to tread carefully about the missing girl. Better not to ask Ursula about it directly. I'll just have to keep my ears open, just like the Prince suggested.

Suddenly Ursula swung the large car into a very long private drive, at the end of which Emma could just about make out a large Victorian house with stone steps leading up to the front door. Blinding security lights came on as the car came to a stop. Ursula got out and slammed her door shut.

'We're here! Now, out you get, girl. Move!' Ursula ordered harshly in a sudden change of tone. It was as if the real Ursula had suddenly come out again – now that she had got Emma here and in her power again. 'Leave your case – you won't need that here!'

'What?' Emma cried, but before she could say another word, the front door opened and a middle-aged Irish housekeeper came down the steps and, ignoring Emma, greeted Ursula and took her bags.

Then suddenly, Emma was astonished to see a slim and strikingly pretty girl who looked to be in her teens burst out through a side door. She had long blonde hair, plaited into two schoolgirl pigtails, and was dressed in white socks and a white blouse under a black gymslip. On top of her head, in her blonde hair, was a black satin bow that matched her gymslip and which set off her schoolgirl look charmingly.

Goodness, thought Emma, what on earth is Ursula doing with a schoolgirl? She looked at the girl with astonishment, for Ursula had not said anything about a girl staying in the house. Indeed, she had understood that she and Ursula would be alone.

The girl ran up to the car and flung her arms around Ursula. 'Welcome back, Madam,' she cried in a strong foreign accent. 'Welcome back!'

Who, Emma wondered jealously, was this girl who called Ursula 'Madam' – just as she herself did?

The girl was followed at a more sedate pace by a tall, thickset woman, dressed like a governess in a plain tweed suit. Hanging from a belt around her waist was a bunch of keys, like those of a housekeeper – or a jailer.

Brushing aside the girl's clinging arms, Ursula turned to this woman. 'I hope she's been good, Miss Peabody,' she said.

'Oh, quite good, Miss de Vere,' the woman replied, in a precise and very educated English tone of voice that somehow sounded rather strange here in Ireland.

She clapped her hands authoritatively, and obediently the girl fell back. 'Now, Ingrid,' she said, 'that's quite enough. Show Miss de Vere how I've taught you to greet a lady.'

Blushing, the girl curtsied prettily, lowering her beribboned head demurely, the very picture of well-disciplined young girlhood.

'That's better,' Miss Peabody said and then, turning to Ursula, added, 'You'll have to excuse her, she's been so excited at the thought of your return!'

'Good,' Ursula said. Then she nodded knowingly

towards the girl, and lowered her voice so that the girl would not hear. 'Has she been taking the pills Doctor Anna prescribed for her?'

Doctor Anna! What, thought Emma, has that terrible lady doctor friend of Ursula's been up to with this young, innocent girl? She shuddered at the thought of how close she herself had come to being one of the Doctor's so-called patients. It was probable the she had only been saved from this fate by the fact that she was a married woman.

'Oh yes, Miss de Vere, she's had them every day.'

'And?' asked Ursula, with a quizzical look at the girl.

'I think they're just about ready now,' came the whispered reply, 'but she still doesn't seem to understand what's happening.'

'Good,' whispered Ursula. 'Then I'll try her out later this evening and see if we can get things moving! Meanwhile it'll be amusing to keep her in the dark about it all. Of course, once the flow's properly established and she realises what's happened, she'll be thrilled and proud. But mum's the word for the moment.'

'Right, Miss de Vere,' laughed Miss Peabody.

What on earth, Emma wondered, were they whispering about? Then Miss Peabody clapped her hands again. 'Now run along, Ingrid! Back to the nursery wing!'

Nursery wing! The very words made Emma wince. But at least she wasn't going to be treated as young girl. Ursula had invited her as a proper guest.

But Emma's confidence was short lived.

'Here's the other girl I said I'd be bringing to you, Miss Peabody,' said Ursula with a laugh. 'Now, Emma, run along and join your little friend in the nursery wing.'

'But you said I was going to be your guest,' protested Emma, tearfully.

'Don't you dare argue with me, young woman,' said Ursula angrily. 'Here you do as I say – and as Miss Peabody says.'

'But what about the special project you said I was going to help you with?' Emma cried, feeling as if her entire world was suddenly collapsing around her.

'Oh, you're going to help with that all right!' said Ursula with a cruel laugh.

Emma felt herself being seized by one ear by the powerful Miss Peabody who then led her away to the side door through which the other girl had disappeared.

'I'll probably come and look at them at bathtime,' she heard Ursula call out as the door closed behind them with a click.

'Now, girls, get undressed for your evening bath before being put to bed,' said Miss Peabody in an authoritative tone of voice, as she led them into a well-heated, old-fashioned bathroom, with a large bath in the centre of it.

'And Ingrid, you can leave on your pretty satin bow,' added Miss Peabody. 'You know how Miss de Vere likes to see you wearing one at all times – it makes you look so nice and young.'

Nice and young! Was the girl not really a schoolgirl at all? wondered Emma. Was she a grown woman whom Ursula made to dress and behave like a schoolgirl? This was, after all, one of her Mistress' favourite methods of humiliation.

'And you, Emma, can tie this satin bow in your hair too,' said Miss Peabody, 'and make sure that it is nice and big and right on top of your head, just like Ingrid's. Miss de Vere will want to see her two schoolgirls always looking as identical as possible.'

'But I'm not a schoolgirl!' cried Emma. 'I'm a young married woman!'

'No, Emma!' answered Miss Peabody tartly. 'Here you are what Miss de Vere says you are – a schoolgirl. Now undress and get into the bath with your little friend, and then you can put on your nightdress and go to bed.'

'Go to bed now?' said Emma, dismayed at having to go to bed so early. 'But it's only six o'clock!'

'Don't you start arguing with me, young Miss Emma,' said Miss Peabody angrily, as she ran the bath, 'or you'll be punished, just like young Ingrid was this morning when she answered me back during lessons.'

Punished! Ingrid was already taking off her gymslip and blouse. Emma saw that she wore nothing under them and, more to the point, saw the distinctive marks of a cane across her bottom.

'I'm your governess now, young Emma,' Miss Peabody was saying, 'and I decide what's best for you. Do you understand?'

Dismayed, Emma nodded. 'Yes,' she said. This wasn't at all, she told herself, how she had expected to be treated when, thrilled, she had accepted Ursula's invitation to come and stay.

'And I don't stand for any impertinence – so just remember, you always address me as Miss in future. Right?'

'Yes M–miss,' Emma stammered.

'Young girls of your age need plenty of rest,' went on Miss Peabody primly, 'and anyway, the Mistress doesn't want to be bothered in the evening with young girls running around the house whilst she is painting or entertaining her friends at dinner – unless, of course, she sends for you to come downstairs in your nightdresses to say goodnight. Now, put on your ribbon and tie it nicely, like a good girl.'

Too astonished and too scared by this unexpected turn of events to argue, Emma did as she was told.

'Is that all right, Miss?' she asked.

'Not quite. I'd like to see it tied right up on the top of your head and in a big schoolgirl's bow – yes, that's better, Emma. Now into the bath with you both,' Miss Peabody said briskly, rolling up her sleeves and picking up a large face flannel. 'I always like to wash my girls all over before putting them to bed.'

Blushing, Emma started to undo her blouse. Ingrid was already naked and, as she climbed into the bath, Emma saw that the very pretty blue-eyed girl had no hair on her mound or on her body lips. But then, to her astonishment, she saw that Ingrid had a very well-developed pair of breasts. Indeed, they were were heavily marked with blue veins and the nipples were strangely prominent.

Goodness, thought Emma, remembering the whispered conversation between Ursula and Miss Peabody, and their talk about the dreaded Doctor Anna. Surely the girl wasn't a young mother? But there were no signs of any stretch marks on the girl's flat belly. So . . .

'Hurry up, Emma!' came Miss Peabody's voice. 'Now, off with your clothes and get into the bath with Ingrid before Miss de Vere arrives.'

Hesitantly Emma began to undress. As she did so, Miss Peabody took her well-cut travelling suit and blouse and her slip to a wardrobe. Then, taking a key from the bunch hanging from her belt, she unlocked it and hung them up. She put Emma's smart London shoes away too.

'You won't be seeing these again,' she laughed, closing the wardrobe and locking it up again. 'Miss de Vere doesn't like to see young girls like you dressing up like grown-ups. From now on you'll just be wearing the same white blouse and black gymslip, white socks and sensible shoes as Ingrid. Now, off with the rest!'

She held out her hand and with a disapproving look took Emma's panties, bra, stockings and suspender belt and locked them away in a drawer. 'Nor,' she said, 'does Miss de Vere approve of her young girls wearing grown-up underwear. You won't need anything under your gym slip.'

She turned back to the embarrassed Emma, who was now crouching stark naked by the bath, one hand over her breasts and the other hiding her intimacies – and, of course the rings and the bar.

'Now let's have a look at you, Emma,' she said briskly. 'Stand up properly and hands to your sides. Head up!'

Emma blushed as she obeyed the governess' orders.

'Well! What's this?' Miss Peabody exclaimed, as her eyes took in the golden rings and the curved golden bar with the little padlock hanging down between Emma's legs. 'I must go and fetch Miss de Vere. Meanwhile, into the bath with you.'

Nervously, Emma climbed into the large warm bath so that she was sitting facing Ingrid. With their big black satin bows on top of their heads they looked like two innocent young girls about to be bathed by their governess.

'Now be good girls and behave properly – and no

splashing,' said Miss Peabody. 'I'll be back in a moment with Miss de Vere!'

She turned on her heel and left the room, closing the door behind her. Emma heard the noise of a key being turned in the door.

'She always keep door locked,' whispered Ingrid in a strong foreign accent.

'Quickly, tell me what you're doing here,' Emma whispered urgently, looking around nervously, as if expecting the door to be unlocked again at any moment.

'I am language student from Norway,' replied Ingrid in a whisper.

'But how old are you, really?'

'Twenty.'

'Twenty! But why are you being treated like a twelve year old?'

'For same reason as you,' laughed Ingrid. 'Because Miss de Vere knows it is best way to keep me in my place.'

'You mean Ursula?'

'I not allowed to call her Ursula, only Miss de Vere or Madam. I think that applies to you too, now.'

'Oh!' exclaimed Emma. 'But how did you meet her?'

'In a club in London. I having great time, but not learning much English. But Ursula – Miss de Vere – she very kind. She take me back to her hotel. We have a lovely time together. I fall in love with her! So I delighted when she invite me to come and work for her as – as research assistant.'

'Research assistant,' said Emma, laughing to herself. It all sounded very familiar!

'And when I say I must improve my English she say she will pay for a teacher, whole time. But she say that to learn properly, I must dress properly and behave as a real schoolgirl. So here I am! All very exciting, no?'

Emma's heart sank as she listened to Ingrid. And she had thought that she would be alone with Ursula. What a fool she had been to think that Ursula would ever be without at least one young woman in tow – and now she had two!

'And what about your family in Norway?'

'My parents dead. I just have aunt. She speak perfect English and she very beautiful,' Ingrid added wistfully. Then her voice became more self-assured. 'But now I have Miss de Vere. She look after me.'

'Oh yes?' said Emma.

'She offer me contract to work for her, I think she call it "enter her service". Lucky me!'

'And for how long is the contract?'

'Three years, I think,' replied Ingrid. 'It not matter as long as Madam looking after me.'

Three years! A lot, thought Emma, can happen to a pretty young woman, even one dressed up as a schoolgirl, in three years.

'And anyway,' continued Ingrid, 'if I am good, Miss de Vere can extend contract.'

'So it can be extended whether you like it or not?' asked Emma.

'Yes,' replied Ingrid, 'but why should I not want contract extended? I happy in Madam's service. I love her!'

'Good! I've loved her too,' said Emma cautiously before asking, 'but did the contract say anything about it being transferable to a third party?'

'Yes, I think so, but I not understand what transferable mean – and what is a third party? Madam gives lots of parties. I not understand.'

Just as well, thought Emma. Ursula certainly seemed to have the girl in her power. But what about the beautiful aunt back in Norway, who apparently spoke perfect English? Wouldn't she make a fuss if her niece did not return? But these thoughts were soon driven from her mind by the girl's next words.

'Miss de Vere kindly send me to see her lady doctor, Doctor Anna, to make sure, she say, I am properly well. She say she investing much money in me, as research assistant, and she want to be sure I not fall ill!'

Ingrid was patting her breasts proudly. 'Doctor say I need special injections and pills – to make them bigger. And yes, my breasts much bigger now. But also strange and heavy, sometimes I wonder if . . .'

No, thought Emma, surely Ursula had not had her . . .? However, before she could comment, the girl changed the subject. 'And now two girls in school room. And Miss Peabody says a third girl joining us soon. She says she has seen a photo of her and she looks just like me. I wonder who she is?'

Three girls! Emma was, she thought in dismay, just going to be one of three pretty young women, being treated as schoolgirls. Then a thought suddenly struck her. Could getting this third girl into the class be part of the mysterious special project that Ursula had brought her here to help with? Goodness!

'But anyway,' Ingrid went on, 'Madam promise that I shall be head girl. I shall be class prefect. You going to be under me now! For I know best how to please Madam! You and this other girl will call me Miss, and walk behind me – or I report you to Miss Peabody for punishment!'

A feeling of intense jealousy surged through Emma. How could Ursula have put this young chit of a girl over her? What did she really know about how to please Ursula? But her thoughts were interrupted by the rattle of a key in the door.

The door opened and in strode a furious looking Ursula, followed by Miss Peabody. Emma, feeling very naked and helpless, cowered down in the bath.

'Ah, Madam!' cried Ingrid happily as she stood up respectfully, her black bow wobbling prettily on top of her head. But Ursula ignored her. She pointed a finger at Emma.

'Stand up, girl!' she shouted. 'I want to see what this is all about.'

Oh, thought Emma with a little sob, how different things now seemed from the happy time they had spent together on the journey here.

'Stand up, I said!' repeated Ursula. 'I warn you, I shan't say it again!'

Terrified, Emma felt her ear being gripped again by Miss Peabody. She was jerked up on to her feet, still standing in the bath, the water running down her naked body. She was aware that Ingrid was watching the scene with a smirk on her face.

'Hands to your side!' ordered Miss Peabody. Reluctantly, Emma obeyed. She had expected a scene, but in private – not like this.

'What's this?' demanded Ursula, pointing down at Emma's hairless body lips, which were held tightly squeezed together by the rings and bar.

'I – I ...' stammered Emma, trying to remember the words that Paddy had told her to use.

'Who did this to you?' asked Ursula coldly.

'No one, Madam. I can show you the bill, if you like – It's in my suitcase. I – I had it done because I thought ... it would please you, Madam.' The well-rehearsed words came tumbling out.

Ursula peered down more closely. 'Yes, little girl, perhaps it will,' she said. She put her hand down and traced a finger along the line of interwoven golden rings. 'Yes indeed, perhaps it will!'

There was a pause as Ursula ran her hand further down, over the rings and the curved gold bar to the little hanging padlock.

'Where's the key?' she demanded abruptly.

'I couldn't find it when I was packing to come here,' lied Emma, desperately hoping that she sounded convincing.

'What?' Ursula exclaimed. 'You stupid girl!'

'Yes,' cried Emma, secretly delighted that Ursula seemed to have believed her. She would much rather be thought to be stupid than be thrashed! 'I know it sounds silly, but I must have mislaid it. I looked everywhere and there wasn't time to try to get another one, and anyway, it was all too embarrassing.'

There was another, longer pause, then Ursula burst out laughing, stroking the rings knowingly. 'Well, little girl, that little bar isn't going to prevent you from carrying out the role I've brought you here to perform!'

What role? thought Emma, what was this strange special project?

'Nor,' Ursula went on, 'is it going to stop you giving me

a lot of pleasure – and without you receiving any yourself! I don't know why I didn't think of using this technique myself! It will certainly be all the more exciting, knowing that you are being kept pure and innocent, so don't expect me to take you to a locksmith!'

She turned to the governess with a smile. 'Well, I mustn't hold you up from giving our two young teenagers their evening bath and putting them to bed.' She paused and then pointed to Emma. 'And put her hair into two little schoolgirl pigtails like Ingrid's. I don't want her getting any grown-up ideas.'

3

Ursula Takes her Pleasures

'Now, you young girls, time to spend a penny!'

Emma and Ingrid were standing naked beside the bath after being carefully washed and dried by the brisk Miss Peabody. Now the governess strode across the room and drew back a curtain, disclosing a loo. Ingrid ran across the room and stood waiting by it.

'Come on, Emma, stand behind Ingrid,' Miss Peabody called out. 'Remember, she's the monitor and as such always goes first.'

Angrily, Emma ran across the room in the girlish way upon which Miss Peabody insisted they always move, and stood behind Ingrid. Why should this girl take precedence over her? she thought jealously. Emma had known Ursula for far longer!

'My young ladies only go to the loo at the fixed times,' Miss Peabody said to Emma, 'so that I can supervise them properly and make sure they're properly clean.'

She nodded to Ingrid who went in and sat down. Miss Peabody followed her in, a packet of cotton wool in her hand, leaving a bewildered Emma standing outside. It all seemed very strange, being treated as a young girl and being made to look and behave like one as well. But, she had to admit, it was all rather exciting – just as Ingrid had said when they were in the bath together.

Moments later, it was her turn to sit on the loo and then be dried by Miss Peabody's cotton wool.

Miss Peabody now led them into the sparsely furnished

dormitory where three truckle beds had been placed in a row in the middle of the large room. They were small and low and some six feet apart from each other which, Emma realised, would make whispering difficult.

On the walls were large posters – just as in the bedrooms of many ordinary teenagers. But, Emma saw, they were all huge, blown-up photographs of Ursula, looking very dominant and stern! Each poster was lit up by a special picture light.

'As you've both got such a strong schoolgirl crush on Miss de Vere,' explained Miss Peabody to Emma, 'she's very kindly agreed to let you have these posters, so that you can look at them and think of her at night and when you're resting – for the picture lights are kept permanently switched on. She doesn't want her young girls having naughty thoughts about anyone else.'

What a clever way of brainwashing us, thought Emma.

'Now watch Ingrid carefully –' Miss Peabody's voice interrupted Emma's thoughts '– and make sure you know what you have to do.'

Emma watched as Ingrid carefully folded up her blouse and gymslip and put them on the floor at the foot of her bed, next to her shoes and white socks. Then Miss Peabody gave Emma a similar set and she had to lay them out neatly in the same way.

'Everything here must always be neat and tidy,' said Miss Peabody. 'Now girls, put on your nightdresses!'

Emma saw Ingrid take from the head of her bed a carefully folded long cotton nightdress. It was pink and decorated with pretty little yellow and blue flowers and looked like a typical young girl's nightdress except that the neckline was cut low to expose the top of the bosom.

'Go on, Emma!' ordered Miss Peabody, pointing to an identical nightdress neatly folded on her own low truckle bed.

When the two girls were standing by the sides of their beds Miss Peabody pointed to a door through which Emma could see a comfortably furnished bedroom with a large bed.

'That's my room – so I can always keep an eye on you

at night,' she explained. 'And hear any whispering – for I don't allow any talking in the dormitory.'

Miss Peabody was certainly strict, thought Emma ruefully.

'Now kneel down, girls, and say a little prayer for your kind Mistress.' Emma found herself praying to catch her Mistress's eye – instead of that beastly Ingrid.

Miss Peabody clapped her hands. 'Now, into bed, girls, and I'll come and tuck you up.'

Moments later Emma was lying in the half-dark of the dormitory, the only light there was coming from the picture lights over the poster photos of Ursula and from Miss Peabody's room. There was complete silence except for the noise of Miss Peabody moving about in her room. Emma heard her choose a book and then settle down to read it in a large comfortable chair from which she could keep an eye on the row of little beds next door.

What an unexpected turn of events, Emma kept thinking, as she lay half-dozing in her hard little bed.

Suddenly, it might have been an hour or more later, Emma was startled to hear a telephone ring next door in Miss Peabody's bedroom.

'Yes, Miss de Vere,' she heard the governess say, 'they've had a little rest so I'll bring them straight down to say goodnight.'

Emma heard the house phone being put down. Moments later, she was blinking in the light that Miss Peabody had switched on.

'Up you get, girls, your Mistress wants you to go down and say goodnight.'

Emma found herself eagerly following Ingrid through the large door that separated the nursery wing from the main house, and down an imposing staircase. Miss Peabody knocked on a door.

'Come in!' Emma heard Ursula call out. She now followed Ingrid into a large country-style drawing room – all brightly coloured chintzes and comfortable furniture. Large wooden logs burned in a fireplace.

Ursula was sitting in a large armchair. She was dressed in a black velvet suit that contrasted sharply with the simple cotton nightdresses that the girls were wearing. Emma watched jealously as she held out her arms to Ingrid who, with a little cry of joy, ran forward and, sitting on Ursula's knee, put her arms around her neck.

'Oh, what an affectionate little girl she is!' Ursula said and smiled at Miss Peabody who was watching approvingly. Emma again felt a surge of jealousy sweeping through her as she stood watching Ursula petting and stroking the Norwegian girl. She saw Ursula put her hand down into the low-cut front of Ingrid's nightdress and lift out a full breast. Her Mistress gave it a little squeeze and there was a cry of delight from Ingrid. Was it her imagination, Emma asked herself, or did she really see a little white drop emerge from the girl's now reddened nipple?

She saw Ursula give a significant nod to Miss Peabody and then put the girl's breast away again beneath her nightdress.

'And now let's see how Emma is settling down to her new life as a schoolgirl,' Ursula laughed, patting her other knee.

At last, thought Emma, as she too ran forward and, sitting on Ursula's knee, put her arms around her Mistress' neck, nuzzling and kissing her, desperate to show that she could please her Mistress more than Ingrid ever could.

'Oh yes,' she heard Ursula say to Miss Peabody. 'I can see that this one's going to be a lovely young girl, too.'

Emma felt Ursula's hand dip down into the low-cut front of her nightdress and gently pull out a breast, just as she had done with Ingrid. She felt her squeeze the nipple and a sudden thrilling shock ran down her body to her compressed beauty lips. Like Ingrid, she too gave a little cry of delight. Then she felt her Mistress' lips on her nipple, sucking. Oh, the excitement!

'I think I'll have them both in my bed tonight, Miss Peabody,' Ursula said. 'It'll be a new experience for them both. I want them both quite helpless so that they don't spoil it. However, I'll leave all that to you.

'Of course, Miss de Vere,' said the governess.

* * *

Ursula looked down at the two slim, naked figures lying on their backs in her bed. Each was blindfolded by a black leather half-hood that covered her eyes and the top of her head. Shiny, wide black plastic straps were fastened around the girls' thighs, and to these their wrists were fastened by small straps, effectively pinning their arms down securely to their sides.

Even more striking were the large white plastic ball-gags in their mouths, held in place by a strap that went through a hole in the centre of each ball. The straps were fastened behind their necks.

Yes, Ursula thought, they looked a perfect picture of helplessness – of excited and helpless young womanhood offered up for her pleasure.

She also knew from experience just how excited the girls would be as they lay in their Mistress' bed, bound, blindfolded and gagged, and not knowing what was going to happen.

Ursula lay down between the two girls and started to play with their nipples. Soon little moans of pleasure came from behind their gags. It was time to move on to the next phase.

She unfastened Ingrid's wrists from the shiny straps around her thighs. 'Kneel up on all fours, Ingrid,' Emma heard her order. Oh, she felt so jealous – guessing the reason for the order.

Ingrid's breasts were now hanging down prettily with the nipples nicely presented. Ursula stroked the breasts and squeezed the nipples until they were hard, and the girl moaned in delight. Then Ursula began to suck noisily first at one and then the other of Ingrid's nipples.

Suddenly she was rewarded by a little jet of sweet-tasting milk.

Oh, she thought, the delight of a young woman's milk! Oh, the feeling of power that this girl had been brought into milk at her command, using the clever Doctor Anna's latest treatment – and, it seemed, without the girl realising just what was being done to her! The miracles of modern medicine! Perhaps she would keep the girl ignorant for a little longer, until the flow was greater. Doctor Anna, she knew of old, liked to see the way in which the milk would gradually build up as the pills took effect on the body of the at first astonished, and then increasingly delighted young woman.

'Aren't you a clever girl, Ingrid?' Ursula laughed mysteriously to the helpless young blonde.

The still blindfolded Ingrid did not realise just what her Mistress meant, though the feeling in her breasts was so strange, so exciting. She longed to ask her Mistress what was happening, but her gag kept her silent.

'Relax your breasts, like a good girl,' Ingrid heard Ursula whisper encouragingly. What did she mean by this? But she tried to do so as she knelt over her Mistress with her breasts still hanging down beneath her. Soon she was rewarded by her Mistress giving her a little pat on the cheek as she redoubled her sucking. 'Yes, little girl, that's much better now!'

Oh, thought Emma jealously, as she heard the sucking noises, surely . . .?

Ursula laughed as she heard Emma, who was still lying helplessly on her back alongside them, make little muffled noises from behind her gag in an attempt to distract her attention from Ingrid. Oh, thought Ursula, the delight of a young woman's hanging breasts. Oh, the feeling of power that came from having a girl only too anxious to please – and indeed, from having two blindfolded and gagged young women at her mercy.

She turned and unfastened Emma's wrists. 'You kneel up too, Emma!' she ordered.

Thrilled, Emma hastened to obey.

Moments later another pair of soft breasts, perhaps not quite as large as Ingrid's, were hanging down above Ursula. Again she stroked and squeezed the nipples until they were hard, whilst Emma moaned in delight and Ingrid made little jealous protests from behind her gag.

Then it was Ingrid's turn again, whilst the now frustrated Emma tried to cry out to her Mistress from behind her gag, begging her not to stop – not now!

Laughing, Ursula now began alternately to suck the nipples of one of her girls and to stroke those of the other. Then, when she was satisfied, Ursula made the two now happily moaning young women lie on their backs again, and refastened their wrists to the straps around their thighs.

Soon she would train these girls to work together to please her, but for the time being she would take her pleasure from each of them separately.

She knelt over Emma's supine body, her hands holding the girl down and keeping her quite still. Then she gently lowered her own aroused beauty lips down on to the line of little gold rings. Gently she began to move up and down, the rings rubbing her beauty bud in a quite delightful way. Oh, the thrill of knowing that the girl's own pleasure was very limited. Oh, the feeling of power!

'Wriggle, Emma,' she called out in ecstasy. 'Wriggle properly or I'll call Miss Peabody to thrash you with her cane.'

The mere threat of the cane was enough. Ursula was soon riding a violently wriggling and plunging young woman, riding her and pressing her beauty lips down on to the girl's exciting row of rings.

With a hoarse cry Ursula climaxed, but that was not enough. Quickly she knelt over Emma's masked face and pressed her beauty lips to the smooth white plastic ball in the girl's mouth.

'Move your mouth up and down,' she commanded.

Oh, the excitement! It was an excitement made all the greater by knowing that the girl was feeling nothing – all she had to do was move the ball in her mouth up and down her Mistress' beauty lips and over the excited little bud itself.

'Now sideways!'

The well-trained Emma obeyed, bringing even greater thrills to her delighted Mistress. But Ursula wanted more – and she knew just how to get it!

Deftly she unfastened Emma's gag. Now she could feel the girl's mouth underneath her mask.

'...gue!' she screamed, and was rewarded by feeling a ...tle tongue pushing its way in between her beauty lips ...nd her beauty bud. Clearly Emma had not forgotten her training in pleasing a woman. Ursula looked down at the blindfolded face – it was time to see the girl's eyes. Hastily she reached down, undid the straps and pulled off the leather blindfold, and then lowered herself down again.

'Tongue!' she ordered again, and again she felt Emma's soft little tongue carefully stroking her now highly sensitive beauty bud. But this time she could also see Emma's apprehensive eyes looking helplessly up at her. Oh, the feeling of power was now overwhelming and she exploded again in a violent climax.

But still she wasn't properly satisfied and she moved across to the now similarly supine Ingrid and straddled her face. Soon she unfastened Ingrid's gag too. Again came the cry of 'Tongue!' and this time it was the equally well trained tongue of Ingrid that brought her to a final convulsion.

Minutes later, she rang the house phone. 'Yes, Miss Peabody, you can come and collect them now and put them to bed. They've both performed well so I'll be giving you your usual bonus. But they're both still frustrated, so make sure they don't try to play with themselves!

4

Startling Developments and Pleasures

It was the following morning and Emma, now dressed for the first time in her black gymslip, with a white blouse and socks, and flat-heeled sensible shoes, was sitting at a desk in the small classroom. Her long honey-coloured hair was no longer swept up into a sophisticated style, but was plaited into two schoolgirl pigtails that hung down her back – just like Ingrid's.

The girls were supposed to be reading, aloud and in turn, parts of Shakespeare's *King Lear*, and Miss Peabody was angrily striding up and down between their desks. 'Concentrate, girls!' she kept saying.

But Emma's thoughts were far away – on the goings on, the previous evening, in Ursula's drawing room and in her bedroom. What an extraordinary woman she was. Did Emma hate her for having tricked her into coming here to be put under the control of a governess together with at least one other girl, or was it all rather exciting?

But, she thought sadly, it didn't look as though she was going to get the chance to learn anything about the missing girl. Goodbye to the reward! Ah, well!

It had, of course, been very frustrating for her – but what else could she have expected, with that damned little bar locked in place? But at least Ursula had kept Ingrid unsatisfied as well. Emma had seen the Norwegian girl in their little dormitory, writhing with frustration and not daring to put her hands below the bedclothes, for the picture lights were on all night and the door to Miss Peabody's adjoining bedroom was also open.

Ingrid, however, had been called back to the Mistress' bedroom that morning to serve to her her usual breakfast of coffee, grapefruit and toast. Then, with Ingrid blindfolded once again, so that she did not know what was happening, her Mistress had, unbeknownst to the girl, coaxed a little milk from her breasts – fresh milk for her coffee!

Jealously Emma had wondered what the two of them had been getting up to. Ingrid had looked so smug when she had returned! Had she been allowed to make herself climax in front of her Mistress whilst she nibbled her toast? Or had she been rewarded after pleasing her Mistress yet again? My God! Emma felt consumed with jealousy. Then again, she thought, perhaps another day she too might be summoned to take breakfast in to her Mistress – and give her much more pleasure ...

'Emma!' She jumped as she heard her name being called. 'That's the second time you've missed your cue. Now go up to my desk and bend over.'

'I'm sorry, Miss Peabody,' said a now terrified Emma, 'but please don't punish me. I'll try harder, I promise.'

'Yes, you will in future – after you've been caned,' replied Miss Peabody.

Caned! Caned in front of that smirking young Ingrid!

'But I've come here as a guest,' protested Emma.

'And you'll get another stroke for arguing. Now run to my desk and bend over! At once! Do you hear?'

Hastily Emma stood up and ran to Miss Peabody's desk.

'Not like that!' bellowed Miss Peabody. 'I've told you that you are always to run like a young girl with your arms out straight and your fingers outstretched. You'll get another stroke for that mistake. Now go back to your desk, and when I call you again do it properly – or you'll get ten for your disobedience.'

With her head down like a whipped cur, Emma went back to her desk. Ten strokes! My God, she'd do anything to avoid that – no matter how silly it might make her look. She saw that Miss Peabody had rolled up her right sleeve. Terrified, she saw her pick up the long whippy cane with a curved handle that had lain across her desk. She trembled as she saw her give it a trial swish through the air.

'Emma! Here!'

This time Emma made a delightful picture of young girlhood as she ran prettily up to the desk and, gripping the far end of it, bent over. Her short gymslip now rode up, exposing her naked bottom and, Emma knew, her hairless and ringed little beauty lips.

'Ingrid!' called out Miss Peabody. 'As head girl you may come and hold Emma's hands still.'

Emma could see Ingrid smirking as, holding Emma's wrists in her strong hands, she looked down on the humiliation of her rival. Oh, how Emma hated her. She remembered the stripes she had seen on Ingrid's own bottom. How pleased she must now be to be head girl. How unfair that was!

'Four!' announced Miss Peabody. 'Two for inattention in class, one for arguing and one for not running properly when called.'

She raised her arm. 'One!' There was a swishing noise and Emma gave a little cry as she felt what seemed like a line of fire across her bottom. Desperately she tried to free her arms to rub her bottom, but Ingrid held her tightly.

'Two!' Again there was a scream.

'Three!'

'Four! Now run back to your desk!'

Sobbing, Emma sat back down at her desk, only to jump up again immediately with the pain from her now well-striped bottom. She would, she realised, be sitting down very carefully for the next couple of days – and she'd be doing anything to avoid getting more of the cane!

'And tonight,' said Miss Peabody, 'you're going to learn by heart thirty lines from *Hamlet*. You'll have to write it out tomorrow morning and there'll be a stroke of the cane for every mistake – except, of course, for Ingrid, as she's now the head girl and class monitor.

Bloody Ingrid, thought Emma jealously. What's so clever about her? She thinks she's the best thing since sliced bread just because she's been here longer and is younger.

'And,' Miss Peabody added with a mysterious little laugh, 'she's soon going to be a new secret source of pleasure for her Mistress.'

What new secret source of pleasure? Emma asked herself jealously. She remembered the suspicions she had had when she had first seen the girl's blue-veined breasts and heard about Doctor Anna's treatment. She remembered the way that Ursula had so excitingly played with their breasts and sucked them the previous night.

Emma knew of old how Ursula and her lesbian friends loved the idea of having a girl in milk – a pretty little animal that they could enjoy and show off to each other. Was this what was happening to Ingrid? She'd be even more insufferably superior when she realised the truth.

Damn her! But perhaps one day Emma herself might also be able to offer her milk to her Mistress – and it would be a damned sight sweeter than Ingrid's!

She looked down at her full, firm breasts – there'd be more of it, too, so she thought, sucks and yah-boo to stuck-up Ingrid!

Suddenly Ursula swept into the classroom. Ingrid immediately rose to her feet.

'Stand up, Emma, when Miss de Vere comes into the classroom,' called out an enraged Miss Peabody. 'That'll be two black marks!'

Emma's heart sank again. Two black marks! She had already learnt about Miss Peabody's system of black marks – each earned you a stroke of the cane at the end of the week, unless countermanded by a red mark for especially good behaviour or scholastic achievement. Moreover, if she was the bottom girl at the end of the week, she'd get another six strokes on top of those given for the black marks.

How embarrassing it was for a grown-up married woman to be treated in this absurd way, as if she really was a much younger girl. Or, on the contrary, wasn't it all rather exciting? Either way it was jolly unfair that Ingrid, that damned Miss Goody Two Shoes, was given a head start, simply because she was head girl, by being given ten red marks at the beginning of each week.

'Now, girls, I've come to tell you that Ingrid's aunt Norah, a beautiful young widow, will be arriving tomorrow to see how her niece has been getting on.'

'What?' cried Ingrid. 'My aunt Norah is coming here? But she'll see me as a schoolgirl, as your . . .'

'Yes, Ingrid,' Ursula replied with a smile, 'I saw your photograph of her and as she is so beautiful I called on her when I was in Norway the other day on business. We got on well and now she's coming here to see if she would like to work for me as a research assistant.

'Work for you? As a research assistant?' cried Ingrid. 'But I'm your research assistant.'

'Yes, so then I'll have two,' laughed Ursula. 'Perhaps she'll soon be wanting to join your class, too – as another young schoolgirl!'

'Join our class?' cried Ingrid in astonishment. 'As one of your schoolgirls? 'But she's not a – she's not got –'

'Lesbian tendencies?' queried Ursula with a smile. 'Well, I certainly found her most attractive and she clearly liked me too. Many women secretly have such desires, even if they are dormant. Yes, I think I detected a little spark of mutual interest that might well be fanned into a flame, so we'll just have to see whether we can arouse her feelings here. It will be an exciting challenge!'

'But she's thirty-five!' cried Ingrid, suddenly becoming very jealous of her beautiful aunt. Clearly, she was worried that Norah might supplant her in Ursula's affections.

'All the more of a challenge,' laughed Ursula. 'You young girls are just too easy to seduce.'

'Oh!' gasped Ingrid. My God, she thought, Ursula, her own beloved Mistress, was planning to use the all-female atmosphere of this house to seduce her aunt. How awful! Hitherto Ingrid had regarded Emma as her only rival. Now there was to be her aunt as well!

'She's very beautiful and young-looking, with lovely soft

eyes,' replied Ursula, seeking to fan Ingrid's jealousy further. 'Like you she seems to be at rather a loose end with no ties to keep her in Norway, so I thought I'd bring her here to see if she would make another little schoolgirl for Miss Peabody to control. Aunt and niece! Both trying to avoid getting Miss Peabody's cane! Both competing for my favours. It really will be very amusing.'

'Oh no! No!' Ingrid was crying over and over again.

My God, thought Emma. So, getting this girl's beautiful young aunt into this school room and into Ursula's bed must be the special project that Ursula had spoken about – the one that she wanted Emma to help her with.

'But, of course, your aunt may just be very shocked and insist on taking you away with her.'

'Take me away? Away from you, Madam? No! No! I want to stay with you!'

'Then we'll just have to persuade her to stay on, won't we?' said Ursula with a little laugh. 'We'll have to make her madly jealous of you and make her realise that the only way she can get into my good books will be by joining your little class.'

'But I hate her,' cried Ingrid, becoming increasingly overwhelmed by jealousy.

'Then you will enjoy making her jealous and lording it over her all the more,' laughed Ursula. Yes, it was all going to be very exciting – and she'd have Emma as well!'

'But you can't – you can't be serious!' stammered Ingrid.

'Oh, but I am,' replied Ursula. 'She'll make a lovely young schoolgirl – and you'll still be head girl!'

'But I – I love you!' sobbed Ingrid, running up to Ursula and crying on her breast.

'And I'm very fond of you too,' replied Ursula, smoothing the girl's long hair.

'More than you are of her?' cried Ingrid, pointing an angry finger at Emma. 'I hate her too!'

'And I hate her!' cried Emma who had been listening to this conversation with increasing dismay. It was bad enough having to compete against this chit of girl, without having to take on the reputedly beautiful aunt as well.

'Now, now, girls, no more outbursts like that, or I shall

have to ask Miss Peabody to use her cane,' said Ursula, trying to disguise her delight at these signs of intense mutual jealousy. 'No, because you both love me, you must learn to love each other too. You're both here to please me – and I hope Norah will soon be doing so too. Meanwhile, I'm very fond of you both, especially when you work hard at your lessons and when you both work together to pleasure me – and I'm sure I'm going to be equally fond of Norah. In any case, a little competition never did love any harm!'

Later that morning the two girls, holding hands like little friends, were taken by Miss Peabody for a walk in the lovely park which surrounded the large and isolated house.

Under Miss Peabody's approving gaze they had to hop around like excited little girls, using little nets to catch newts and tadpoles in the pond in front of the house. Then they had to put them into jam jars and bring them back to the schoolroom for their Natural History lesson. Each played her schoolgirl role faultlessly, but secretly both girls' thoughts were on the arrival the next day of Norah.

"Oh, Miss Peabody,' said Ursula that evening as the governess turned to usher her charges back upstairs again after they had said goodnight to their Mistress. 'Just make sure that Emma is washed out properly.'

Miss Peabody smiled.

'You see,' went on Ursula, 'the arrival tomorrow of the innocent and beautiful Norah has made me feel like taking a rather more masculine role tonight in preparation for her seduction. And, as Emma can't offer me her normal facilities I'll have to use the alternative one – and we like to keep things nice and clean, don't we?'

An hour later, a nervous and empty-feeling Emma was lying naked on her Mistress' bed, her eyes almost popping out of her head as she looked at the tall slim figure of Ursula coming towards her, followed by Ingrid. Ingrid was wearing her cotton schoolgirl's nightdress, but Ursula was wearing a lovely long white satin negligée, beneath which her small firm breasts scarcely swayed as she walked towards the bed.

Emma, however, was looking at the large rubber manhood protruding from between the folds of Ursula's negligée. She gasped in horror and then gasped again as Ursula untied the silken sash of her negligée and pulled it open, exposing her firm belly and thighs, and the black double dildo strapped around her waist.

The slightly smaller of the two rubber manhoods that made up the double dildo had been inserted inside her, giving her intense pleasure as she walked. Further intense stimulation was provided by a rubber pad, covered with small rubber knobs, which joined the two manhoods together at the base and rubbed against her already aroused beauty bud.

Hanging down below the manhood that jutted out in front of her belly were two very realistic heavy testicles. Emma eyed them nervously as she remembered that Ursula went in for loading her dildo with a mixture of warm milk and menthol – and she had doubtless told that bitch Ingrid, as head girl, to make sure that all was properly ready for the sodomising of her rival.

A slight squeeze of the rubber testicles, Emma knew, and a little of the mixture would jet out – not up inside Ursula, but inside the girl she was using. At first the warm milk would provide a reassuring feeling, but soon the menthol would start to take over and give the girl an increasing burning sensation. Soon she would be wriggling and writhing desperately, giving her Mistress untold physical and mental pleasure as she held the girl down underneath her.

Ursula came over to the bed and lay down on it, then made Emma squeeze and suck her nipples, causing little shock waves to run down her body to where the dildo was already arousing her.

'Kneel!' she finally ordered. 'On all fours!'

With a little sob of despair, Emma did as she was told. Ursula came and knelt behind her, whilst Ingrid now knelt by her side and took over the task of squeezing her nipples.

'Head down!'

Emma's forehead was now touching the sheets, between the outstretched fingers of each hand.

'Bottom higher!'

Suddenly Emma felt the firm rubber manhood probing at her rear orifice. After washing her out, Miss Peabody had greased her well. Now she knew her puckered little ring would be so slippery as to almost invite the thick manhood to penetrate her. But still Ursula was not satisfied.

'Hold her cheeks apart!' Emma heard her say to Ingrid.

Emma felt the cheeks of her bottom being pulled wide apart. Oh, the shame of having this done by that little upstart of a head girl! Then, moments later, she gave a little scream from her still-lowered head as she felt the large manhood forcing its way up inside her. It was withdrawn slightly, only to move up a little more with Ursula's next thrust.

She could hear Ursula's panting breaths behind her, and soon, Ursula's cries of pleasure as the rubber buds at the base of the dildo moved up and down against her beauty bud. Once again, however, it was not only the physical pleasure that was proving so exciting, but also the mental pleasure of sodomising Emma, of making her accept the humiliation, and of making her feel utterly dominated.

Emma saw that Ingrid was watching her humiliation with a smug look of contentment. Oh, how she hated her. But worse was to come.

'Kiss me, darling Ingrid,' she heard Ursula order from behind her, 'and let me suck your breasts.'

Emma's hatred was now mixed with jealousy as she saw the happily smiling Ingrid bend down to obey her Mistress. Suddenly Emma felt a little warm jet inside her. Oh, how exciting! Then, a minute later, the burning sensation began and she soon found herself writhing and screaming with Ursula and Ingrid gripping her hands to prevent her from trying to pull out the manhood. The excitement for Ursula was now even more intense. She could feel herself climaxing again and again.

The burning sensation eased and with it Emma's

writhing and wriggling. Ursula took advantage of this respite to recover her breath, then she dropped her hand and gave the testicles another little squeeze. The whole cycle recommenced.

Satiated at last, Ursula gave the testicles a really hard squeeze and was gratified to hear a scream from Emma announcing the arrival of a huge jet of the mixture. Moments later Emma's buttocks were writhing as never before, and this brought on a final and exhausting climax for Ursula.

Oh yes, she told herself, the little curved bar might prevent Emma from receiving pleasure, but it certainly did not prevent her Mistress from taking her own pleasure.

And, she thought, these two girls might be very jealous of each other, but they could clearly be made to act as a team in her bed.

5

Ursula Seduces Another Woman

Norah's eyes were shyly lowered as she sat on the same sofa as Ursula. Soft music was coming from a record player in the corner of the room.

Peeping out from under her eyelashes, she could not help but admire the casual elegance of Ursula's country suit and, equally, the country elegance of her drawing room. How she had admired Ursula, ever since she had met her briefly in Norway a few weeks before.

She had decided, almost at once, that Ursula was one of the most fascinating and intelligent women that she had ever met. No wonder her niece seemed to have fallen under her spell! Ursula seemed to have been everywhere, to know everyone and even to speak half a dozen languages.

But, Norah knew, there was even more to her than that. She had also instantly recognised Ursula – by the look in her eyes, by the way she walked and by her voice – as a potentially dominant woman. She had found herself becoming moist and excited at the idea that Ursula might perhaps be someone who would stand no nonsense from another woman in her power. Would Ursula, she had privately wondered, enjoy having her in her power? More to the point, would she secretly enjoy being in Ursula's power?

Ever since her dynamic and gorgeously masterful husband had died, Norah had, secretly and so far unsuccessfully, been seeking another Master who would command and take charge of her – and who was rich enough to shelter her from the day-to-day problems of modern life. She was, she now realised, a born masochist, a born slave. Oh, if only she could find a reasonably gentle sadist to take charge of her life!

She had never been involved in a lesbian affair, and indeed the very idea had rather repelled her. Meeting Ursula, however, had made her wonder whether she should perhaps be looking not for a Master but a Mistress – an older, richer and commanding Mistress!

There had been no opportunity during their brief meeting at a drinks party to explore matters further, and Ursula was leaving for London the next day. But when Ursula, with a firm look in her eyes, had invited her – no, commanded her – to visit Ireland 'to come and see how her niece was getting on', she had found herself accepting with alacrity.

And now here she was! Alone at last with Ursula! But in the same house as her niece. Oh, how embarrassing, she kept thinking.

'I'm so glad,' Ursula was saying to the well-dressed, beautiful, blue-eyed blonde sitting alongside her on the sofa, 'that you've been able to come and see for yourself the progress that young Ingrid has made in her English. You mustn't be surprised, but I told her she'd have to accept being treated as a schoolgirl if she wanted to come here.'

'A schoolgirl!' exclaimed Norah, raising her head and looking at Ursula in surprise. Her English was very good – much better than her niece's. 'But she's twenty!'

'Oh, women much older than that can make very convincing young schoolgirls,' laughed Ursula, looking Norah in the face. What a beautiful woman she is, she was thinking – and what a lovely young skin. With her hair in pigtails and ribbons, and with a little discreetly applied make-up, she would indeed make a delightful, and very convincing schoolgirl.

Grown-up women treated as schoolgirls? Norah was meanwhile thinking. How strange! But also, perhaps, how exciting! What a simple way for the dominance of one woman over another to be established – and accepted. It could even be achieved in public, without strangers suspecting what was going on. Well!

'And as for Ingrid,' went on Ursula, 'you'll soon be able to see for yourself how being treated as a schoolgirl here under the eye of a governess, and working long hours in the schoolroom, has enabled her to make so much more progress than just running around London as a student – for I like my young ladies to be under strict discipline.'

'Strict discipline!' cried Norah, secretly wondering what it must be like to be under Ursula's strict discipline.

'Yes indeed!' continued Ursula. 'She seems to have had far too much freedom in the past – perhaps because her parents are dead. But, as I said, she is being treated here as a schoolgirl and no longer as a young adult.'

'But what made her ever agree to it?' Norah asked, this time secretly wondering if she herself would have agreed.

'Oh,' replied Ursula airily as if it was one of the most natural things in the world. 'It was simply one of the conditions that I laid down if she were to come here. I'm certainly not going to waste my time and money on training her if she still feels free to do whatever she likes.'

'Training?' queried Norah. 'You mean the English lessons?'

'That and a good deal more!' replied Ursula with a laugh.

Goodness, Norah thought, surely Ursula wasn't using Ingrid for – her pleasure? Was she shocked or a little jealous? Hastily she collected her thoughts. 'It's terribly kind of you to have taken her under your wing – but why have you bothered?'

'Oh, it always amuses me to have one or two young women in my house,' replied Ursula enigmatically. She smiled at Norah. There was something soft and gentle about this attractive young widow. She thought she had recognised a secret masochist when she had first met her in Norway – and hence her invitation. Did Norah perhaps miss being under her husband's control? The problem was that she was obviously nervous about forming a relationship with another woman. Perhaps the time had come to push the door a little further open.

'But doing what?' asked Norah, though she already knew the answer.

'Oh, sometimes they might be studying,' Ursula replied. 'Or –'

'Or?' persisted Norah intrigued.

'Or working in my – my service.'

In her service! Norah had once been in the service of another person – a man, her husband. She had been his secret slave. It had been their great secret, the bond that had held them together.

'I think we can all become friends, great friends,' Ursula said, looking Norah in the eye and making her blush and then look down again. Then she reached forward and took Norah's hand. 'And, of course, some of my girls are slightly older.'

'Oh!' cried Norah feeling a thrill of excitement running through her as Ursula, delighted to find that Norah did not withdraw her hand, gave it a little secret squeeze that sent more thrills of delight running through Norah's body.

'And,' Ursula went on, now speaking in a sexy, soft and deep tone of voice. 'I'm sure you'd love to be in my service too. You're such a beautiful and charming young woman.'

'Hardly young now!' laughed Norah nervously, not knowing where to look. Ursula was such a delightful woman! She seemed to know just what to say to have Norah hanging on her every word.

'Nonsense!' came Ursula's well-practised flattery. 'With hardly any make-up at all, you could easily pass yourself off as a schoolgirl again – just as Ingrid does.

'And you've got such lovely long legs as well,' she said, now running her hand down Norah's thighs and then back up again.

Again Norah blushed, dismissing any idea of pushing Ursula's hands away.

'Let's dance,' whispered Ursula, as the slow strains of 'Night and Day' filled the room. She pulled Norah to her feet then, clasping the lovely Norwegian to her, she led her in a swaying version of the romantic dance.

'So why is it,' murmured Ursula, pressing her small hard breasts against Norah's soft ones, 'that such an attractive and intelligent woman as yourself has not married again? Men must be mad about you!' Ursula was indeed well-versed in using flattery as a preliminary to seduction.

'Oh, I think I'm off men now,' laughed Norah. Since her husband's death she had never found a man in whom she could confide her secret longing to be dominated.

'Really!' exclaimed Ursula. 'I wonder why? Well, you'll be glad to know that you won't find any men here. This is an all-female house.'

'Oh!' exclaimed Norah, blushing. 'I hope you didn't think that I am a lesbian.'

'No, of course not,' replied Ursula in an even tone, looking Norah in the eye. Then she pressed her lips against Norah's and was delighted to feel her mouth slowly opening. Next, she put her hand to Norah's breast and was equally delighted to be rewarded by a further relaxing of Norah's mouth. She gave Norah's soft cheek a gentle caress with the back of her hand. 'But we women can still be such understanding friends, can't we?'

'Oh yes!' Norah heard herself cry out. 'Oh yes!'

It was time to hold back, Ursula decided – to hold back just when Norah clearly wanted her to go on. Holding back would make Norah all the more desperate for her embraces! But to bring things to a head, she decided, she would eventually have to use more physical means rather than sheer seduction. But that would come later, after a little more physical frustration and mental preparation.

'Well, Norah, do you want to get into my good books?'

'Er ... yes!' Norah murmured, not quite sure what Ursula was driving at.

'Then you'll have to join my class of schoolgirls!'

Norah's mouth fell wide open. Oh no! Not that! But before she could say a word of protest, Ursula had quickly added, 'So, let's go and see how your niece is getting on – as my favourite schoolgirl.' She looked Norah in the eye again and gave her hand another little squeeze. 'Favourite for the moment, that is!' Then, taking the still gasping

Norah by the hand, she led her up the stairs and along the corridor.

'Ingrid's got another little friend studying with her now,' said Ursula as she unlocked the door to the nursery wing. 'We keep the door locked so that their lessons won't be disturbed. Indeed, rather than interrupt their present lesson, why don't we just look in from behind a two-way mirror?'

Ursula drew back a small curtain, and there before them was the schoolroom with two girls, dressed in black gymslips, sitting at their desks with their backs to them. They were, it seemed, reciting with some difficulty, their thirteen and seventeen times tables, under the watchful eye of a governess.

'Miss Peabody's such an experienced teacher of young girls,' murmured Ursula, still holding Norah's hand. 'Well, do you recognise your niece?'

At first Norah did not realise which of the two girls, each with long blonde pigtails hanging down her back and a big black bow perched on top of her head, was Ingrid. Then the girls turned to look at something Miss Peabody had written on a blackboard on a side wall.

'Yes, there she is!' she exclaimed excitedly.

'And a very pretty and obedient schoolgirl she makes too,' laughed Ursula.

'Obedient? You mean that . . .?'

'That she has been punished for being lazy or impertinent? Oh yes! And as a result, she now works much harder – and is much happier. She knows just where she stands now. I think most young women are happier and work better if they are strictly disciplined.'

Again Ursula looked a blushing Norah in the eye. 'And so too, often enough, do beautiful and slightly older young women.'

Norah gave a little shiver, but was it of fear or excitement? She did not know. Could, she wondered, being disciplined by a woman like the governess, or indeed by Ursula herself, really be as exciting as she had found being disciplined by her husband?

Ursula gripped Norah's hand more tightly, and felt it become soft and yielding. She smiled. It was time to go a little further. 'Yes,' she said, 'I always say that the cane is a great leveller.'

The cane! The word reverberated around Norah's head. Her husband used to cane her sometimes as part of their fun and games together and would then leave it hanging up in their bedroom as a reminder of his authority over her. It had, she remembered, been very arousing.

'The cane! You mean these girls ...?'

'Get the cane from time to time from their governess? Oh yes!' Norah saw that Ursula's eyes were glistening. 'And sometimes from me.'

'From you?'

'Oh yes, I think it does a servant girl good to be disciplined occasionally by her Mistress.'

Her Mistress! A servant girl! Norah blushed and again lowered her eyes, remembering how her husband had, during their love making, often insisted on her calling him Master.

'Anyway, you'll soon see how my methods, and my discipline, have improved Ingrid's English – and made her a much more pliant young woman.' Ursula paused for a moment. 'Of course,' Norah heard Ursula continue, 'as I said, it's not only younger girls who respond well to the cane.'

Norah blushed yet again. Had Ursula guessed her secret desires?

'And of course,' Ursula went on, 'Ingrid is much more than merely my star pupil.'

'Oh!' said Norah in an angry tone of voice that brought a little smile to Ursula's face. Norah, she realised, was beginning to feel a little jealous of how such a wonderful, rich and intellectual woman seemed to take such an interest in her niece. Surely, she was clearly thinking, she herself was much more interesting – and more her age?

It was now two days after Norah's arrival, and today she had found herself becoming increasingly frustrated and jealous of her niece's evident success in winning the affection and attentions of the fascinating Ursula.

She had been thrilled by the very warm and exciting way in which Ursula had initially greeted her, stroked her, danced with her – and yes, she had to admit it– aroused her. But then, to Norah's dismay, Ursula's interest had seemed to switch back to Ingrid, and she had found herself being increasingly ignored.

Her jealousy had grown as she had seen Ursula taking Ingrid for walks alone in the park, or inviting her for intimate chats in her drawing room. Even worse was when she had asked the housekeeper where Ursula was, only to be told, 'Miss de Vere is having her usual afternoon rest with Miss Ingrid.'

Having an afternoon rest with her niece? Did that mean that Ursula was ... but why not with her?

Now at last, though, she had been invited to dine alone with Ursula. Oh, how romantic! And what a chance to show herself off to Ursula as a sophisticated woman and not a mere schoolgirl like Ingrid.

She had made herself look quite exceptionally beautiful, with her blonde hair up in an exotic Edwardian style, her nails freshly polished and her body scented with Miss Dior. She was wearing a lovely long satin dress that showed off her slender figure and her full breasts.

Suddenly there was a knock at the door of the guest room and the rattle of plates on a tray.

'Come in,' cried Norah. She had just finished dressing for dinner with Ursula and was now sitting on the edge of the curtained four-poster bed.

'Miss de Vere sends her compliments,' said the friendly housekeeper in her strong Irish brogue, as she swept into the room with a loaded tray, 'and wonders if you would mind having dinner in your room this evening. Instead of you, she's invited Miss Ingrid to dine with her – alone.'

'What?' gasped Norah. Ingrid dining alone with Ursula! Instead of her! Just when she was half expecting Ursula to make love to her, she had been dismissed at the last moment – and, in favour of her niece. My God! And after all that she had done to make herself irresistible for Ursula! What a snub! She felt like weeping. A rage of jealousy of her niece swept over her.

She'd go downstairs straight away and give Ursula a piece of her mind – and her niece, too. She rushed to the door. It was locked! The housekeeper had locked her in her room whilst Ursula used her niece for her pleasure!

These thoughts went around and around in her mind for the next hour as she paced up and down her room. She could hear faint sounds of laughter and gaiety filtering up from the dining room which was immediately below her bedroom. She heard the strains of 'Night and Day'. Was Ursula dancing with Ingrid? Was she fondling and arousing Ingrid, just as she had fondled and aroused her when they had danced? As she listened to the music she began to feel more and more jealous of her niece.

She remembered how, when Miss Peabody had first brought Ingrid to the drawing room to meet her, Ingrid had almost ignored her and had instead flung herself, like a child, into Ursula's arms. Ingrid had kept repeating how happy she was to be able to give pleasure to Ursula, whom she kept calling Madam as if she were a servant. They seemed to be sharing a secret, one from which Norah was excluded.

But what, she thought jealously, could Ursula see in Ingrid? What could Ingrid offer Ursula that she, Norah, did not have more of? Wit? No, Ingrid was not as quick-witted as she was! Attractiveness? Well, Ingrid might have the advantage of youth, but she herself was still, she knew, a most attractive woman – as indeed Ursula herself had told her. And yet she was being shut out and given dinner in her own room, like a naughty child.

So, she wondered, just what was it that Ingrid was offering to Ursula that she was not? She remembered the way Ursula's eyes had glistened when she had mentioned using the cane herself. Was she using it on Ingrid even now? My God, was that whistling sound she suddenly heard the noise of the cane?

Goodness! Was Ursula signalling to her that, despite her

beauty and attractiveness, she could only be admitted to her private coterie if she also submitted to the cane, to the classroom, and to being treated as a schoolgirl? Was that why Ursula had suddenly and inexplicably broken away in their loving dance?

She remembered how, just afterwards, Ursula had suggested she join the class. Norah had taken this as a joke. But perhaps Ursula had meant it seriously!

Just then, there was a rattle of keys in the door, and the housekeeper re-entered the room.

'Oh, I'm so so sorry,' she said, 'I thought you might be finished by now. I'll come back later. But I can see you're upset – perhaps about your niece not being in Miss de Vere's good books? But don't you fret! It's all right now, I just heard Miss de Vere tell Miss Peabody to bring your niece to her bedroom later tonight. She'll spend the night there, no doubt.'

'Oh!' gasped Norah.

'So you see, you've got nothing to worry about,' the housekeeper added as she turned to go out again, groping for the doorkey in her pocket. 'Your niece is back in favour again. So don't worry.'

'Don't worry!' Norah wanted to scream at the retreating figure. 'Don't worry because she prefers my niece to me!'

And to think she had been thinking of joining the class! She must have been mad to have thought of doing any such thing! No, in the morning she would leave – and she would take Ingrid with her! Yes, that's what she would do! She'd had enough of being humiliated!

It was with these thoughts racing round her mind that she gulped down the hot drink on her tray. It tasted surprisingly nice and soothed her nerves a little. She allowed herself to relax and all the anger and resentment she had been feeling inside her seemed to melt away. She suddenly realised just how tired she felt – it had, after all, been a very long and exciting day – and so she undressed, went over to the large four-poster bed and slipped in between the sheets. Within moments she was fast asleep.

* * *

Some time later, she was woken by the sound of her bedroom door being opened. On seeing Miss Peabody enter the room she decided that, for the time being at least, feigning sleep might be the wisest option. The governess walked over to the bed, peered down between the curtains and smiled. Then she turned on her heel and left the room.

Moments later the door opened again, and again it was Miss Peabody who came in through it. This time, however, she was accompanied by Ursula. Ursula was wearing her long white satin negligée, but this time there was no black manhood pushing out from between the folds. Instead she was carrying some strange-looking sets of shiny black plastic straps. Norah suppressed a shiver of excitement. Let Ursula and Miss Peabody think she was asleep – and let them do whatever it was they wished to do with her.

Quietly, Miss Peabody pulled back the bedclothes and lifted up Norah's nightdress. Ursula handed two of the sets of black plastic straps to Miss Peabody. Each consisted of one long strap to which was connected another shorter one. As Miss Peabody began to fasten one of the longer straps around her thigh, Norah knew this was her last chance to speak up, to protest, even to struggle, and yet she did not make the slightest sound or movement. This, she knew, was just what she wanted, just what she had been searching for ever since the death of her beloved husband and Master.

Deftly, Miss Peabody fastened the other long strap around Norah's other thigh and then, using the short straps, secured each of her wrists to the corresponding thigh strap. Next, Ursula handed the other two plastic straps to the governess. They were smaller, but each had a short length of chain fastened to it, with a snap fastening at the end of the chain. Miss Peabody fastened these straps around the beautiful woman's ankles. Then she gently pulled her legs apart and snapped one chain on to each of the rings which had been set into the two posts at the foot of the bed.

The sleeping Norah was now lying helpless with her hands tied down to her sides and her ankles fastened wide apart. Gently, the two women slipped two pillows under her hips. Her mound and beauty lips, both covered in silky blonde hair, were now raised as if they were some kind of an offering.

Ursula looked down on the now bound Norah. It had been an amusing game, getting her excited and then keeping her at arms length. She lowered her head and kissed her softly on the cheek. Norah did not respond to this so Ursula nuzzled her neck, then whispered sharply into her ear, 'I know you're awake.' She smiled to herself as she felt Norah start in shock. 'So you can stop pretending to be asleep, if you really want to stay in my good books.'

'B–but,' protested Norah, 'the drink. I–I thought–'

'A herbal nerve tonic,' said Ursula, 'no more potent than a mug of milky cocoa.' She turned to Miss Peabody. 'Well, now that our guest is fully awake I think it's time we introduced her to Emma.'

Dressed in just her simple cotton nightdress, Emma nervously followed the satin-clad Ursula into the guest room. She had just been roused from her bed and was wondering why. She saw the large four-poster bed with its curtains drawn back on one side. Standing by the bed and looking down on it, was Miss Peabody. Emma gave a little gasp as she saw that Miss Peabody had her cane in her hand.

She gave an even louder gasp when she saw that lying on the bed was a beautiful bound woman. The woman was blonde and bore a certain facial resemblance to – Ingrid! My God, Emma thought, this must be Ingrid's aunt!

'Now lie down between her legs and use your tongue and fingers to excite her,' ordered Ursula. 'I want you to get her properly aroused for when I'm ready for her.'

Just like Ursula, thought Emma rebelliously, to make someone else prepare a girl for her pleasure. But why should she bother?

As if reading Emma's thoughts, Ursula added, 'And do it quickly and properly. Just remember that Miss Peabody will be standing over you with her cane!'

With a little sob of despair Emma climbed quickly on to the bed and lay down between Norah's outstretched legs. So this was Ursula's special project and this was why she had brought Emma here – to help her seduce a beautiful woman! Out of the corner of her eye Emma glanced up nervously at the cane hovering over her bottom. Hastily she began to lick and tickle.

Norah stirred testing the strength and tightness of her bonds. She was wide awake, and yet she was content to keep her eyes closed and enjoy everything as it happened to her. She felt herself being kissed – she opened her eyes a tiny fraction – kissed by Miss de Vere! Oh, how lovely!
  Between her outstretched legs, her strangely raised beauty bud was also being kissed and tickled. She was, she realised, wet with arousal.

6

Three Schoolgirls

Still kissing Norah, Ursula put her hand down to touch the Norwegian woman's beauty lips. 'Out of the way,' she murmured harshly to Emma, who was still lying between Norah's outstretched legs, diligently licking her beauty bud with her tongue and tickling it with her fingers – just as she had been told to do by Ursula.

It was a pity, Ursula thought, about the hair on Norah's intimacies. She liked a woman to be completely hairless down there. But that was something which could quickly be corrected by Miss Peabody as soon as Norah had agreed to become one of the schoolgirls – or, better still, had begged to do so. Nevertheless, the beauty lips were now nicely moist and soft.

Ursula lowered her own beauty lips down on to Norah's. Oh, how lovely they felt rubbing up against her own.

'Wriggle!' she said and smiled as she felt Norah move obediently under her.

'More!' she ordered. Norah was now moving, excitedly, in time with her own gyrations. 'That's better!'

Norah found herself responding wildly to being tied down for Ursula's pleasure. How it had all happened she did not understand, but she was in no doubt as to how thrilling it was to feel utterly subjugated. She found herself responding passionately to Ursula's kisses and writhing madly under her pressing beauty lips.

It was the first time, she realised, that she had made love since her husband had died. Oh, what a fool she had been, not to have realised before the immense pleasure she could derive from being mastered not by a man, but by another woman. She wanted it to go on for ever.

Ursula, too, was finding it all most arousing but in her case it was the feeling of power that was really turning her on – power over a beautiful and helpless woman, who clearly had never before been made to pleasure another woman, but was finding it all very exciting.

'Do you love your Mistress?' she cried hoarsely. 'Do you, Norah?'

'Yes! Oh yes!'

'Then say it!'

'I – I love my ... Mistress.'

'Say it again!'

'I love my Mistress,' sobbed Norah.

'And she loves you, too. And you've made her come very excitingly. But before you can be allowed to come, you've got to enter her service, haven't you?'

Enter Ursula's service! Ursula understood her secret longings!

'Well, Norah? Go on, say it!

'I – I ... no, I can't,' whispered Norah.

'Go on! Say it!' cried Ursula.

'I – I want to enter the service of my Mistress!' cried Norah, suddenly but fervently.

'And you know what that means, don't you?' There was a pause. 'Well?' said Ursula.

'I must ... join ... the other girls ... in the classroom.'

'Yes!' said Ursula triumphantly. 'You must! And you're going to make such a pretty little schoolgirl in your pigtails and gymslip – and, of course, with all your body hair removed. Your beauty lips will be completely smooth. You'll love that, won't you?'

'Yes.'

'Yes what?'

'Yes ... Madam.'

'And every time I drive my sharp nails into your arm like this, I want to hear you begging to be a little schoolgirl again. Go on, say it!'

'I want to be one of Madam's little schoolgirls,' screamed Norah, as she felt Ursula's nails again pressing cruelly into her arm. She might, she told herself, be being seduced into accepting it, into begging for it, but it was still what she really wanted.

'Good girl,' cried Ursula enthusiastically. Then she turned around. 'Emma!' Get down on your back and please me!'

With another nervous look at Miss Peabody's cane, Emma lay down on her back and wriggled up under Ursula's legs and between Norah's outspread ones. Ursula slipped down a little and was rewarded by the delicious feeling of Emma's tongue on her hot moist beauty lips.

Moments later she raised herself slightly, and then pressed her aroused pleasure bud down on to Norah's beauty lips. Oh, the sheer thrill of having two beautiful women in her power and pleasuring her!

Alternating between the two, and sometimes thrusting her now erect nipples down to be sucked by an eager Norah, she reached a plateau of almost continual climaxes – climaxes that were only interrupted by Norah begging again to be taken into her service and to be put into the classroom.

'Very well, Norah, I'll let you join the class,' said Ursula suddenly, getting up off the bed, 'but first Miss Peabody has a little present for you!'

A present, thought Norah – what could Ursula, now her Mistress, mean?

'Yes, a little present! If you're going to be allowed more pleasure, then you must also suffer a little pain for your Mistress' delight. Yes, it's time you met Miss Peabody's cane!'

Cane! The word reverberated once again around Norah's brain. This was to be her present! She was going to be beaten in front of her Mistress to give her further pleasure! My God! But her thoughts were interrupted by Miss Peabody going to the door and calling out, 'Ingrid! You can come in now!'

Overcome with embarrassment, Norah saw Ingrid,

dressed in her simple nightdress, run into the room, fall on her knees in front of Ursula and put her head under her long negligée.

Meanwhile Miss Peabody, her cane again raised, had gone back alongside the bed.

'Turn over on to your tummy, Emma!' ordered Ursula as she parted her legs and felt Ingrid's hot little tongue running up and down her soaking wet beauty lips. 'And now lick Norah and make her come!'

To emphasise this order, Miss Peabody brought her cane down across Emma's bottom. With a little cry, Emma began to lick Norah's beauty lips. Soon Norah was crying out in ecstasy.

'Now the pain!' cried Ursula, nodding to Miss Peabody.

Suddenly Norah gave a scream as Miss Peabody brought the cane down across her belly – just above Emma's nodding head. Desperately, Norah tried to turn over, to get away from the terrible cane, but with her ankles secured to the bottom bedposts there was nothing she could do except wait for the next stroke, her eyes fixed on the raised implement. Oh, the shame of being beaten in front of her niece! Meanwhile Emma's little tongue was driving her on to greater and greater delights.

'Stop, Emma,' cried Ursula. She paused. There was a little gasp of disappointment from Norah as, just as she was at last about to climax, the exciting little tongue was removed.

'Are you ready for the cane again, Norah?' laughed an excited Ursula, holding Ingrid's head to her loins under her negligée. 'The cane and the tongue. You can't have one without the other! Well?'

Oh, the embarrassment of all this happening in the same room as her niece! But her need overcame her shame.

'Yes, yes!' she cried.

Down came the cane, and again Norah screamed and writhed. Seconds later Emma's head was again bobbing up and down between her legs, and at the same time Ursula, overcome by the erotic scene, gave another hoarse cry and erupted into the eager little mouth of Ingrid.

* * *

Next morning Ursula raised the curtain that covered the two-way mirror that looked into the schoolroom.

Three blonde teenagers, all dressed in black gymslips, white socks and flat-heeled shoes, were sitting quietly at their desks, working at sums.

Any suggestion that they might really be a little old to be dressed in such girlish attire was cleverly hidden by make-up and the effect was completed by each of them having her long blonde hair plaited into schoolgirl pigtails.

The girl sitting on the right was proudly wearing a red ribbon tied in a pretty bow around her neck to show that she was the head girl of the class.

As Ursula watched, Miss Peabody called the girl on the left up to write her answers on the blackboard. There was a close similarity between her and the head girl – they might have been sisters. How amusing it was, Ursula thought, to have a pretty aunt and her niece to play with, together with another grown-up girl, Emma, who was also having to pretend she was a schoolgirl. And the fact that they were all so jealous of each other made it all the more exciting – as did the idea of the niece now coming into milk, though she still scarcely seemed to realise it. Should she, Ursula wondered, have the aunt treated, too?

Perhaps it was time for Doctor Anna to pay a little visit. She could check on how Ingrid was coming along, and get started on Norah!

She smiled approvingly as the aunt reached up to write her answer, disclosing, under her short gymslip, three recent marks of the cane across her naked bottom. Clearly Miss Peabody was standing for no nonsense from her latest charge.

It was all a very arousing sight. Yes, Ursula decided, she would tell Miss Peabody to bring all three of them to her bedroom at rest time that afternoon.

Three young schoolgirls were lined awkwardly at the foot of Ursula's bed. They were all wearing identical long cotton nightdresses. Each of them had been allowed to take her hair out of its pigtails and brush it down her back.

'Thank you, Miss Peabody,' said Ursula from the large bed. 'They look very nice and fresh. You can leave them all with me now.'

As the door closed behind the governess, Ursula turned to the girls. 'Now, all of you, turn and face the wall and when you hear your name called, run over to the bed and use your imagination to show how much you love your Mistress. There'll be a prize of a little sweet for the best girl and the worst one will get a note to Miss Peabody.'

A note to Miss Peabody! Emma's heart sank as she turned to face the wall. She could imagine what that would mean – six strokes of the cane for laziness!

'Norah!' she heard Ursula call out.

The girl standing next to her turned and ran to the bed. Moments later she heard a slurping noise, mixed with little cries of contentment from Ursula. They seemed to go on forever. Then suddenly she heard her own name.

'Emma!'

Quickly, she too turned and, remembering to keep her arms out straight and her fingers outstretched, ran to the bed. Ursula was lying on her back, her satin negligée open, her long slim body exposed and her beauty lips hidden by a mass of blonde hair – not for her the depilated look that she imposed on the women in her service!

Norah was kneeling between Ursula's legs, her head bowed and bobbing up and down. As Emma approached the bed, she saw Ursula kick poor Norah down to the foot of it.

'Suck my toes!' her Mistress ordered harshly.

Then she reached up and, grabbing Emma by her hair, pulled her down between her legs.

'Now let's see what a trained licker can do,' she said.

Emma thrust her tongue between Ursula's beauty lips, seeking out her beauty bud whilst Ursula still held her down by her hair.

'That's good, little Emma!' she heard Ursula say. She gave her tongue an extra little sideways wriggle in grateful acknowledgement of her Mistress' praise. Then to her dismay she heard Ursula call out, 'Ingrid!'

To her surprise, Emma was not kicked down to join Norah at the foot of the bed. Instead her head was still held firmly in place. She saw Ursula blindfold Ingrid, and then slip off her nightdress before making her kneel down at her side, her milk-laden breasts hanging down over her Mistress' mouth. Emma saw that Ursula was now alternating between squeezing and releasing Ingrid's nipples with one hand and tickling her beauty bud with the other.

Was Ursula, Emma wondered, getting the blindfolded girl to associate letting down her milk with sexual excitement – or even with relief? Lucky girl, she thought jealously, for just then she would have given her right arm to have her beauty bud tickled by her Mistress.

'Oh!' cried Ingrid. 'Oh!'

How unfair, thought Norah, as she glanced up and saw what was happening. Was her niece mysteriously coming into milk to please her Mistress? But how? Might Ursula have her done too?

'Norah! Come here and kneel up on the other side – and offer me your breasts too.'

Oh, how cruel it was, thought Norah as Ursula switched between sucking one of Ingrid's nipples, from which little white drops could be seen emerging, and then one of Norah's fuller but dry teats. Oh, the excitement when she felt Ursula's tongue on her nipples.

'And would you also like to be able to offer your milk to your Mistress?' Ursula whispered teasingly into Norah's ear. Ingrid, still innocently unaware of just what was happening, could not hear.

'Oh! Oh yes, Madam,' Norah could not help crying. There, she'd said it. 'Oh yes, Madam.'

'Very well, then,' laughed Ursula. Then, speaking again in a little whisper, she added, 'I'll tell Doctor Anna to see to it. She's coming here on a short visit next week. Soon we'll have a little competition as to which of you can give your Mistress the more milk, and the sweeter!'

Next week, thought Emma, as she strained to keep her tongue working hard. How lucky that she would have left by then! She knew only too well that by then, as had already happened with Norah, the temptation for her to beg to be treated by Doctor Anna would be almost irresistible.

Ursula lay back. Oh, the sheer bliss! Emma's little tongue on her pleasure bud, the taste of Ingrid's milk, and the sight of Norah's lovely breasts swaying in front of her eyes – all were competing to bring her to a peak of ecstasy.

How brilliantly she had succeeded with the aunt and her niece. What a clever idea it had been to bring Emma over whilst she was seducing the aunt. And now here they were, all three of them, each desperately trying to outdo the others in giving her pleasure. This was indeed the life!

It was bathtime that evening and three young girls were happily splashing and giggling in the large bath under the watchful eye of Miss Peabody when Ursula entered the room.

There was a sudden silence and all three girls stood up in the bath, their hands clasped behind their necks in the way in which Miss Peabody had made them practice.

Silently Ursula looked them up and down. They were hers, she was thinking, hers to do with as she pleased! She was particularly pleased to see that the beauty lips of all three of them were now entirely bereft of hair – as befitted women in her charge.

She nodded to Miss Peabody. 'Good! I'll see them when they come to say goodnight.'

It was mid-morning two days later. The three schoolgirls were lined up in front of Ursula's desk in her office.

Miss Peabody had just made her routine morning report. In front of the embarrassed young women, she had recounted the most intimate details of their toilet, telling Ursula whether or not they had eaten up their simple food, together with a detailed review of their work and above all their general attitude.

There was a long pause as Ursula considered what she had just heard. All three of them were trembling. Even Ingrid was worried lest her position as head girl, and hence her relative freedom from the cane, might be under threat.

'Norah,' said Ursula finally. 'I will not stand for any dumb insolence towards Miss Peabody. You are very lucky to have her as your governess – Six strokes!'

'No, please!' Norah sobbed.

'Six strokes!' said Ursula angrily. 'Another word and it'll be eight!'

'All right, but please, not in front of my niece! Please!'

'No, on the contrary, you're going to be beaten in front of her as a lesson to you. And you, Emma, can come and please me under my dress as I watch. And do it well – or you'll get the cane too!

7

Emma Overhears a Strange Conversation

It was towards the end of Emma's stay that she overheard a strange telephone conversation.

All three girls, once again wearing just their printed cotton nightdresses, were silently lying on their little beds in the dormitory, having their afternoon rest.

Ingrid was by now aware of the nature of the strange changes in her breasts, and longed to ask Miss Peabody how it had happened. But Miss Peabody refused to discuss it, saying simply that curiosity killed the cat. Nor had Emma or Norah been any more forthcoming when Ingrid had whispered to them about it, for they had been warned by Miss Peabody not to say a word to her – or they'd get a thrashing. Once she had got used to the idea, however, Ingrid was pleased and proud to be in milk.

Miss Peabody was now sitting in her comfortable adjoining room, with the door open so that she could see them all.

She was reading, however, whereas the girls were not allowed to read whilst they were having their rest. They had to lie down, half-asleep, with their hands always where Miss Peabody could see them – above the bedclothes. The punishment, as Emma had learnt to her cost, for being caught with your hands beneath the bedclothes was six strokes of Miss Peabody's cane for 'attempted naughtiness'.

Suddenly the house phone in Miss Peabody's room rang.

All three girls stiffened in their beds. It was what they had been waiting for. Often Ursula felt like having a girl after her lunch. Which one of them was going to be chosen?

'Yes, of course, Miss de Vere, I'll send one of them down straight away. Only one? ... Very well, which one would you like? ... You'd like to keep the aunt and her niece until later on tonight? ... Then I'll send Emma down. ... Yes, straight away. ... You'll send the housekeeper up to the door of the nursery wing to escort her down? ... Yes, I'd rather stay here and keep an eye on the other two. I don't want them being naughty together!'

Emma heard the phone being put down.

'Emma!' called out Miss Peabody, coming into the dormitory. 'Miss de Vere wants to see you. So, up you get and check your pigtails and make sure you look like a pretty young schoolgirl. And aren't you a lucky little girl?'

Ingrid and Norah watched in jealous silence as their governess looked Emma up and down and then, nodding in approval, beckoned the girl to follow her. 'Keep your hands above the bedclothes,' she warned them. 'I shall be back in a moment and I'm leaving the door open!'

The governess took Emma by the hand to the strong main door to the wing and unlocked it. There, standing in the corridor waiting for her, was the housekeeper.

'Go with her, Emma,' Miss Peabody ordered and then turned back through the door. Emma heard it being locked again. Nervously, Emma followed the housekeeper down the stairs like a schoolgirl suddenly summoned to the headmistress' study. Just what had she been summoned to do? She gave a little shiver of fear as she remembered that Ursula kept a cane in the drawing room.

The housekeeper knocked on the door of the drawing room, pushed Emma in and shut the door behind her.

Emma saw that Ursula was sprawled in her favourite armchair. She was wearing a shiny blue housecoat made of heavy satin. It was open down the front. There was a cushion on the floor between her parted feet. Lying on a little table by the side of the chair was the cane – and a telephone.

Ursula was engrossed in a glossy up-market magazine.

There was a picture of a half-naked girl on the cover. Emma recognised it as a German publication which catered for lesbian tastes. Not knowing German, she had never been able to read it, but she had seen the erotic pictures of helpless young women, bound and chained, that illustrated the magazine's stories.

Without looking up or speaking, Ursula pointed down to the cushion.

Scared by the sight of the cane, and anxious not to annoy her quick-tempered Mistress, Emma ran over and knelt down on it. She saw Ursula, still enthralled by the magazine, reach out absent-mindedly for the cane. Hastily she lowered her head, thrust out her tongue and began to pleasure her Mistress. She felt a tap of the cane on her bottom, and wriggled her tongue sideways in the way that Ursula so enjoyed. Not a word had been said.

Suddenly the telephone by the chair rang. Ursula put down her magazine and picked up the receiver. Emma could not resist raising her head a little to hear what was being said.

'Hello? Francesca! What a lovely surprise!' Emma heard Ursula say.

She was able, vaguely, to hear a woman's voice on the phone. Whoever Francesca was, she was certainly talking nineteen to the dozen about something very exciting.

Intrigued, Emma paused in her licking to hear better. She heard Ursula say, 'Well, I think it's very clever of you to get hold of her again . . . Yes, I know you sold her for a very good price . . . And now she's back with you again! . . . Yes, these Arab Masters can be very cruel . . .

Arab Masters! What, Emma wondered, could Ursula be talking about?

'Yes, and the higher up they are, the more cruel they can be . . . Yes, no wonder she's happy to be back with you again! . . . Yes, I think a playpen would be a very good idea, I always think they make a pretty sight in a playpen . . . And how clever of you to have found a suitable nanny . . . A proper wet-nurse! Even better . . . Yes, I'd love to come and see Brigetta. What a pretty name.'

Emma's natural curiosity was stretched to its limits. A

playpen? A wet-nurse? For a baby? A baby called Brigetta? She knew how Ursula and her friends were fascinated by pregnant girls. It was as if, through them, they experienced the thrills and pangs of the maternity that they themselves eschewed. It sounded as though this Francesca had such a girl, and was making plans for a forthcoming birth – or, to judge from the talk about a playpen, perhaps one had already taken place. Goodness! How fascinating!

But hang on, she suddenly thought, what was that she had heard about the girl's Mistress getting her back from her cruel Arab owner? She remembered that the Prince had said that the Crown Prince's former girlfriend, Renata, might be pregnant. Could this Brigetta be her baby? No, it was all mere coincidence ...

Suddenly she screamed as the cane came down across her bottom.

'Get on with your work, and don't you listen in to my private telephone conversations,' shouted Ursula angrily.

Quickly, Emma lowered her head again and thrust out with her tongue.

'I'm sorry, my dear, for the interruption,' She heard Ursula say into the telephone. 'I've got a disobedient and inquisitive little girl here. But do go on. She won't hear any more now!'

Emma felt Ursula position her head carefully and then close her thighs to hold her in place. With Ursula's thighs now pressed against her ears she could no longer hear a word of what was being said.

It was a long conversation. It must also have been an exciting and arousing one, for Emma could feel her Mistress becoming increasingly wet and soft, and she periodically tapped Emma's bottom to keep her working with her tongue.

Suddenly, still holding the phone, she erupted into Emma's mouth.

Moments later, she kicked Emma away and closed her housecoat. Cringing at her Mistress' feet, Emma heard a bell being rung and then the housekeeper opened the door. Still speaking on the phone, Ursula waved Emma away, dismissively, with one hand. She then pointed to the door and to the waiting housekeeper.

Feeling like a used whore, Emma ran over to the door with a little sob of disappointment, and allowed herself to be led up the stairs again to the big locked door. The housekeeper pressed a bell.

Whilst they were waiting for Miss Peabody to arrive and unlock the door from the other side, Emma was thinking – not only about the humiliating and anonymous way in which she had had to please Ursula, but about also the strange conversation. Who was Francesca? And who exactly was little Brigetta?

These two questions were still running around her mind as Miss Peabody took her back to the dormitory and put her back into her little bed to continue her rest. She did not dare to ask Ursula, who would just have her thrashed by Miss Peabody for being inquisitive.

It was Emma's last day. Her eyes were still red from crying from the 'farewell thrashing' that Miss Peabody had given her, 'to remember her by'. Oh, it was all so unfair!

What an extraordinary ten days it had been. It had certainly been a totally unexpected 'special project', she told herself – a mixture of shame-making fear and high excitement. Ursula had simply used her to help her achieve her aim of bringing a beautiful aunt and niece willingly under her control – and of using them not only for her physical pleasure, but also for her mental pleasure.

Did she resent being tricked by Ursula into coming to stay? Not really. It was true that she hadn't had much pleasure herself – but then, nor would she have done if she had simply stayed at home. The whole object of the Prince's rings and bar was to make sure that she couldn't play with herself or climax until he returned. But, she had to admit, giving pleasure, or being made to give it, was also pretty exciting

Of course, she was disappointed at not learning anything definite about the missing girl, but being treated as a schoolgirl had been pretty exciting. And at least Ingrid and

Norah had come up and commiserated with her as she lay in pain on her tummy in her little bed after her farewell thrashing. She would miss them! They were, after all, all three of them victims of their own longings to be controlled and disciplined.

To make sure she got away, Emma had repeatedly told Ursula that she had to go home because her husband was coming back soon.

It was a lie, of course, but she did not dare to tell Ursula about the Prince. Ursula would have had her thrashed, just as the Prince would, if he ever learned about Ursula.

She was certainly living dangerously! How exciting!

8

The Prince Returns

Emma peered down through the bars of the attic window, anxiously trying to catch a glimpse of the Prince as he stepped out of his car.

Yes! There he was – dressed like a fairytale Arab Prince with a gold-threaded black cloak over his long white robe, and a gold rope around his white headdress. Yes indeed, there he was with his tall, slim, virile-looking figure, his pointed beard, his hawk-like nose and his cool, piercing eyes.

Oh, what a thrill! She could feel herself becoming moist with excitement. Women's bodies were lovely and soft, but there was nothing like a man! All the more so when the man was a cruel and ruthless brute of a man like the Prince, with his irresistible aura of wealth, and his veneer of Western sophistication – a veneer that lay lightly over his Arab attitude of unchallengeable male superiority.

Or, she laughingly asked herself, was it simply that he had the key to the padlock that had kept her beauty lips tightly closed for what seemed to have been weeks and weeks? Oh, how she longed to feel a hard manhood penetrating her again!

For two whole days she had been driven mad by being kept locked up in this small attic room – ever since, two weeks after her return from Ireland, the Prince's private secretary had rung her from London to say that His Highness would shortly be arriving. A car would fetch her the following morning, to take her to his country house outside London to await his arrival.

The Arab chauffeur had been non-committal during the journey. Emma had wondered whether it was because he felt that speaking to a mere woman was beneath his dignity or because he did not like to chatter to a woman who belonged to the Prince. Belonged to the Prince! Yes, the little gold rings, the curved bar and the tiny padlock that held it in place all reminded her of that fact.

Similarly, the two monthly allowances, paid in advance, had also reminded her that she was the Prince's kept woman. They had been paid into an account in her name at Harrods, and eagerly, she had embarked on a spending spree. Her status as a kept woman had been further underlined when she had received a letter from a Swiss bank saying that future monthly allowances would be paid into an account at their bank in her name. However, they warned her that they had received instructions to keep each payment on deposit for three months before releasing it to her – if the Prince authorised the transaction. She might, she realised, be the Prince's prize paid whore, but she was still under his strict control!

The Prince's large country house was set in beautiful grounds and enclosed by a high wall. An electronic security gate ensured that only approved visitors could enter. Emma had seen little of the house, for the car had driven up to a back door and she had then been taken, in a special lift, up to the top floor, by a silent, sallow-skinned man dressed in a long white Arab robe and white headdress. He did not, it seemed, speak English and had merely smiled at her anxious questions about the Prince's arrival.

He had led her out of the lift and into a corridor. At the end of the corridor, apparently leading to the rest of the house, was a massive door, strengthened with iron bars and fitted, she saw, with an electronic lock. It rather reminded her of the door in the Prince's palace, the door that had led into the harem.

The Arab had courteously shown her into a comfortably furnished bedroom. She saw that it, too, was fitted with an electronic lock – on the corridor side only. The Arab had smiled, turned, and silently left the room, shutting the door behind him. She ran to it and tried the handle – it was locked.

She turned to the windows and saw that they were all barred. Once again she was struck with the similarity to the Prince's harem.

Other similarly dressed Arabs had silently brought her light meals and a number of pills which seemed to have no noticeable effect on her. Indeed, she seemed to be the only woman in a household which was entirely male, just as Ursula's had been entirely female.

The only pictures in the room were a large photograph of the Prince in Arab dress hanging on the wall facing the bed, and another, smaller one on the dressing table. They would, she knew, ensure that he was never out of her thoughts whilst she was locked up in this room.

However, she had been thrilled when she had found, hanging in a wardrobe, a selection of lovely dresses, suits and nightdresses. Eagerly, she had tried them on. Oh, how they really showed off her blonde beauty and long legs! She was wearing one of them now. It was a white suit of shot silk with a tight fitting jacket, which showed off her slim waist and ample cleavage, and a wide skirt. To match them she wore a pair of white high-heeled shoes. She looked yet again in the mirror. Yes, she looked gorgeous!

She had been equally delighted to see that on the dressing table was a selection of expensive French scents and make-up. Oh, how lovely! She was, she knew, now irresistible!

The small bedroom had a bathroom off it, but every time she had tried to explore the rest of the house, she had found that her door was locked.

Astonished, she had seen that high up in the corner of both the bedroom and the bathroom were small, remotely controlled, closed-circuit television cameras. Goodness, she had wondered, would the Prince amuse himself by secretly watching her every movement? There would be no privacy at all.

And now the Prince had arrived!

As she paced anxiously up and down, she heard a slight

humming noise coming from the corner of the room. The television cameras had suddenly come alive, and were following her. They must have been switched on for the Prince. Was he even now watching her? Goodness, what should she do?

I know, she said to herself, I'll show him what I think about being spied on. She turned and faced the camera, which was now pointing directly at her. Then, slowly and very deliberately, she put out her tongue at it.

Moments later she heard footsteps running along the corridor and then the click of the electronic lock. Well, she thought, putting out my tongue at the Prince's television camera certainly got a reaction, all right!

Then she gasped in astonishment as two pretty young men, dressed like pageboys in tight-fitting coats with a long line of shiny buttons, entered the room. She recognised them as the Prince's Romanian white eunuch pageboys, his personal attendants, whom she had last seen in his palace in Arabia.

Quickly, one of them came up behind her and held her hands, whilst the other embarrassingly lifted up her dress, pulled down the silken panties she had found in a drawer in the wardrobe, and inspected the rings and the bar. He also ran his hand over her hairless mound. Thank heavens, Emma thought, she had kept herself as depilated as she was able with her beauty lips tightly compressed.

Apparently satisfied, he said something in what Emma presumed was Romanian to his companion, and let the hem of her skirt fall back down. Without a word, they left the room. Emma heard the electronic lock click again behind them. Had they gone to report their findings to the Prince?

For what seemed like hours, Emma was again left alone in the room. Coming, presumably, straight back from his harem in Arabia, was the Prince too satiated to need her? Was he instead dealing with his English racing affairs? Goodness, might Paddy even now be downstairs discussing racing plans with his employer? Might he even now be secretly wondering if she were locked up in the attic, awaiting the Prince's call?

Suddenly, she again heard footsteps and the click of the electronic lock. One of the pageboys beckoned her out of the room. Eagerly, she followed him out into the corridor and into the lift. The other pageboy followed behind her. Goodness, she thought, she was under close escort!

She was taken into the front of the house and ushered into a large room that was decorated and furnished in a simple Arab style with huge sofas, brass trays on slender tables, and tiled walls. To her surprise there were several Arab men sitting in the room in groups, sipping little cups of Turkish coffee. They had, Emma presumed, come to welcome the Prince back to England. Were they, she wondered, his subjects, fellow racehorse owners or businessmen?

There was not a single woman in the room and her entrance caused quite a stir.

'Why,' she suddenly heard the Prince ask the leading pageboy, in an angry tone of voice, 'is this paid servant woman not wearing proper Moslem dress? Take her away! And scrub her face!'

Paid servant woman! Scrub her face! Poor Emma was overwhelmed. She had spent so much time and thought on making herself look beautiful for the Prince. She stood there speechless until, blushing at the Prince's anger, the two pageboys gripped her arms and rushed her out of the room and back up to her own room.

Once there, they took off her suit and underclothes and replaced them with an even more revealing costume. This consisted of half-transparent silken harem trousers, and a stiff embroidered bolero that did not meet at the front, so that her nipples were peeking cheekily around its edges. Her arms were covered by long black silken gloves, and her feet were encased in little Turkish slippers. She had been transformed into an Arabian houri!

She blushed as she saw that the voluminous silken trousers were cut away in front giving, as she moved, occasional glimpses of the golden rings and curved bar that guarded her beauty lips.

Then, to her dismay, the pageboys produced an ugly,

tight-fitting cotton chador that went over her head and down to below her neck. It covered her entire head except for a small cutaway strip over her eyes, and even this was divided in half by a piece of black elastic that ran down from the bridge of her nose to hold the chador in the correct position. Her lovely blonde hair, smooth forehead, cheeks, ears, mouth and chin were all completely hidden.

These chadors, thought Emma, made women look strangely alike and almost featureless – as indeed they were intended to do.

'We thought you had special permission to wear English clothes,' explained one of the pageboys in halting English. 'When Prince with Arab friends you must always wear chador and long robe.'

He draped over her a shapeless black robe that came down to her ankles. Emma looked in the mirror. She saw that she now looked just like one of those anonymous, veiled Arab women whom she had seen in Earls Court, shuffling along behind an Arab man. She wondered were they too dressed, under their hideous black robes, in an excitingly revealing harem costume?

Next the pageboys rubbed off her eye make-up carefully leaving on her rouge and lipstick, which would, of course, be hidden under the chador.

But still the pageboys had not finished eliminating from view anything about Emma that might interest a watching male. They made her put on ugly black leather boots to hide her ankles, and thick black gloves to hide her silk-clad hands.

'You lucky Prince not make you wear this,' one of them said, holding up another chador that would completely cover the face, except for a narrow strip of black lace over the eyes. 'Because you here in England, Prince not make you hide all face behind veil.'

Again she was taken downstairs and into the room in which the Prince and his visitors were sitting. This time he nodded in Emma's direction, and waved her away to a corner of the room. Here she was left to stand alone, except for one of the pageboys who stood by her side, gripping her arm. She now noticed that none of the men was so much as glancing at her. Dressed as she was, she was simply a non-person.

'You keep eyes lowered,' murmured the pageboy. 'You wait like Arab paid whore for Prince to finish his business!'

At last, one by one, the Prince's guests left. At last she was left alone with him – except, inevitably, for the pageboys.

The Prince looked up. He snapped his fingers. The pageboys removed the black shroud. The Prince laughed at the sight of Emma who was, from the neck downward, the epitome of Eastern eroticism, but equally the model of rectitude from the neck up.

'All right!' he cried. 'Paint her up again and let's have that ghastly chador off!'

One pageboy lifted off the ugly chador, and turned Emma round to face his companion who produced from his pockets the hairbrush and cosmetics from Emma's bedroom. Two minutes later, they turned Emma around again to face the Prince. Her long blonde hair hung down glistening, her blue eyes sparkled, her cheeks were gently rouged and her lips were painted scarlet.

'Yes,' said the Prince reflectively, stroking his beard. 'Yes, that's better, much better!'

He beckoned the two pageboys to bring Emma forward so that she was now standing right in front of the sofa on which he was seated. One of the boys held Emma's hands behind her back and the other, gripping her hair, pulled her head back so that her belly was thrust out towards the Prince. Emma could not now see down properly, but she felt the Prince's hands part the slit in the front of her diaphanous trousers. Seconds later she felt them brush the rings on her beauty lips and then reach down to feel the little padlock.

She felt like a prize heifer being inspected by a buyer. She longed to cry out, to say that she was so glad that her Master was back, and that she longed to serve him. But with her head stretched back, she could hardly speak. 'I – I . . . Master,' was all that she could get out.

Oh, how she longed for a kind word from the man in whose power she was. But all she heard was the Prince saying to his pageboys, 'Good! Now here's the key. Wash her out and get all the remaining hair off her. Then bring her to my room – and get that bar polished up and put back in place again.'

As she was taken out again, Emma realised that the Prince had still not yet addressed a single word to her.

Half an hour later the pageboys brought Emma, now wearing just her harem trousers, and with her bare nipples entrancingly painted scarlet, to the Prince's large bedroom.

She was marched up to stand, waiting, at the foot of a large four-poster bed. The curtains at the bottom of the bed were parted. She noticed that the bedclothes were not tucked in at the bottom of the bed. She caught a glimpse of the Prince lying in the bed, wearing a silken sleeping robe, his head half-hidden behind a book. She could feel herself becoming moist with excitement and anticipation.

Then, looking down, she caught sight of what seemed to be a leather dog collar lying on the floor by her feet. It was, she saw, attached to a dog lead that disappeared up between the bedclothes.

'Keep your head up,' whispered one of pageboys. Nervously, Emma looked straight ahead at the wall above the head of the bed.

Then the pageboys pulled down her harem trousers. Shyly, she put her hands over the now gleaming bar – it had been temporarily removed while they had depilated her beauty lips and had then, as the Prince had instructed, been polished before being locked back in place again.

'Hands to your side,' whispered the pageboy.

Blushing with shame, Emma stood to attention in silence for what seemed like hours, wondering when the Prince was going to deign to notice her and put down that damned book! Then, suddenly, she heard him snap his fingers.

'Kneel down,' whispered one of the pageboys urgently, 'and on all fours.'

She felt the leather collar being fastened around her neck. The bedclothes at the foot of the bed were lifted up. She could see the chain lead – now her chain lead – disappearing up between them. Suddenly her head was thrust in between the bedclothes, and then they were dropped down again. Her head was in darkness.

Still kneeling on the floor, she recognised the scent of the unguents which the Prince used on his well-kept body.

Silently, she waited. And waited.

Suddenly she heard the Prince snap his fingers again. She felt the two pageboys reach down behind her and unlock the little padlock hanging between her legs. She blushed again in the darkness, as she felt the curved gold bar being gently withdrawn. Suddenly, her moist but tightly compressed beauty lips were free. She could feel them opening like a flower in the coolness of the bedroom.

Then she felt a podgy hand delicately tickling her beauty bud. Oh, the excitement! Then, as if she were not already soaking wet, she felt another podgy hand rubbing a little oily cream up inside her. She had been made ready for the Prince – ready to be penetrated for his enjoyment!

Then the hands were taken away and there was silence. She could imagine the two pageboys bowing to their Master – to her Master. She heard their footsteps going away and the sound of the bedroom door closing behind them.

She was alone with the Prince – alone at last! The thrilling feeling of anticipation was now overwhelming. She caught her breath under the bedclothes. Memories of Ursula, of the house in Ireland and of Miss Peabody now seemed very remote and unsatisfactory. Oh yes, this was what life was all about – kneeling naked and helpless at the feet of a rich, cruel and ruthless man!

Once again, she waited and waited, her head still in darkness under the bedclothes.

Suddenly she felt herself being drawn up by the chain attached to her collar. Eagerly, she put out her tongue to lick the Prince's manhood, but her head was drawn up further. Soon she was in the fresh air again, her head on his shoulder.

She cried out with joy, but almost immediately felt the Prince's bearded and moustached lips on her mouth, and at the same time his strong hands on her breasts. Oh, the excitement! Oh, how different this felt to the touch of Ursula's soft, womanly skin and hands. Vive la différence!

Moments later she cried out again, as the Prince moved down to suck her nipples. Then she felt his hand brushing aside the golden rings and finding her beauty bud. Happily, she snuggled up to him and licked him under the chin.

She dropped her hand and found his strongly erect manhood. Oh! Oh! Moments later she found herself flung onto her back as the Prince held her down and forced his way into her. Oh, the thrill! Once again she found herself reaching up to lick his chin and then bringing her parted legs up over his back so that he could drive deep, deep down into her.

It was not long before she screamed with delight as she felt his seed gushing into her.

'Master!' she cried. 'My Master! . . . Oh . . .!'

9

The Stallion

'I'm taking you with me today to a rather special event,' said the Prince, with a winning smile.

'Oh, how exciting!' cried Emma, thrilled that her beloved Prince, her cruel and dominating Master, wanted her company. 'Where are you taking me?'

She never seemed to know where they might be going next. Sometimes it was to a race meeting where one of the Prince's horses was running and where the Prince would be entertaining his friends in a private box. Sometimes it would be to go shopping in Harrods or Jermyn Street, for the Prince was a well-dressed man. Sometimes it would be to visit his trainer, Paddy, in which case Emma and Paddy would both be careful to treat each other as purely platonic acquaintances.

She was used to travelling incognito with him, as one of his entourage – the only female member of it. Then she would have to wear the black chador, the shapeless black robe, the ugly black boots and the thick black gloves.

On these occasions she was, to the outside world, just another uninteresting looking Arab woman walking respectfully behind her man. It was all rather shame-making and when she saw friends at race meetings, she was delighted that they did not recognise her. How astonished they would be to know that under the black shroud was a white woman, dressed in the height of fashion – or occasionally, to indulge the Prince's whims, dressed in transparent harem clothes.

She was never allowed to speak to a man. She was generally ignored. She never travelled in the same car as the Prince and was accompanied everywhere she went by at least one of the pageboys. And always, before they left, a pageboy would embarrassingly check that her golden bar was still firmly locked in place.

Back in the Prince's house she would be locked up in her room again, never knowing when the pageboys might come to take her to please the Prince.

Why did the Prince bother to take her around with him, she often asked herself. But, of course, she already knew the answer – power! It clearly gave him a great feeling of power to have a beautiful white woman traipsing along behind him, forbidden to speak to anyone other than the pageboys, and guarded at all times by them. This feeling of power was further heightened by his keeping this beautiful Irishwoman hidden from the public gaze – hidden for his own private enjoyment.

But this degrading treatment made it all the more wonderful when the Prince was visiting the houses of English friends. Then she was allowed off the hook. She was able to shed her black shrouds, to appear in the lovely dresses and suits that hung in her wardrobe, to talk and laugh with other men, and to feel that the Prince was enjoying showing her off.

She and the Prince would occasionally exchange glances across a room, and always she would be reminded that in his top left-hand pocket was the key to the padlock that kept the golden bar in place. He in turn would be thinking how delightful it was to have control, secretly, over the sexuality of such a lovely European creature.

Wherever they might end up for the night, whether it was a hotel, a private house or, more usually, back at the Prince's own large country house outside London, there was always the likelihood that he would send his pageboys to unlock the little padlock and prepare her for his pleasure. Then, beautifully made-up and wearing a scarlet silk negligée that set off her pale skin and blonde hair, she would be draped from head to toe in a black shroud – for, except when staying with European friends of the Prince, it was the rule that she must always be hidden under a shroud when taken out of her room.

Gripping her by the arms as if to prevent her from escaping, the two pageboys, one on either side of her, would lead her to where the Prince was waiting for her. There, trembling with excitement under her shroud, she would often be kept waiting standing in a corner of the room whilst he finished a chapter of his book or a telephone call.

Only then would they bring her forward, remove the shroud and draw back her negligée to reveal her naked body to the smiling Prince. Then they would wait for him to toss them the key to the little padlock.

But these were the lucky days for Emma. Often the Prince did not intend to take his pleasure by penetrating her and so the bar was kept locked in place. Her pleasure then came only from the feeling of being his slave forced to excite him. She would feel herself wet and aroused under the bar but quite unable to climax – a fact that increased the mental pleasure for her cruel Master.

Instead, she might find herself kneeling at his feet between his knees, his strong manhood in her mouth and her hands reaching up to squeeze his nipples and thus send little thrills down to his groin until he finally erupted into her mouth. On other occasions she might find herself simply lying alongside him in his bed, once again squeezing his nipples and playing with his manhood, until with a cry of pleasure he reached a climax – a climax that he found all the more enjoyable for knowing that she was being kept frustrated under her golden bar.

She had also learned that the Prince also much enjoyed being licked from underneath, as he half-knelt, half-squatted, over her, looking down on her exciting body and stroking the bar that kept her pure. It was again frustrating, but she derived an intense pleasure from having to reach up with her tongue to please him. The very fact that she was an anonymous slave, her face hidden underneath him, somehow made the frustration all the more exciting.

Oh, the thrill of anticipation as she waited, naked under her negligée, scented and irresistibly beautiful, for the sound of the pageboys' keys in the lock of her door! Oh, the excitement as she waited, wondering whether this time they had orders to remove the little golden bar!

Emma was now well aware that the Prince, like other Arab men, did not normally discuss his private affairs with a mere woman. Nevertheless, it did sometimes amuse him to talk to Emma as a confidante and as someone with whom he could discuss his racing plans.

Even then, Emma soon learnt, she had to be careful not to overstep the mark. Always she had to show great respect and to address him as Master or Sir. On one occasion, when she rashly failed to do so, the result was the pageboys being summoned and told to take her away and give her six strokes of the cane for her lack of respect.

Poor Emma did not know which was worse; the actual pain, the humiliation of being given a formal thrashing by two mere pageboys, or the embarrassment, when she was brought back with her bottom still on fire, at the way in which the Prince had nonchalantly continued with their conversation as if nothing had happened. But never again did she fall into the trap of not treating the Prince as her superior and Master.

'Yes, I'm having one of my fillies brought over from my brood mares' stable,' said the Prince enigmatically.

Emma was intrigued, the Prince had never told her where he kept his brood mares – just that he kept them in secure stables with Arab grooms in charge and a full-time Arab vet in attendance. Clearly the Prince did not entirely trust anyone who was not an Arab and, equally clearly, he wanted to keep his breeding of racehorses private and secret.

'Oh, I'd love to see where you keep your prize brood mares,' enthused Emma.

'Oh, you will, and very shortly, I promise you,' said the Prince, with a rather sinister laugh, 'and today you're also going to see one of my most promising young fillies being covered for the first time – and by a very much sought-after stallion.'

Oh, how exciting, thought Emma. But what did the Prince mean by 'also'? She knew, of course, that brood mares were taken to be covered at the stud at which a stallion was standing. Was the Prince going to take her back to his secret stable of brood mares?

'Which filly will be covered?' asked Emma. She was by now quite knowledgeable about the Prince's racehorses.

'Arabian Slave,' replied the Prince.

Arabian Slave! Yes, what an outstanding runner she had been. Crossed with the right stallion she could well produce a Derby winner. It would be well worth the Prince spending a large sum to get an early nomination for her to a top stallion.

Arabian Slave! She was, Emma remembered, a light grey – almost white – in colour. And what an appropriate name for a filly belonging to the Prince, whether of the four-legged or two-legged variety, she thought ruefully.

'Yes,' went on the Prince, 'I'm sending her to the stud of my racing rival, Sheik Faruk. He hates me but all my bloodstock advisers keep telling me that I must put Arabian Slave to his stallion, Sand King.'

'Sand King!' exclaimed Emma, showing off her Irish knowledge of racing. 'But there's a waiting list as long as your arm for his nominations, and you'd have to pay through the nose!'

'Yes, and I failed to get a proper nomination for him in time. So, as the filly is now in season, I've had to do a special deal with the Sheik.'

'But how on earth did you arrange it? The Jockey Club would come down hard on you both if they thought there was any underhand payment.'

'Oh no, it wasn't a question of money. Not at all!'

'What, then?' asked the astonished Emma.

'Ah, little girl,' replied the Prince with a mischievous and mysterious air, 'that's something that you're going to learn for yourself before the day is done! Suffice to say that Sheik

Faruk drives a very hard bargain, but I've been able to satisfy his little whims. So, thanks to you, we struck a deal and my filly will be covered today – and something else is going to happen there as well!'

'Thanks to me?' cried Emma with a shudder. She had seen the cruel-looking Sheik Faruk at race meetings, always surrounded by a posse of huge, tough-looking, black bodyguards. 'You mean you're going to give me away to him in exchange for his prize stallion covering your prize filly? Oh no! Please, no!'

'No, no, little Emma, I promise I'm not planning to give you away to anyone. I've got far too many special and exciting plans for you!'

Dressed as usual in her chador and black shroud, Emma arrived at Sheik Faruk's stud in the car behind the one carrying the Prince. She noticed that a smart horsebox was also just arriving. In it was Achmed, the Prince's head stud groom and devoted servant – a stern looking Arab who often travelled with the Prince between his stables in England and Arabia.

Moments later the ramp was lowered and the Prince's future prize brood mare, the young thoroughbred Arabian Slave, was led down. The filly was jumping about skittishly. Does she, Emma wondered, have any idea why she has been brought here today? Or for that matter, she laughed to herself, have I any idea why I have?

She saw the Prince being greeted effusively by his arch rival, the fat, waddling, Sheik Faruk, who seemed to be gloating over something, rubbing his hands. Moreover, whereas she was used to being completely ignored in her unbecoming black chador and shroud, now she saw that the Sheik kept glancing at her in a strange anticipatory way.

Knowing that in the Arab world, even here in England, women, like children, were seen but not heard, she kept in the background, escorted by one of the Prince's pageboys. But he too, however, seemed to be looking at her in a strangely anticipatory way.

The pageboy led her up to the comfortably furnished small gallery overlooking the straw-covered mating box and told her to sit down at the back. It was, she knew, a gallery designed, traditionally, in the days when owners wanted to be sure that their precious prize brood mares were covered by the actual stallion for whose services they had paid.

The gallery had remained, though these days, of course, few owners bothered to attend a mating themselves. She supposed that on this occasion, having struck a special deal with the Sheik, the Prince wanted to be sure that the Sheik kept to his side of the bargain – especially as they were such bitter rivals.

Sitting in the front of the small gallery were the Prince and his unsmiling host, the Sheik. Behind each was standing a good-looking white youth. The youth standing behind the Sheik, also wearing the tightly buttoned uniform of a pageboy, had the same smooth and boyish cheeks as the Prince's pageboys.

She noticed him bending down to whisper something into the Sheik's ear. When he spoke, his voice seemed strangely high-pitched, like those of the Prince's pageboys – and under his skin-tight trousers his buttocks, like theirs, were almost girlish. Goodness, did the Sheik also go in for white eunuch pageboys? How terribly cruel!

Emma could never get over the fact that these young European men went, quite willingly to Arabia where there were gelded and then sold to rich Arabs as their personal attendants. White eunuchs had a reputation for being dedicated and loyal servants. Certainly the Prince's ones seemed happy enough serving him, and obviously he had complete confidence in them. Anyway, she thought with a shiver of fear, they were not so frightening or cruel as the traditional black eunuchs who had been in charge of the Prince's harem.

She noticed too that several of the Sheik's burly bodyguards were also eyeing her in, she thought, a rather lascivious fashion, particularly one huge great brute of a man.

Down in the mating box the young filly stood tethered. Achmed was fastening a strong-looking strap around her neck. Two chains hung down from this big strap, each terminating in a smaller strap. Achmed now fastened one of these to each of the filly's hind fetlocks. Then he tightened the chains by turning a little bottle screw in the middle of each of them.

From the days of her country upbringing in Ireland, Emma recognised them as mating chains – designed to prevent a mare being mated from kicking out at the valuable stallion who was going to cover her.

A gelding, known as the teaser, was now led in. Sniffing the scent of the mare's heat he immediately started to take an interest in her, and she responded to him, twitching her hindquarters and whinnying as the teaser sniffed and licked her.

After a while Achmed clapped his hands and nodded to the groom holding the teaser. The filly was now ready for the stallion and the teaser was led out.

The stallion, Sand King, was now led in by the Sheik's stud groom. He made a magnificent sight, his neck proudly crested and his mane flowing. He also quickly picked up the filly's scent, and began nuzzling her. Then things began to move very quickly, and suddenly the Sheik's stallion duly mounted the Prince's filly.

Emma found it a fascinating and even an arousing sight, with its overtones of human behaviour. When it was over, the Prince, to her astonishment, turned to speak to her.

'And now, my dear, as my friend Sheik Faruk has kept his part of our bargain, I must let you keep my part of it.'

10

Covered!

At first Emma had not understood what the Prince had meant. He had specifically said that he would not be giving her to Sheik Faruk. What did he want her to do? She stood up and smiled at the Sheik, who gave a sign to his bodyguards.

Suddenly Emma found herself seized and gagged. Desperately, she looked towards the Prince, expecting him to order her immediate release, but he now had his back to her and was busy talking again to the Sheik, apparently indifferent to what was being done to her.

Screaming under her gag and wriggling in the arms of the brawny bodyguards, she was frogmarched down into the mating box which was now empty except for the Sheik's stud groom. She saw that a strange wooden apparatus rather like an old-fashioned pillory had been set in the middle of the box. She had, however, no time to wonder what its purpose was, for the bodyguards then proceeded to strip her. She looked up to the gallery. Surely the Prince would not allow this outrage? But his gaze was averted as he had now turned round to speak to his pageboy. She saw that the Sheik, however, was looking down at her with a cruel smile.

First her black chador and shroud were taken off, and then her dress was ripped open and her underclothes were pulled off. She now found herself being displayed to the smiling Sheik up in the gallery, stark naked apart from her boots and gloves, and the little gold rings, bar and padlock nestling between her legs.

She must, she realised with mounting horror, be a very erotic sight. But why was the Prince allowing her to be treated like this? Was this part of his deal? And if so, what was going to happen to her?

The Sheik nodded again and his bodyguards led her towards the strange-looking pillory. Her neck was thrust down into a cutaway half-circle and her hands into two smaller ones. Then the top half of the pillory was brought down, holding her prisoner by her neck and wrists.

Desperately, Emma looked around her. She could see up into the gallery, but not behind her, because of the high top of the pillory behind her neck. With her feet still on the ground and her neck and wrists held down in the low pillory, she was, she realised, now bent over invitingly. The bodyguards then bowed to the Sheik, left the box and went back up into the gallery.

Mystified at what was happening, Emma saw Achmed come into the box, look up at the Prince and bow. He said something in Arabic. Then she saw the Prince throw down to him a little key attached to a leather fob. Horrified, she recognised it as the key to the little padlock that kept her gold bar in place.

Achmed moved in behind her, and moments later she felt his hands between her legs as he unlocked the padlock. Then, gently, he slipped the gold bar up through the gold rings. As he did so, she once again felt her hitherto compressed beauty lips open like the petals of a flower.

Oh my God, she thought. No, it can't be true. No!

But then she saw Achmed coming towards her carrying a smaller version of the mating chains that she had seen him put on to the filly before she was mounted.

She felt a leather collar being fastened round her neck just behind the pillory. Then she heard the rattle of the chains being outled back and then felt them being fastened to her ankles. The chains were tightened, making her bend her knees and raise her buttocks, thus opening herself even more invitingly. At the same time, she too would be prevented from kicking back at her mate.

Her mate! Oh no! No! She too was going to be covered

like a mare! She was to be mated as an amusing spectacle for the Sheik – all part, presumably, of the deal on which he had insisted as part of his price for agreeing to let the Prince have his filly covered, out of turn, by his prize stallion.

Watching a European woman being covered like a mare must have been that 'little whim' of the Sheik's that the Prince had said he could satisfy! Yes, he could, using her! But her feelings had not even been considered. She was, in the eyes of these men, just a woman – something to use as required.

Her gag was now removed and she cried out in dismay, but her cries were greeted with laughter by the Sheik.

She calmed down a little when she realised that the Sheik's good-looking young attendant had also entered the mating box. He came up to her and started to stroke her face just as the teaser had nuzzled the filly. He kissed her and reached down for her hanging breasts, playing with them and rubbing her nipples. Soon Emma felt her body reacting – oh, the shame!

But worse was to follow, for as the teaser had done to the filly, so too the young eunuch went behind Emma. She heard him kneel down and again he started to play with her hanging breasts. Then she felt his tongue on her ringed beauty lips. The rings made it feel all the more arousing. Soon she felt his fingers gently find and then stroke her beauty bud.

Oh, the thrill! She could feel her body wriggling excitedly behind the pillory. Oh, but also the shame, too! She could not bear to look up at the Prince.

Then suddenly she heard Achmed clap his hands, just as he had done when he had been satisfied that the filly was ready for her stallion. She felt the eunuch boy's tongue and hands being withdrawn and saw him, his task as a human teaser now completed, go up to rejoin his Master in the gallery.

Now she felt Achmed's hand on her beauty lips. He parted them and thrust a little ball of grease inside her – making her ready for her mate.

But who was to be her mate, her stallion?

She heard the rear door of the mating box being opened and footsteps approaching the pillory which held her. Desperately she tried to look behind her, but the high plank of the pillory behind her neck prevented her from seeing who it was.

Suddenly she noticed that the particularly huge brute of a bodyguard, whom she had earlier noticed eyeing her so lasciviously, was no longer up in the gallery.

She heard someone undressing. She heard the Sheik's excited little giggles of admiration as whoever it was presumably turned, doubtless stark naked, to face the gallery. She saw the Sheik's fingers pointing, most likely to his powerful manhood.

Then she felt hands, strong hands, on her body. She smelt a man and smelt his arousal. Soon this scent made her feel even more aroused than she had been by the attentions of the teaser. Bent over as she was, she could feel the grease, now melted by her own heat, running up inside her, preparing the way.

Mortified, she felt Achmed part her beauty lips for her mate, her unknown mate. Then she felt a huge manhood being thrust into her, stretching her as she had almost never been stretched before.

She could hear her mate's laboured breathing as he moved in and out of her and the slap of his belly against her buttocks. Against her better judgement, her own arousal soon made her push back in time with his thrusts forward – much to the amusement of the Sheik.

'This filly of yours is certainly responding better than the four-legged one did!' she heard the Sheik say humiliatingly to the Prince, but now she was too carried away by own excitement to care. She could feel her own climax building up.

Suddenly, she felt her unknown mate's seed shooting up into her. It was enough to trigger her own orgasm. She gave a little cry of intense pleasure and then, moments later, one of sheer unbelieving disappointment, as she felt the now soft manhood slipping out of her body. She wanted more! But it was not to be.

She heard the Sheik's sardonic laugh and little bursts of applause. How she had hated him! How she hated the Prince! How could her beloved Prince, her Master, have been so cruel as to allow her to be treated so appallingly? She had heard that Arab men were keen on sexual exhibitions, but never had she thought that she would find herself performing in one.

She heard footsteps going down the stairway that led down from the gallery, and then leave the building. Still secured in the pillory she was now left alone with Achmed.

She saw him go to a corner and return with a douche. He appeared to wash her out. Thank God for that, she thought, but had he done it properly? Was it her imagination, or could she still feel the seed of her unknown partner where he had planted it deep inside her? Oh God! But surely, in any case, some of those pills, that the pageboys gave her every day with her breakfast, were contraceptive ones? But were they? It was, she realised, the Prince who now had complete control over her body, just as he had over that of his filly.

It was with these thoughts racing through her mind that she felt Achmed squeezing her beauty lips together again, and then slide the little gold bar down through the now overlapping rings. She heard a little click as the padlock was closed, locking the bar in place. Was her purity just being preserved for the Prince as usual, or was the seed also being locked in place?

Then Achmed picked up what looked like a black chador, but made of thick felt. Quickly, he slipped it over her head, but whereas the chador at least left her eyes uncovered, this one was more like a hood. From the outside she might merely look like a totally veiled woman, with a lace slit over her eyes through which she could peer without being seen. But recessed behind the lace, and in front of her eyes, was another piece of thick black material through which she could not see. There were several tiny holes below her nostrils to allow her to breathe, but she could see nothing at all. She was in darkness. She tried to cry out in protest but found that the thick hood muffled her cries.

Her hands were now freed from the pillory and tied behind her back, and then Achmed stood her upright. She felt her black shroud being draped over her. Unable to see where she was going she let Achmed guide her out of the mating box and out into the yard.

She felt herself being guided up what seemed to be a wooden ramp and then along a wooden floor. Then she heard a little whinnying noise alongside her. She was in a horsebox! It must be the Prince's horsebox, the one in which Arabian Slave had been brought to be covered. Now, both covered, both drenched with the seed of their mates, they were being taken – where? And why was she being treated like a filly?

She felt a headcollar being strapped over her head and round her neck. It seemed to be fastened to the side of the horsebox. She heard the noise of a partition being closed, then there came a thump as the ramp was raised and the bars were fastened in place. She heard the noise of a padlock being closed. Goodness, security was certainly tight! Was it only because of Arabian Slave – or was it also because of herself?

She remembered what the Prince had said about having special and exciting plans for her. My God, was one of them to have her covered and treated as a filly – as a pony girl? Was that the real reason why the Prince had brought Achmed with him to England?

She heard the engine of the horse box being started and felt it moving off. Now where was she being taken – and why?

11

Stabled!

At last the lorry stopped. Emma heard Achmed's voice – talking in Arabic to a younger man. She heard the ramp being unlocked and lowered. She heard them enter her part of the horsebox.

She felt her headcollar being untied, and the partitions being opened. She gave a little encouraging moan from under her hood. She wanted them to treat her kindly. It was answered with a little whinny from Arabian Slave and a stable lad's laugh.

She let herself be led down the ramp. She could hear the filly following her down it. She tried again to peer down through the little holes in the hood over her nostrils, but still she could see nothing. She felt herself being led across a concrete yard and into a building. There was the familiar pungent smell of stables. She could not make out what was happening to her, but then suddenly she was stopped and made to step up into something.

Emma felt her rope headcollar being taken off. Instead a thick leather collar was fastened around her neck. There was a clanking noise as if it were attached to a thick chain. She could feel its weight dragging on the back of the collar.

Her heavy boots were taken off and she felt cobblestones beneath her feet. Where was she? Why had she been brought here? Then she felt gloves being strapped on to her hands. They seemed strange, with the fingers all sewn together and only the thumb free, making it impossible for her to use her fingers. Then her now-helpless hands were unfastened from behind her back.

She felt the thick shroud being slipped off her shoulders. She shivered at the realisation that she was now barefoot and stark naked, except, it seemed, for her hood, and for the collar and the gloves. And, she remembered, blushing, except for the rings and gold bar which now held her beauty lips as tightly compressed as they had done before her mating.

Her mating! She felt so ashamed at what had occurred earlier at the Sheik's stud. It had been as awful as it had been arousing. She had been covered, in the same way as the Prince's young filly – and in the same mating box.

And this had happened in front of the Prince and his rich Arab rival racehorse owner – for the Sheik's amusement. And all just as payment for a special nomination – or, she thought bitterly, was it also a chance for the Prince to show off his power over a helpless European woman?

And now what?

She felt a short, rough jute rug being strapped over her shoulders. Then her thick felt hood was lifted off. She blinked in the sudden unaccustomed light.

She was facing, she saw, the brick back wall of what seemed to be a narrow stall, some four feet wide and six feet long. On either side of the stall were wooden partitions some six feet high. The stall seemed to be inside a well-lit barn-like room with a high ceiling, like a stable block. A curtain had been drawn behind her, across what must, she realised, be the front of the stall. She wondered what was beyond the curtain.

Then there was a rustling noise from behind the wooden partition on one side of the stall. To her astonishment, a horse's head appeared over it, looking at her. It was her friend, Arabian Slave, the filly who had also been covered that day. What was going on? Where was she? Was she in the Prince's secret stable complex for his brood mares?

Before she could say anything Achmed and an Arab youth, presumably the stable lad she had heard talking when she and the filly were being unboxed, thrust a rubber bit into her mouth.

'No talk in stables!' muttered Achmed in his broken English.

Emma saw that the bit was part of a cleverly designed bridle that went over her head and was fastened behind her neck. She felt a flat piece of stiff rubber, attached to the bit, pressing down on her tongue. It served both, she realised, to keep her silent and to prevent her, as with real horses, from avoiding the bit by getting her tongue over it,

The two Arab grooms stood back and admired their new charge. Emma tried to unfasten the bridle but found that her cunningly designed new gloves prevented her from gripping anything. The two grooms laughed cruelly at her efforts.

Emma now looked about her. She tried to scream in horror, but again, thanks to the bit, all that came out was a little moan. Then she gasped when she saw, fastened to the wall, high up at the back of her stall, was a nameplate which read, IRISH SLAVE.

She saw she was wearing a pretty cape, fawn-coloured with red and black stripes, and made of horse blanket material. The Prince's crest was embroidered on the right breast and the cape was fastened by a leather strap around her throat. It opened down the front, revealing her breasts, and was cut away at the bottom to expose her ringed beauty lips. At the back it finished just above her buttocks. It must, she realised, make a very pretty and erotic sight.

The other end of the heavy chain fastened to the back of her collar was secured to a ring set halfway up the wall at the back of the stall. It was about six feet long – long enough to allow her to stand up or lie down, and to come to the front of the stall when called. Its mere weight would, she realised, serve to exercise her muscles constantly whenever she was standing up.

Next to the ring holding the chain was a mirror. It was placed, she saw, so that a groom inspecting her as she stood at the front of her stall could also see the back of her body. She peered into the mirror and gasped at what she saw.

A strap ran down across her forehead and divided on the

bridge of her nose into two cheek straps, each of which was joined to a small ring at one end of the rubber bit. Inside the metal rings, just as she had often seen on real horse bridles, were flat rubber ones which would protect the corners of her mouth from being rubbed.

From the metal rings, two more thin leather straps ran back and were fastened behind her neck. Another two were fastened tightly to what looked just like a horse's curb chain and which, as with a real horse, went under her jaw. These all combined to hold the bit and its tongue piece firmly in place – thus muzzling her very effectively. Try as she might she could not spit out the bit, nor relieve the pressure pushing down her tongue, which ensured that she was reduced to the level of a dumb animal.

She saw in the mirror that the beautifully polished bridle was set off by several long, bright red plumes attached to the top of the strap that went over her head. The plumes swayed to and fro with every movement of her head. How beautiful they made her look, she thought proudly.

But, she realised, just as a groom has to comb a horse's mane and use a body brush to keep its coat gleaming, so she, too, would be dependent on a groom to keep her hair neatly combed under her bridle and her body clean and healthy.

The stable lad tapped Emma on the shoulder and pointed to a drinking trough on one side of the stall. She would, she realised, be able to suck up water without needing to have her bit removed. Then he pointed to a feeding trough on the other side. She saw that it already contained a small feed of muesli-like oats floating in milk, and realised that she would be able to suck up this food too.

Now he pointed down to the floor of the stall. She looked at it and saw that the cobblestones sloped slightly down to a little channel which had been cemented into the centre of the floor. Shocked at the channel's obvious purpose, she saw it ran down to the front end of the stall where the curtain was hanging, and disappeared under it. Where to? she wondered.

She saw that straw had been pushed back to the walls of the stall. Presumably, Emma thought with a little tremble, it would, when spread over the cobblestones, serve, as in a real stable, as bedding. Then the boy pointed to a small pile of straw in a corner of the stall. It had been arranged in a little circle like a bowl. Emma blushed as the boy explained its purpose.

'Your droppings – here,' he said. Like Achmed's English his was rudimentary and crude, but his meaning was only too clear – and humiliating. Then he pointed back to the cobblestone floor of the stall. Waving an admonishing finger, he added, 'Not there!'

Emma gasped. She was being treated just like a horse or pony! But why?

Achmed and the stable lad now pulled back the curtain at the end of Emma's stall. She caught her breath as she saw that it faced, across a lowered passageway, a line of stalls just like her own. She could see the hindquarters of various horses in several of the stalls. She must, she realised, be in the secret stable where the Prince kept his valuable brood mares.

What had really caught her attention, however, was that in between the stalls holding the horses – in two stalls opposite her own – were two young women. Their stalls, like hers, were narrower than those of the horses and were raised some two feet above the passageway. Was this, she wondered, to allow the grooms easier access to the women's bodies? Once the woman was standing or kneeling at the front of the stall, a groom standing in the passageway would not even have to bend down to examine her. How shame-making!

Both women were dressed, like Emma, in short capes made of rough jute, like horses' stable rugs, and each, like her, was chained by the neck to a ring at the back of her stall, to prevent her from escaping. Each had also, like her, been bitted and bridled – and silenced.

They made an appealing picture as they knelt up on some straw near the front of their stalls and silently looked at Emma across the passageway, their heavy collar-chains hanging down behind them.

She saw that fastened to the rear wall of one of the stalls was a name plate which read ORIENTAL SLAVE. She could also see that the girl in that stall did look half-Oriental, indeed she looked rather like the half-Vietnamese, half-French girl she had seen in the Prince's harem. Surely she could not be the same girl?

With a shock Emma saw that the Prince's crest of crossed scimitars and a star had been neatly and prettily tattooed in red and green on the girl's taut little belly. My God, was she going to have her belly similarly tattooed?

The nameplate in the other stall read POLISH SLAVE. Emma remembered the Prince's liking for Eastern European girls for his harem. Perhaps he also liked them for his stables! The woman was certainly very pretty, with long blonde hair piled up under her bridle and hanging down her neck. She too had the Prince's crest tattooed on her belly, but it seemed a little larger than on the Oriental girl's and strangely stretched. Was it her imagination, or was the girl's belly distinctly swollen.

Goodness, she thought, has this girl, too, been covered? But where and when? And why? And if this was the Prince's special stable for his brood mares, did he also use it for his two-legged fillies in foal? She remembered her doubts in the mating box. Was she herself now in foal? Was this the fate that the Prince intended for her? Was that why she was here? Oh no!

She saw the girl smile as she looked down proudly at her belly. Obviously she was happy to have been put into her present state for the Prince. If the same was being done to her, Emma wondered, would she too be proud? Would it be just the maternal instinct taking over, or would she, as was apparently the case with Polish Slave, be thrilled to be serving the Prince in a new way? And if, in her case, it was all imagination, would she be relieved, or perhaps secretly sad?

She saw Achmed and his young assistant groom disappearing down the passageway. Then the lad reappeared with a stiff stable broom in his hand and started to sweep up any straw that might have dropped into the passageway from the raised stalls.

She went to the end of her open stall and looked down.

It, too, was raised up nearly two feet from the passageway. She saw that a little rubber flap stuck out from end of the channel running down the centre of the stall to enable any liquids to trickle down into the usual open stable drain, which ran down each side of the lowered cobblestone floor of the passageway like a gutter.

She saw that another, older Arab groom was now sweeping straw into the open drains on the far side of the passageway, whilst another Arab lad did the same on her side. Then, with their sturdy brooms, they swept the drains clear, down to the end of the passageway. Was the older groom normally in charge of the Prince's brood mares when Achmed was away in Arabia? Was the lad another member of his staff, like the lad who had seemed to be in charge of her? Did the Prince only employ Arabs in this stable for security reasons? Certainly, it held some valuable animals – and valuable women!

The scene reminded Emma of the routine of 'evening stables' when she had worked for a time in a racing stable. How many times had she similarly swept the stable's passageway spotlessly clean before the evening inspection of the trainer himself?

Emma's thoughts were suddenly interrupted by a bell ringing. The two other girls opposite her jumped up and stood at the front of their stalls with their legs apart and their knees bent. Emma saw that their feet were placed neatly astride the rubber lips of their drains, with their toes gripping the edge of the floor of their stalls.

The women's collar-chains were now taut behind them and they were leaning slightly forward to stop themselves being pulled over backwards by their weight. They were looking straight ahead and clasping their gloved hands behind their necks. It was a position that opened their woollen capes, disclosing their firm breasts.

A shocked Achmed rushed down the passageway towards her, pointing to the other two girls and shouting in his poor English, 'Position for inspection! Veterinary inspection! You copy other women! And, this time, Prince coming!'

12

A Veterinary Inspection – and the Prince Explains

A veterinary inspection! How awful! How shame-making! But on hearing that the Prince was coming too, Emma decided that she had better take up the same embarrassing position as the other two women. Perhaps the more obedient she was, the sooner the Prince would take her out of these awful stables and back into his bed!

Out of the corner of her eye, she saw the Prince strolling down the passageway behind Achmed, who was now carrying what seemed to be a rather terrifying carriage whip.

The Prince was dressed in a dinner jacket, as if he were about to go out to eat. The contrast, Emma felt, between his sophisticated dress and her own nakedness – and that of the other two bridled and bitted girls chained in their stalls – was dreadfully humiliating. Even worse, he was accompanied by an Arab man in a white medical gown with a stethoscope hanging around his neck – his Arab vet! Achmed's young assistant was following along behind, pushing a trolley with a large monitor, like a television screen, upon it.

Ignoring the chained girls, they stopped at the stall of Arabian Slave. The Prince was talking to the vet, and to Achmed, in Arabic, and stroking the nose of the prize filly. Clearly, they were discussing her recent mating.

Then he broke off and went across the passageway to

Polish Slave, pointing to her belly and speaking to the vet.

'Belly out for inspection!' shouted Achmed in his broken English, and cracked his whip.

Blushing under her bridle, but with a conceited look in her eyes, the girl proudly thrust her swollen belly right forward over her bent knees and parted legs, leaning back slightly in order to keep her balance. Standing as she was on the edge of the raised stall, her proffered belly was now almost level with the Prince's face.

Then, whilst the girl kept quite still, her eyes fixed straight ahead looking over his head, the Prince reached forward to stroke the swollen tummy. With his finger tips, he proudly traced his now neatly stretched crest.

Then he nodded in agreement as first Achmed and then the vet knowingly cupped the swollen belly in their hands. The vet put his stethoscope to it and listened carefully. Then he took something from the trolley that the young groom was pushing. With the woman still obediently looking straight ahead, he ran it over her belly. As he did so he was pointing at something on the screen and explaining something, in voluble Arabic, to the nodding Prince.

Gosh, thought Emma, they must be using an ultrasound machine to look at the state of the little progeny that the girl was carrying!

The girl lowered her head as if trying to catch a glimpse of what was on the screen.

'Head up!' shouted Achmed angrily, cracking his whip menacingly. 'Eyes to front!'

Clearly, Emma realised with a little shiver of fear, the girl was not allowed to see what she was so proudly bearing. That was not her business. Hers not to reason why, hers but to do and deliver!

The vet now ran his hands down between her parted legs and felt up inside her, saying something to Achmed in Arabic as if advising him of the precautions to be taken to prevent an accident. Then, with the woman still standing stock still and looking over his head, the Prince ran his hands down the muscles of her legs and thighs, and then up over her arms and shoulders, discussing each in turn with Achmed.

Then he stood back. The vet nodded to Achmed.

'Prepare to perform!' shouted Achmed, again cracking his whip.

There was a pause. Emma saw that whilst still keeping her head raised and her eyes fixed ahead, the blushing girl was alternately making little thrusting and relaxing movements with her swollen belly. It was an erotic sight. Suddenly she froze, and Achmed gave an order to his assistant. Emma watched as the boy quickly reached forward and, using both hands, held the woman's beauty lips apart. How embarrassing for the poor girl. But obviously she had been trained to do this. Would Emma, too, be similarly trained to perform to order?

Again Achmed cracked his whip. Seconds later, there was a tinkling noise and, as Achmed and the vet nodded approvingly and exchanged comments in Arabic, a flow of amber-coloured liquid ran down between the woman's parted legs and into the open gutter below her.

Satisfied with his inspection, the Prince moved on to the next stall, that of the half-Vietnamese girl, Oriental Slave. Once again there came the crack of Achmed's whip and the humiliating order, in broken English, 'Belly out for inspection!'

Emma watched with mounting dismay. Was this girl also pregnant? But the ultrasound machine was not brought into action. Instead, the Prince had a long conversation with Achmed and the vet as they felt the girl's firm little breasts and then her thighs and arms – and down in between her legs.

Then, once again, Achmed cracked his whip and gave the humiliating order, 'Prepare to perform!' This time it was the turn of the slight Oriental girl to alternately suck in and then relax her tummy. Then, finding herself ready, she too had to stand quite still whilst the boy groom held her beauty lips apart. Yet again the whip was cracked and, seconds later, a trickle of liquid ran down the open drain on the other side of the passageway.

Then the vet turned to the young assistant groom and

asked him something. With a long, four-pronged pitchfork, the boy expertly reached into the corner of the stall, picked up the now slightly soiled little pile of straw, and brought it back to show to the vet. Emma saw that like her own, it too had been arranged in a little bowl-like shape.

All the men looked down at what was nestling in the bowl and discussed it. My God, thought Emma, even the Prince is being shown the girl's wastes!

The Prince again nodded approvingly, and the wastes were put back into the corner of the blushing girl's stall. Leaving the two girls standing rigidly in the position for veterinary inspection, the Prince and Achmed moved on down the line of stalls holding the prize brood mares.

After a while, Emma saw out of the corner of her eye, as she tried to remain looking straight ahead, the Prince coming back up the passageway, discussing the horses in the stalls on the same side of it as hers. The strain of keeping still in this degrading position, and of leaning forward to overcome the constant backward tug of her heavy collar-chain was tiring her, but she did not dare to move. Was this being done intentionally, she wondered, to improve her muscles – and those of the other two women? But why?

All Emma could think of, as she stood on the edge of her stall with her knees still bent and her legs apart, was whether she, too, would be degradingly ordered to 'prepare to perform'. After the long journey and all that had happened, she was, she knew, longing to spend a penny – but not like that! Not in front of all these people. Not in front of the Prince!

At last the Prince reached her stall.

'Belly out for inspection!' Again the humiliating order. Like the other two girls, Emma now found that she had to lean back slightly to avoid overbalancing forward, but not too much or the heavy chain would have pulled her over backward.

Oh, how she longed to call out to her Master! How she longed to ask him why he had sent her here – what had she done to deserve it? She also wanted to ask him whether there was any connection between her own so-called 'mating' and the present condition of Polish Slave.

As if sensing her concern, the Prince laughed and moved forward to stroke her bridled cheeks and then her breasts and nipples.

'What a very pretty pony girl you're going to make. You and your little friends here are going to make a splendid team for your Master. One has to be blonde, one from the Far East, and one a girl well on her way to expecting a happy event, as we call it.'

A pony girl! Were she and these other pretty girls really going to kept as pony girls? She had read some rather exciting and very erotic novels about pony girls, but had never imagined that she might one day be one herself. Goodness!

'Yes,' the Prince continued, 'I shall be driving all three of you. You'll be pulling a little chariot, like a Russian troika, against another team driven by Sheik Faruk. And the race will be in three weeks' time.'

Three weeks! With her chained up here, Emma wondered, what on earth would the Prince do for sexual relief for three whole weeks?

'It'll be a long race, over a mile. That's forty laps of the large indoor manège. So we've got to get you really fit!'

A race over a mile! Forty laps! That might be all right for a horse, thought Emma, but not for a woman – and especially not if she's pulling a chariot being driven by a grown man.

'And,' continued the Prince, 'if I lose, I will have to pay the Sheik a million dollars for my filly being covered out of turn by Sand King.'

A million dollars! Crikey! No wonder the Prince was taking it all so seriously.

'Yes,' the Prince went on, 'that's what he wanted to charge me for jumping the queue for nominations for his stallion. When I remonstrated, he offered me the services of his stallion free of charge – provided I met two conditions. Of course, he never thought that I'd be able to meet them.'

The Prince laughed. 'The first condition was to be the mating of a blonde society woman, to be provided by me, and to be covered by one of his body guards in his mating box. Thanks to you earlier today, I met that condition!'

Her mating had just been part payment for services of the Sheik's stallion! How she hated the Prince for his callousness! But, she quickly told herself, perhaps she really only half-hated him, for she could feel the thrills running through her body as he almost absent-mindedly rubbed her nipples with his experienced hands. Oh, those wonderful hands! She looked down at him, half in a rage, half understandingly, as he stood in the low passageway.

'Keep head up,' Achmed cried out, cracking his whip. Hastily, Emma raised it again, until she was looking straight ahead over the Prince's head – just as she had seen the other women do.

'The second condition,' went on the Prince imperturbably, 'was a good deal more complicated – a race against his team of pony girls. To prevent any cheating and the use of hefty professional athletes, there's a total weight limit for the whole team and the pony girls must be kept properly stabled for only three weeks before the race – starting now! To ensure that I abide by this rule, and that I'm not giving you any performance-enhancing drugs, his vet can visit my team at any time and, by the same token, my vet can visit his. His vet might even be coming tomorrow – so you've got to learn the ropes quickly.'

The Prince's hands had dropped to Emma's well-displayed beauty lips. Now she was panting as she felt them arousing her even more, as he played with her beauty bud. Desperately, she tried to overcome her increasing excitement. How wicked it was for the Prince and the Sheik to use live girls to make such a callous bet.

'Yes,' the Prince went on, 'I don't suppose the Sheik thought I'd be able, in the short time available, to put together a team of two-legged fillies that would meet his strict criteria. He thought he had me over a barrel! But the team's here! Of course I had you, and the Sheik didn't know about my secret harem of European girls – or that there was an Oriental one there, too. And luckily, I'd decided some months ago to have one of them put into the family way by one of my guards. We have a saying in my country: "A harem without a girl expecting a happy event is like a bowl of fruit without any grapes – dull to look at and dull to enjoy!" And provided that it is clear that the Master is not the father of her progeny, it presents no threat to his legitimate sons.'

A frightening thought struck Emma – did the Prince want, as a precaution, more than one girl in the team to be expecting a happy event? She shivered as she remembered the Sheik's huge bodyguard who had apparently been used on her. Was she also . . .? My God!

Again the Prince laughed cruelly and went on, 'All this may sound a bit callous, but the fact is that the girl concerned soon thoroughly enjoys being the centre of attention and quickly finds herself taking a pride in her swelling belly.'

Emma remembered how, indeed, she had been struck by the proud way in which Polish Slave had displayed her belly.

'So,' continued the Prince, 'I took the risk of bringing over the requisite girls from my harem in my private jet. Of course, they were travelling on Arab passports and disguised as heavily veiled servant girls – and, of course, under the strict supervision of my black eunuchs. They arrived only yesterday. At the airport, they were handed over to Achmed to be brought here, and soon after their arrival at the stables they found themselves bridled and bitted and chained up in their stalls – just like you did!

'I like to boast,' he continued, 'that all the women in my harem enter it voluntarily, and that they're fully aware that they will be mine to do with as I please. Anyway, most women rather like being under strict control, and certainly Ali Efendi who, you will remember, is chief overseer of my harem, makes sure they can't just walk out whenever they want to. And here, in my breeding stud, security is also very tight – as tight as in my harem. Few outsiders know about it. None are let in and none of the inmates can get out. So, there'll be no chance of these two girls being seen or of them escaping – nor of you doing so, either!'

Indeed not, thought Emma despairingly, as she felt the weight of the heavy chain that was fastened to the back of her collar.

'After the race,' the Prince went on, 'they'll be put back into my private plane, handed back over to my waiting black eunuchs, and flown back to Arabia to be locked up in my harem again – as if nothing had happened.'

'But you, I think, I'll keep over here,' he said. 'And meanwhile, you can take your turn with the other two at pleasing your Master.'

Taking her turn with the other two! Furiously jealous, Emma remembered how she had innocently wondered what the Prince would do for sexual relief over the next three weeks. Oh, how naive she had been!

Clapping his hands in a gesture of decision, the Prince nodded to Achmed. Turning back to Emma, he added, 'Now, let's have a good look at this body of yours. It's going to have to work very hard!'

Achmed reached forward and unlocked the little padlock which was now well on display between her legs. Then, as he had done before her mating, he gently lifted the curved bar up from between the little rings. Once again she could feel her previously compressed beauty lips opening up again.

'I don't think you'll need the bar to protect you from other men here in my secret stables,' laughed the Prince cruelly, 'and you're certainly not going to escape. And with those special gloves kept strapped over your fingers, you won't find it easy to play with yourself, but if you're ever caught trying to do so, then the bar will be replaced! I want all your energies devoted to pulling my chariot. Understand?'

Blushing with shame, Emma nodded.

Suddenly there was a crack from Achmed's whip. 'Prepare to perform!' he ordered. 'Hurry!'

Terrified, Emma began to relax her muscles. After the long day and journey, she was indeed longing to spend a penny. It would not be long, she knew. She remembered seeing how the other two girls had stopped wriggling as a sign that they were ready. Oh, the shame! But worse was to follow as she felt the stable lad's hand on her beauty lips.

'Head up!' came the order.

She blushed yet more as she felt her lips being held apart – just as those of the other girls had been. Oh, how awful! Even worse was that now she could not hold out any longer! She gripped her hands behind her neck as, looking straight ahead, she heard a tinkling noise in the open gutter below her.

Then she felt something hard pressing against her beauty lips. She looked down and saw that the vet was collecting her liquid wastes in a specimen bottle!

'Head up!' screamed Achmed. Hastily, Emma looked straight ahead again as she filled the vet's bottle. Was the vet going to check that she wasn't . . .? She remembered the care with which the Prince's pageboys always gave her her special pills every morning – presumably to ensure that she did not conceive. And thank God, she thought, that the little bar had meant that Paddy had been forced to take her in her rear hole.

So were they just making sure? Or . . . She remembered her earlier fears when she had first realised what had been done to Polish Slave. My God, she thought, was this a first early test to see whether or not her own mating had taken? Had the Prince not told her all? Had the Sheik's first condition secretly required it to be a successful mating? How awful! Or were they, after all, just making sure that it had not taken? God! She tried to scream, to demand the truth from the Prince, but all that came out were a few grunts.

Finally she felt the bottle being taken away. Again, for a moment, she heard the tinkling noise in the gutter below her. Then she had finished.

But the vet had not.

First he took her blood pressure and then, to Emma's embarrassment, he ran his ultrasound machine over her belly, just as he had done with Polish Slave. But this time, apparently, no little progeny was showing on the screen. Not yet, anyway, thought Emma nervously.

Then she felt the Prince's hands running down her thighs and legs. She did not dare to look down again. Soon the Prince was feeling the muscles of her belly, of her arms and of her shoulders.

'She's going to need a lot of exercise to toughen up her muscles,' she heard the Prince mutter before apparently repeating it in Arabic to Achmed.

Suddenly she felt him grip her by her hair and turn her head so that she was facing him.

'Yes, my little Irish Slave,' he said, looking her in the eye, 'you and the other fillies are going to be made by Achmed to really strain your guts out to get fit – and to win for your Master. You'll be put on a special diet, and woe betide you if you don't eat up all that's put into your feeding trough. I shall be coming to see how you're getting on. You're going to be made to show, along with the other girls, just how much you really love your Master – by proving to be a really effective troika team, running in step and achieving both speed and stamina. You're going to work really hard for me, aren't you?'

Unable to speak, Emma found herself nodding hard. Everything was explained now and her Master, her cruel, beloved Master, needed her help.

It would be rather exciting to be strictly controlled and treated like a pony girl for a few weeks. But what a terrifying prospect it was too, she thought, as she looked at Achmed's unsmiling face.

'Meanwhile,' she heard the Prince saying as he turned and pointed to the long whip that Achmed was now holding, 'all you're going to think about, and even dream about, is that carriage whip – it's the one I shall be using on the day of the race, and the one Achmed will be using to drive you on and on during your training. It's what's going to ensure that I win the race!'

Emma looked at the long-handled whip with the little knots at the end of its leather tail. She was so absorbed by it that she scarcely noticed that the Prince had turned on his heel and was leaving the stables. He stopped at the door.

'And if I win, I'll buy you a mink coat!' he called out. Then, turning to Achmed, he added, 'That'll make the lazy slut work all the harder, but nevertheless, don't spare the whip!'

He paused at the big locked door at the end of the passageway and turned to Achmed. 'After dinner I think I'll come and use Oriental Slave for my pleasure,' he said, speaking in English, evidently for the benefit of Emma. 'There's a comfortable couch next to the tack room – have her chained down on it!'

Later on, a highly jealous Emma watched as the feathers were taken from the top of Oriental Slave's bridle and she was unlocked from her collar-chain. Instead, her hands were chained behind her back and a lead was fastened to the ring at the front of her collar. Emma remembered what the Prince had said about them having no chance to escape.

Escape or not, Emma's jealousy reached fever pitch as she watched the pretty half-Vietnamese girl being led, naked but still bitted and bridled, down the passageway to offer herself to her Master.

Passing Emma's stall she gave a contemptuous toss of her head. She, she seemed to be saying, and not Emma or Polish Slave, had been chosen by the Master for his pleasure.

13

In Training

Crack! Emma jumped as Achmed's carriage whip cracked just behind her. 'Keep in step,' he warned.

Desperately, she tried to keep in step with Polish Slave who was in the middle of the three women as they ran up and down the large schooling manège – an arena that adjoined the stables.

Oriental Slave, who was on the other side of Polish Slave, was also having difficulty in keeping in perfect step – something that was made more difficult by the blinkers that had been fastened to the bridles of the outside girls, or flankers, to keep them looking straight ahead and to prevent them from being distracted by anything else.

However, as they got more and more used to running alongside each other, keeping in step with Polish Slave gradually came automatically to them. They learnt to take their time from the feel of her body as it touched their own. Indeed, to keep them close together, two straps – very like the straps used to link carriage horses – went from the ring at the front of Polish Slave's collar to the rings in front of the other two women's collars.

'Push!' she now heard Achmed call out from the troika behind her. Again the whip cracked, making her redouble her effort to push, through her immobilising gloves, the wooden push-bar to which the wrists of all three of the women were attached by straps. Several times she had felt the whip across her backside – not hard enough to draw blood, but painful enough to make her desperate not to get another stroke.

Two shafts, one on either side of Polish Slave, linked the push-bar to the three-horse troika, or racing chariot, in which Achmed was sitting, reins in one hand and raised carriage whip in the other.

The reins were attached to the bit rings on either side of Polish Slave's bridle. This ensured Achmed had complete control over her, for the bit was like a horse's curb bit, with a curb chain going under the jaw. A pull on the reins would not only twist the stiff rubber tongue-piece painfully up against the roof of the girl's mouth, but it would also drive the curb chain up under her chin.

But the success of the driver was not only dependent on the way he used the reins. Much of the skill in driving these troikas came from adroit use of the whip. It could be used to make the right-hand outside girl push harder at the bar, when rounding, left-handed, one of the two markers at one end of the arena. Then, applied equally to all three women, it could be used to make them run flat-out down the length of the arena towards one of the two markers at the other end.

Then, if this time the driver decided to round the chosen marker right-handed, the whip would be used to make the left-hand outside girl strain harder at the push-bar to make the troika swing around, neatly leaving the marker to the right, before setting off back down the arena again.

In the actual race the two troikas could round either of the two markers at each end, either left or right-handed, blocking the way of the rival troika or getting away from it, thus making the race all the more exciting – and potentially dangerous for the women.

Emma had learnt to respond to the little tugs given on the reins to steer her towards the chosen marker, and then to indicate which way it was to be rounded. When she was the outside girl she had learnt to anticipate the whip across her back by visibly straining at the bar, and when she was the inside girl to hold back the bar to swing the troika around behind her.

When rushing down the arena from one marker to another, she had, like the two other girls, learnt to lower her head and shoulders so that she could get the full strength of her entire body behind her now straightened arms. In this position the women's breasts would be swinging down below their outstretched shoulders. Emma was also acutely conscious that, in this position, her carefully depilated beauty lips, with their two lines of little golden rings, would be on display to whoever was driving the troika.

When they slowed to round a marker, the women would straighten up again as they steered the push-bar around it, being very careful not to earn penalties by grazing it.

They were not, however, always taken out from their stalls to be harnessed to the troika to practise racing at high speed down the arena or spinning around one of the markers. From his experience with horses, Achmed was a firm believer in the lunge and in varying the pace as a way of inducing both fitness and obedience.

So it was that Emma and the other two girls had found themselves, twice a day, being taken out of their stalls and placed in a single-file line, fastened together by little chains attached to the rings at the front and back of their collars. Sometimes the petite Oriental Slave would be in front, then Polish Slave – still proud of her stretched belly – with Emma bringing up the rear. Sometimes Emma would be the leading girl, with Oriental Slave at the rear.

Still stark naked except for their immobilising gloves, they would be marched along the passageway to the big manège, goose-stepping, with their now straightened legs being raised high in front of them, and their hands straight down by their sides. Here they would be made by Achmed to walk, run or sprint round and round in a circle, but always on the lunge.

Achmed would hold one end of their lunging reins. The other end would be fastened to the inside ring of the leading girl's bit – the ring on her right cheek when they were being made to go round and round clockwise, and the left-hand ring when they had to go round anti-clockwise.

They all soon learnt the Arabic for walk, trot and sprint,

and also just what each order entailed – for Achmed used a special, extra-long carriage whip to flick their bottoms if they were going too slowly, or their bellies if they were going too fast.

To get them fit and better-muscled, as well as making them goose-step when walking, he made them prance with their knees raised high in the air and their hands clasped behind their necks when they were trotting. When cantering, they had to run fast, taking longer strides and using their now bent arms to pound to and fro under their shoulders.

But it was the order 'Sprint!' that they really dreaded, whether on the lunge or harnessed to the troika, for that meant a desperate, short, flat-out rush, driven harshly by the whip.

Clearly, the art of winning pony girl troika races depended, as in real horse races, on not exhausting the animals too quickly and in conserving their energies for a last-minute sprint to the winning line – or rather, in a troika race, for a last effort to round the final marker at high speed and then make a dash for the finishing line. But there was also the need to make several short sharp sprints earlier on to gain the lead, or to hold on to it, so that the leading troika could block the other troika or, even better, disrupt the pace of its women, by suddenly swerving across it and unexpectedly going for the marker it was aiming at. The blocked troika would then be forced back well behind the leading troika.

But the women had always to keep in perfect step, to keep the troika moving quickly and smoothly, with the flanker fillies taking their time from the centre mare and all three being driven on by the whip or held back by the bits in their mouths.

Their breasts would then sway in perfect time, as would the high plumes attached to the tops of their bridles.

Indeed the plumes served as an immediate indicator that a wing filly was not quite in step – and out would flick Achmed's extra long carriage whip, making the unfortunate girl immediately correct her step. The whip would also be brought into play again should the centre mare slightly stumble – she had to concentrate on giving a steady and regular step just as the others had to concentrate on following her lead. Gradually, whether they were practising with the troika or being exercised on the lunge, Achmed was making them move and think as a unit. No longer were they three individual and intelligent young women, but rather a team of broken-in and unthinking animals, obedient to the bit and the whip.

It was all very exhausting and soon Achmed would have them all sweating and blowing just as he did when he was getting a racehorse fit.

It was, Emma realised, making her very fit. She was, though, very glad she was not Polish Slave, for Achmed made no allowance for her swollen belly and growing progeny. How glad Emma was that there was still no sign that she, too, was in the same expectant state. Indeed it looked as though her fears on that first, awful evening in the stables had proved groundless.

Also from his experience with horses, Achmed was a firm believer in strapping and wisping as a way of improving muscular development. Accordingly each girl would find herself, twice a day, being taken into the tack room and strapped down on her belly on a massage couch.

Then he and his young assistants would set to work with their strong hands, body brushes and wisps of hay, massaging the girl's body all over.

Whilst this was being done to her, Emma could not help glancing furtively and jealously at the large comfortable couch in the corner. Upon this, every evening, either Oriental Slave or Polish Slave, still bitted and bridled to keep them silent, were chained down for the Prince's pleasure.

At first she had been surprised at Polish Slave being chosen so often, but then she remembered that in the Middle East there were no inhibitions about a girl in an expectant state. On the contrary, it was considered to be a state that was both normal and desirable. A swollen belly made a girl all the more interesting.

But oh, how jealous she was of them as she watched them being led proudly down the passageway to await their Master. And then it was even worse to see the smug look of satisfaction on the faces, under their bridles, when they returned. If a swollen belly was what turned on the Prince, then she even began to hope that perhaps her mating had taken after all.

As she jealously watched the Prince spending so much more time inspecting Polish Slave than herself, she found herself secretly regretting that she could not thrust forward a swollen belly when the Prince's arrival in the stables was announced by the order, 'Position for inspection!', followed by 'Bellies out!'.

She remembered the Prince's arrogant remark that, in his harem, a girl whom he had mated loved being the centre of attention and soon became proud of her state. Oh yes, she thought, oh yes!

Emma now realised that these stables must be near the Prince's country house, for, accompanied as usual by his pageboys, he was always looking in to see how the three girls were getting on, inspecting them in their stalls, watching them being lunged by Achmed and trying them out in the troika – as well as taking his regular evening pleasure.

There was now a marked difference in the behaviour of the girls as soon as the Prince appeared. No longer did Achmed have to use his whip to make them go faster when harnessed to the troika, or raise their knees higher when prancing around at the lunge. Now they would be straining every muscle to please their Master and so catch his eye. Each would jealously be trying to outperform the others.

Like the other girls, Emma felt the increased mental excitement of being driven by her Master in the troika – of knowing that he was holding her reins and that she was just his plaything, his animal, and that it would be he who would decide which way they were to round each marker.

There was also the embarrassed thrill of knowing that when she bent down to push the troika along faster, it would be to her Master that she would now be displaying her beauty lips with their little golden rings.

She did not know whether to be ashamed or proud when, despite what she was being put through, she could feel herself becoming moist with excitement, and knew that her Master would see the signs of her arousal glistening on her beauty lips in front of him. Were, she wondered jealously, the other two also shamelessly displaying themselves to him in this way?

14

Used!

At last came the day when she heard the Prince say nonchalantly to Achmed, 'Oh, by the way, leave Irish Slave out for me tonight after dinner.'

Emma was thrilled when, with her hands fastened behind her back, it was her turn to be led down the passageway to the tack room. Oh, at last she could, for once, contemptuously toss her head as she passed the two other jealously watching women.

Earlier on, Achmed had made her swallow some mysterious pills, which looked like the ones the Prince's eunuch pageboys had used to give her. Did they mean, she had wondered excitedly, that the Prince would be climaxing inside her?

She was overwhelmed by a feeling of eager anticipation as, still bitted and bridled, she was fastened down on the big couch. Her hands were momentarily freed and then chained to the couch above her head. A huge bolster was placed under her hips, leaving her beauty lips raised and proffered. Then, to her surprise, her ankles were bound, spread wide apart and, with two red ribbons, tied to the foot of the couch.

For what seemed like hours she lay there, helpless and alone in the darkened room, wondering when the Prince was going to finish his dinner party and come to take her. Would he, she wondered, be dining in Arab dress with his Arab cronies, all expecting him to go off and relieve his pent-up feelings with a waiting concubine? Or would he be dining in a dinner jacket with his cosmopolitan and sophisticated men and women friends from the racing world – people who would never suspect that a naked, married, European woman would be awaiting him, bound, bitted and bridled.

Suddenly Emma heard footsteps and high-pitched voices. The Prince's Romanian eunuch pageboys! They entered the room and, laughing, came over to where she lay. They checked her bonds and then her bridle.

'Yes, you properly muzzled for Prince,' said one of them.

'So now we blindfold you too,' said the other.

Emma did not know whether to be angry or excited as they attached a strip of black silk to her bridle, covering her eyes. She could see nothing.

'Now listen,' she heard one of them say, 'you not climax. Understand? All your energies must be preserved for getting fit for race. You only give pleasure – or you get whip. You come – you get whip.'

Poor Emma was already feeling so aroused by anticipation and frustration that she wondered how she could possibly hide her inevitable climax. But she was terrified of the whip. She knew all about pretending to reach an orgasm, but could she successfully pretend not to have reached one?

'And,' added the other pageboy, 'when Prince arrive you wriggle raised belly to attract him.'

Like a mare in season attracting a stallion, thought Emma, with a blush of excitement.

Suddenly she felt her beauty lips being parted. An oily cream was squirted up inside her.

'We make you ready for Prince to enter you,' said one of the pageboys smugly.

Enter me! Oh, the excitement, thought Emma. Oh the anticipation! It's killing me!

'We still here whilst Prince take you,' said one of the pageboys, 'and when he enter you, we untie red bows on ankles and you then close feet together. You grip Prince's manhood inside you. When Prince put his feet outside yours, we tie yours together. So you stay nice and tight for Prince.'

And nice and tight for me, too, Emma could not help laughing to herself. Really, the ideas of these obstreperous young pageboys!

'But remember, you not climax. You just lie there!'

Like hell, thought Emma. How could she possibly not come? Then she remembered the threat of the whip. Would these young eunuchs, who knew nothing of the thrill of orgasm, be watching her to ensure that on this occasion she did not either? Would the young swine be hoping that she would fail to control herself and that they would then be given the task of whipping her?

'Then, when I tap sole of your foot with whip, you start milking Prince with your inside muscles. You keep quite still. Not move. Just using inside muscles to give pleasure to Prince. For long time. Understand?'

Oh no! That would be too disappointing, too frustrating.

Suddenly she screamed behind her bit as the pageboy brought his whip down across her raised belly.

'Understand?' he repeated.

Desperately she nodded. Yes, she would keep quite still. Yes, she would concentrate on giving pleasure with her internal muscles. Yes, she would take no pleasure herself. Yes, she would spin out the Prince's pleasure.

'Good.'

She heard the pageboys whispering excitedly to each other as they touched the new red weal of the whip across her belly.

'Prince will like sight of that,' one of them laughed. Oh, the cruel swine! But she knew it was true.

'Give her another,' urged the other pageboy. 'Two red lines prettier than one – and make up for no crest tattooed on this one's belly.'

This one! She was just another of the Prince's women!

Suddenly, she screamed again behind her bit as another line of fire hit her across her soft little tummy. She wriggled in her bonds trying to free herself, trying to get away from the whip, but she was held still.

'And three even better,' laughed the first pageboy.

Again she writhed in pain as the whip came down across

her belly. My God, she thought, are they ever going to stop?

Suddenly there was the noise of heavy footsteps.

'The Prince,' whispered one of the pageboys. 'Remember what you do – legs together and just use inside muscles when you feel whip.'

'And remember what you not do,' added the other menacingly. 'Not come!'

Lying there bound, muzzled and blindfolded, Emma could hear the Prince being undressed by his pageboys. Not a word was said.

She could hear them carefully folding his clothes. Were they a simple Arab robe, a dinner jacket or an informal jersey? Were the pageboys pointing to the three red weals across her proffered belly? Was the sight of the lines, coupled with her own helplessness, arousing the Prince's manhood? Oh, how embarrassing it was to be watched by the pageboys.

Suddenly she jumped as she felt something soft and exciting touching her between the legs. She felt her beauty lips being parted and the soft thing running up and down between them. The pageboys! They were arousing her with an ostrich feather, getting her ready for the Prince, ready for her Master. But she must not get too aroused! It was too cruel, too impossible.

Suddenly she felt the Prince get on top of her. She recognised his masculine smell. He said not a word, but his hands were playing with her breasts, rubbing her nipples in the experienced way that always drove her mad with excitement. Suddenly she felt his aroused manhood probing between her legs. She almost came there and then.

Instinctively she raised herself to him, silently begging to be penetrated. And then, suddenly, she was. Oh, the excitement as he drove in deeper and deeper. She longed for a tender word, a word of love, but there was just silence. I am not worthy, she recited to herself. Why should my Master deign to speak to me?

She felt hands loosening the bows that tied her ankles apart. She remembered her instructions and brought her feet together. She felt them being tied again.

Desperately, she tried to overcome her increasing arousal, as she felt the Prince slightly withdrawing and then plunging in again even deeper. Desperately, she tried to make her mind a blank as her Master drove on and on. She must not climax! Mentally she started to recite French irregular verbs, her seven times table, Hamlet's soliloquy – anything, just anything that would make her forget the sheer overwhelming thrill of being taken by her virile Master whilst bound, muzzled and blindfolded. Oh, the excitement!

But I mustn't, I mustn't, she kept telling herself. The whip! And those awful eunuch pageboys watching her, watching her body for signs of orgasm. How awful!

Suddenly she felt the whip on the sole of her foot. The signal! Hastily she lay quite still and, using just her internal muscles, started alternately to grip her Master's manhood and then to relax. It was tiring, but the whip on her foot drove her on and on – on and on interminably.

As the Prince gradually reached a higher and higher plane, Emma managed somehow to slow down.

She was just a whore, a slut, a receptacle, she kept telling herself. She was not worthy. She must lie there, completely still, milking her Master with her muscles, waiting to receive her silent Master's offering.

Suddenly, that was exactly what she did. She heard him cry out with pleasure and she felt his spasms.

And, she thought proudly, she had not come! She would not be whipped! As instructed, she had succeeded in preserving her energies for her Master's troika.

Unbelievably, despite being highly aroused, she had been made to give exquisite pleasure and yet take little for herself. Oh, the frustration! Oh, how she longed to wriggle and, with her Master still inside her, reach a tremendous climax. But she knew she must not do so. Somehow she managed to make herself keep still and inert, as she felt her Master withdraw, leaving her with an acute sense of loss.

She heard him being washed and dressed by his pageboys. Oh, how she longed for a word of love, of thanks. But instead he thanked his pageboys!

'Well done!' she heard him say. 'You've got her well trained. Tell Achmed to give her a lump of sugar when she's back in her stall.'

With that he was gone.

Satisfied or not, Emma felt proud at having served his purpose. She too would go back to her stall with a look of satisfaction on her face, the look of a good and faithful servant who had fulfilled her role. She too would disdainfully toss her head as she passed the other two girls.

And she was going to get a lump a sugar! It would be the first sweet that she had had since entering the stables. Already her mouth was watering at the thought.

15

The Race

The girls had been kept unaware, in their stalls, of the passage of time. They only knew as the tempo of their training increased that the day of the race must be approaching.

Then suddenly it all happened. Into the manège came another troika, to which three women were harnessed, just like themselves. The girl in the middle, however, with a swollen belly just like Polish Slave's, was black, and the two girls on either side of her looked to be Arab or Levantine.

And there, sitting in the troika, was Sheik Faruk.

'Your Highness,' he cried, speaking in English. He looked at the little creatures who made up the Prince's team and, deciding that the day was clearly his, said, 'Would you agree to a small side bet?'

'Why not?' smiled the Prince, guessing what was going through the Sheik's mind, and sure that the Sheik had no idea as to the severity of the training to which his team had been subjected.

'Then I suggest that, as well as our already agreed terms, the winner should also have the right to choose one of the losing team for his harem.' As he spoke his eyes were on Emma.

'Oh no!' Emma tried to cry behind her bit as she eyed the terrifying Sheik.

'An excellent idea,' cried the Prince, knowing that what his team had just heard would make them strain all the harder to win. They might regard him as a ruthless and barbarous Master, but they only had to look at the Sheik's cruel eyes to know that life in his harem would be far worse than anything they had ever experienced in the power of the Prince. 'Done!' he added enthusiastically.

There were a few preliminaries, then suddenly came the crack of the starter's pistol and both teams were off, rushing down the manège towards the two markers at its far end. The other team was obviously well trained, for as the Prince's team made a good quick turn around their marker, so too did the Sheik's. Both teams were neck and neck as they set off back to the other markers.

It was not until the tenth exhausting lap that Emma realised that the Prince's team was gradually getting ahead. Then suddenly Sheik Faruk whipped his team into wresting back the lead, and this time he steered his troika expertly across the track of the Prince's, forcing him to rein back.

Sheik Faruk then forced the Prince's troika yet further back by driving right ahead of it and then going around the same marker that the Prince had been using. This gave Sheik Faruk a clear lead, and when the Prince, following along behind, tried in subsequent laps to get across to the other marker, the cunning Sheik drove his troika down the middle of the manège, weaving from left to right to block his way.

The situation, Emma thought, looked desperate. She was already beginning to envisage her future life in the Sheik's harem. Why did the Prince not let them swerve across and try to get back the lead? She tried as hard as she could to increase her speed, but the bit in her mouth kept her back.

Emma was now beginning to tire. But the Sheik's girls, their energies used up by the burst into which he had earlier whipped them, were even more tired. Desperately the Sheik now applied his whip across the naked backs of his team in an attempt to maintain his lead.

Then suddenly the Prince saw the opening he had been waiting for. He applied his whip ruthlessly, making Emma and the other girls scream with pain behind their bits. But they now shot up alongside the Sheik on the other side of the manège.

The hours of training, of practising rounding the markers either way at speed, now paid off. The Sheik kept guessing wrongly which way the Prince was going to go around a particular marker, and soon the Prince was clearly in the lead.

Five laps to go, and the Sheik was using his whip relentlessly to try to recover his lead.

All that Emma and her companions were thinking about was, on the one hand, avoiding ending up in the Sheik's harem and, on the other, avoiding being whipped into the ground by the Prince. Almost without the need for him to apply his whip again, they strained and strained to maintain their lead. Each was ready to die of exhaustion rather than risk leaving the service of the Prince.

But they were now beginning to totter on their feet. In a daze they rounded, yet again, a marker and, their eyes staring, set off down the manège again. Suddenly they heard the crack of a pistol.

They had won!

Emma stood totally exhausted, the sweat running down her naked body.

She had only a vague memory of what had happened immediately after the race. The Prince had shaken hands with a furious-looking Sheik, and she had experienced an equally furious jealousy, first at hearing the Prince say that he would not insult the Sheik by refusing the choice of one of his girls and then at seeing him pointing to one of them. She remembered being unharnessed from the troika, and marched back to be chained up again naked in her stall. Then she had had a bucket of refreshing water thrown over her by her young groom.

Then, while recovering from her exertions, she had a much clearer impression of being overwhelmed at seeing the Prince, delighted with his win, striding down the passageway, nodding to the three girls in his team and telling them how well they had done. Oh, how thrilled she had been at that moment. All the pain and suffering of the training and of the race itself seemed worthwhile. Oh, what a man! Oh, what a Master!

And under his arm was a mink coat. The mink coat he had promised her if they won. It was a beautiful coat.

'You will not do justice to such a coat here in the stables,' he said, 'but you shall wear it over your nakedness the next time I send for you.'

Her heart was in her mouth as he threw the coat over the side of her stall and strode on down the passageway to the tack room – the room in which he had so cruelly, and so excitingly, used her. Doubtless after the excitement and adrenaline of such a race, he would now be seeking relief. Was this what he had meant when he had said she was to come to him naked under the mink coat the next time he sent for her? Was she now to be put into it and, once again, led down to the tack room to please him? Oh!

She could feel herself becoming aroused with excitement and anticipation.

But then, moments later, her feelings turned to desperate disappointment and jealousy as the pretty girl the Prince had chosen from the Sheik's team was led, on a chain, down the passageway to where the Prince was waiting to enjoy her.

Her head was held high, and as she passed Emma and her two companions, she tossed her hair contemptuously. She had a new life now, as the property of a new Master.

It was, Emma thought, like a scene from the traditional life of the Arab tribesmen, with the victorious tribal leader enjoying the wife or daughter of his vanquished rival. How close she had come to being the Sheik's trophy!

To the victor, the spoils!

16

The Missing Girl

It was two weeks after the race and Emma was again sitting alone in her little attic room in the Prince's large country house. As usual the door was locked, and similarly, the gold bar and padlock were back in place.

She was dressed, as was often the case, in transparent baggy harem trousers, cut away in front to display the bar and the little gold rings, and a stiff, open bolero that scarcely hid her scarlet-painted nipples.

As she moved nervously about the room, the television camera followed her. Who was watching her? she wondered. Presumably it was the two Romanian eunuch pageboys, for the Prince, she knew, had been away for the night, staying with some rather puritanical English friends. He had decided to leave her behind, locked up in her room and under the watchful eye of the pageboys.

Now she was going to be taken to join the Prince on his way to an important race meeting where he had several runners. Wondering how his horses would do, he would be in an excited state – especially as he would not have had any sexual relief during the night.

She wondered how the pageboys would dress her. There on a chair, ready for her to put on, was the hated black chador that would hide her hair and her face, leaving just a small opening around her eyes, which would then have to be well scrubbed. Moreover, to hide her identity, the pageboys often made her wear mirrored sunglasses which hid her eyes completely. She was, in fact, rather glad about the sunglasses, for she was terrified that one of her racing friends would recognise her and ask her what on earth she was doing.

The Prince, however, often preferred to have her heavily made-up as an Arabian houri, but for his eyes only – and, of course, for those of his white eunuch pageboys. Then, in public, she would have to wear, as well as the chador, a black mask which hung down over her face. The eyeholes cut into this were only just big enough for her to see what was happening around her.

There were also two ugly black shrouds, designed to cover her body. One left her face bare, or rather it left bare whatever was not already hidden by the chador and glasses or the mask.

The other one, which the suspicious eunuch boys increasingly preferred to use, was like a combination of the mask, chador and robe in a single garment. It covered her head, face and body entirely, leaving just a little strip of black lace over the eyes through which she could peer without any of her features being visible. The pageboys would then muzzle her by putting a strip of sticking plaster over her mouth. Thus reduced to complete silence, there was then no risk of her embarrassing the Prince by talking to some male friend of hers. Nor would she be tempted to reach for a glass of champagne when in the Prince's box at the races.

Either way, to anyone looking at her she might have been nineteen or ninety, black or white, slender or fat, pretty or ugly. No one would know – except, of course, the Prince and his two pageboys.

She would not, she knew, be the only veiled woman at the race meeting, for she had often seen other black-shrouded figures, also anonymous and silent, dutifully following along behind other rich Arab owners. Were they too European concubines or Arab wives? Who could tell? Only their Master, or their husband, if he was that – and Arab men did not discuss their women outside their immediate family.

On the floor by the shrouds were the ugly, thick-soled

black boots which would hide her ankles from male eyes, and alongside them, the equally ugly thick black gloves which would hide her hands.

It amused the Prince to parade her in public as just another anonymous veiled woman waddling along between his handsome white eunuch pageboys. It was exciting for him to know that underneath the shapeless shroud was a beautiful and sensuous European woman, dressed as a harem houri and ready for his instant use.

It was a feeling made even more exciting by the thought of the little bar threading the two lines of gold rings, which would be keeping her hairless beauty lips tightly compressed, and that of the little padlock securing it – the key to which was in his pocket.

The feeling of being kept hidden from public view by her Master was one which Emma, too, could not help finding rather exciting. Also thrilling, was never knowing when she might be called upon to please her Master.

Emma heard footsteps in the corridor outside, and the sound of fingers pressing the secret combination on the electronic lock to the door of her room. The two pageboys entered the room, dressed as always, in their tightly buttoned uniforms and pillbox hats with black leather straps under their chins.

One of them pointed silently to the chador and then to the mask. Hastily she put them on. Then he pointed to the shroud which would disclose her veiled face. At least, she thought, today her eyes would not be completely hidden.

Emma gasped as a glance in the mirror, through the two little eyeholes, showed a typical anonymous veiled woman. But the pageboys had not yet finished. One of them pointed to the ugly black boots. With another gasp of despair, Emma took off her pretty Turkish slippers and buttoned up the boots. Oh, how heavy they were!

Then came the thick black gloves, and she found herself being bundled out of the room, into the lift and then into the back of one of the Prince's fleet of cars. The windows were tinted black so that, from the outside, nothing could be seen of the occupants.

The pageboys seated her helplessly between them on the back seat. Then, hidden on the other side of the black-tinted partition, the Arab driver set off. Where to? Emma wondered.

Suddenly, the mobile telephone in the back of the car rang. One of the pageboys answered it. Then, pulling back the blackened glass partition to the chauffeur, he said something in broken Arabic.

Minutes later a large limousine, also fitted with opaque windows and carrying the Prince, hove into sight. Both cars stopped in a lay-by.

The pageboys hustled the still shrouded Emma out of her seat and into the spacious rear of the Prince's larger car. They thrust her down to kneel on all fours at the Prince's feet, with her forehead touching the carpet. Then they sat themselves down on little folding seats on either side of her.

As the car drove off again, the pageboys lifted off Emma's shroud and chador, displaying a half-naked but still-veiled houri to the Prince, who as usual was busy talking in Arabic on a mobile phone.

He raised one foot and crossed his knees under his robe.

One of the pageboys gripped Emma by the hair and pulled up her head. She could see the dirt on the sole of the Prince's shoe, now only inches in front of her eyes.

'Say it!' ordered the other pageboy in a whisper.

Emma gave a little gasp, but she knew what she had to say. 'I – I am not worthy . . . to lick my Master's shoe,' she stammered.

'Again!' She felt the second pageboy pinch her bottom, hard.

'I am not worthy to lick my Master's shoe!' she cried. She saw the Prince nod to the pageboy as he continued his phone conversation. Oh, how shame-making this was!

'Purse lips!'

It was, she knew of old, a favourite order of the pageboys. Hastily she pursed her lips as if to kiss. She saw the Prince glance down at her.

'Kiss!'

The arousal of the busy Prince was, she realised, going to be a drawn-out affair.

'Kiss!' came the order again and the other pageboy gripped her tighter. She reached forward and planted a kiss on the top of the Prince's shoe.

'Keeping lips pursed, lick!' came the order. Again it was one of the pageboys' favourite orders. It was one that they had made her practise, pushing her tongue past her pursed lips and wriggling it from side to side, and making an erotic and submissive sight.

But this time it was not the Prince's slippers that she had to kiss. This time it was too awful. She simply could not do it. But, with her hair gripped tighter than ever, and her head thrust towards the shoe, she knew she had no alternative but to obey.

'Up – and down!' The leather tasted foul and Emma almost wanted to retch. But somehow she continued, knowing that the Prince would be looking down at her. At last the shoe was glistening with her saliva. Thank God, thought Emma, withdrawing her head. But the Prince had not yet finished. Slowly, still talking on the phone, he crossed his legs again and raised the other shoe.

Again came the orders, 'Purse lips! . . . Kiss! . . . Lick!' This time it tasted even worse. But at last the other shoe was also shining wet.

Emma felt her head being pulled back.

'Open mouth!'

One of the pageboys carefully cleaned her lips and the inside of her mouth with a scented cloth. Now what? she wondered.

She saw the Prince nod. One pageboy lifted up the front of the Prince's long Arab robe and the other pushed her head down under it. She was able to smell the Prince's male arousal – an arousal brought on, she realised, by the sight of her half naked body and by the mental satisfaction of watching an educated society woman being made to demean herself by licking clean the soles of his shoes.

Ashamed, she felt herself reacting under the golden bar. She felt even more ashamed as she registered the podgy hand of one of the pageboys running up and down the bar, checking the oily liquid which would now be seeping out between her compressed beauty lips.

Like a well-trained performing animal, she reached out with her tongue – reached out to her Master's already half-aroused manhood.

From under the darkness of his robe, Emma could hear the Prince still laughing and probably negotiating some deal. She felt one of the pageboys grip her neck through the heavy material, holding her firmly in place.

Then she felt a fat, well-greased little finger being thrust into her rear orifice. She would, she knew, have to follow with her mouth the movements of the finger, taking her Master's manhood deep into her mouth when the finger was pushed deep inside her, and lifting her head when the finger was slightly withdrawn.

Well trained as she was, she also reached up under the Prince's robe and began to squeeze his small male nipples.

The pageboys would be handsomely rewarded by the Prince, if she gave him real pleasure. But she, if she was lucky, would just get a little piece of chocolate. She was just a woman, and in the Prince's world, as he had so often told her, women existed only for the pleasure of men.

Emma heard the Prince hand the telephone back to the pageboys. There was a tinkling noise as they handed him a glass of champagne from the well-stocked drinks cabinet in the back of the limousine. Oh, how she longed for a sip! She had not had a proper drink for weeks. The Prince did not approve of his women drinking.

'I'm afraid, my little slave,' the Prince said, looking down approvingly at the head bobbing up and down under his robe, 'I must soon return to Arabia.'

Emma gave a little moan of protest as she dutifully sucked her Master's manhood. He would be returning to his harem – to all those other beautiful women! Back to Polish Slave and Oriental Slave! And all their companions! She was so jealous!

'Yes,' went on the Prince imperturbably, 'I must return for discussions with the Ruler.'

Emma's eyes opened wide as she continued to kneel humbly at the Prince's feet, but she did not dare to interrupt her task.

'He wants me to redouble my efforts to locate Renata, the missing girl who belonged to the late Crown Prince. He is still concerned lest she might be tempted to sell her story to the Press, especially as she is said to be pregnant.'

Emma caught her breath under the Prince's robe, as she suddenly remembered the strange telephone conversation she had overheard in Ursula's house. That had been about a foreign girl whom one of Ursula's woman friends had bought back from an Arab. And there had been talk, she again remembered, of a playpen and a cot. Goodness! She had then thought it all so vague that she had not bothered to report it to the Prince. Anyway, she had heard the name Brigetta, not Renata. But might this be the name of the baby? Or, fearing that the girl's former owner might try to get her back again, had her owner simply decided to give the girl a new name?

'But enough of all that,' she heard the Prince say sternly. 'Get on with your sucking ... Take it deep into your mouth ... That's better!'

Moments later, her neck still firmly held by one of the pageboys, she felt, apparently at a signal from the Prince, the other pageboy remove his finger and, instead, reach down between her legs. He parted her thighs and she felt him unlock the hanging padlock, and then reach up and remove the bar. Oh, the relief!

Then she felt him part her now-released beauty lips and insert a little cream.

Next, whilst the Prince, unbelievably, started another telephone call, the pageboys lifted his robe right up and made Emma climb up on to the wide seat and straddle her Master. As the car swayed, the pageboys held her in position, stimulating the tip of her Master's now fully aroused manhood with her beauty lips.

The car slowed down and, with one pageboy holding Emma's beauty lips apart, the other inserted the still talking Prince's hard manhood between them.

'Up and down!' whispered one of the pageboys, again pinching her soft little bottom.

17

The Prince Shows Off his Piety to the Mullahs

A few days before the Prince was due to return to Arabia for the family meeting to choose a new Crown Prince, he had two visitors – fundamentalist mullahs who had come to check that he had not, whilst in England, fallen, like the late Crown Prince, into what they regarded as the shameful ways of the West.

The Prince was well aware, as his visitors were ushered into the drawing room, of the power of the fundamentalist movement that was sweeping the Middle East. He well knew that these mullahs taught that women should be made to stay indoors, that they must never go out or travel alone or without permission, that they should not be allowed the freedom of driving a car, that they must never be alone with a man who was not a close relative, and that their education should be limited to being taught to be satisfactory wives and mothers.

Fundamentalists, therefore, regarded with particular disapproval what they felt to be the unbridled immorality of Western women, with their freedom and brazen ways, and their immodest behaviour and dress, which tempted men to indulge in extra-marital sex.

He also knew that, as the fundamentalist mullahs had great power in Arabia, the ruling family of his country was anxious to placate them and to go along with their strict preaching. With the death of the Crown Prince, it would be doubly important to impress on them his acceptance of their ideas.

'In the name of the Prophet, may he rest in Paradise forever,' began the Prince formally in Arabic, as he waved the two bearded mullahs to comfortable armchairs, 'you are very welcome to my humble abode.'

Dressed in long robes with small black turbans, they would have looked extraordinary in England fifty years before, but now they would pass almost unnoticed in the streets of many towns.

'As a brother fundamentalist,' the Prince continued suavely, his tongue slightly in his cheek, 'I am always delighted to greet those who devote their lives to upholding the strict tenets of the true faith in this materialistic age.'

The Prince saw the two men exchange glances of approval. He clapped his hands and the two pageboys came in and obsequiously offered little cups of Turkish coffee to the mullahs.

'These Christian boys have, of course, been castrated,' he murmured. Again he saw the mullahs exchange approving glances.

The Prince gave an order to the pageboys who then withdrew.

'Doubtless, the sad death of my cousin, the Crown Prince, may his soul be saved, has made you all consider just how strict a Moslem I am.'

'My son,' said the older mullah, 'your generous gifts to our mosques are well known. So, too, is the strictness with which you treat the Christian sluts in the privacy of your harem. All this we approve of. You are indeed regarded in Arabia as a true believer.'

'But,' said the younger mullah, 'now that you are so close to the throne itself, we are concerned lest you might have allowed yourself to be tempted into the ways of Satan here in England where you have so many interests.'

'And must be exposed to so many temptations,' added the older mullah.

'We believe that the late Crown Prince actually allowed

an unveiled Christian woman to accompany him here in public,' said the younger mullah in a horrified tone.

'Well, I think I can quickly reassure you that I do no such thing,' laughed the Prince. Then he picked up a house phone and gave a brief and clearly expected order.

Moments later, the two pageboys led in a black-shrouded figure. Nothing could be seen of her face, not even her eyes, nor could her figure be made out. She stood there, gripped by the two pageboys and apparently peering through a small strip of opaque black lace.

'An Irishwoman,' explained the Prince to the astonished mullahs. 'A member of my household.'

'An Irishwoman!' exclaimed the older mullah.

'See for yourself,' laughed the Prince. 'Show her head and face to the holy men!' he ordered.

Deftly the pageboys slipped the shroud off over Emma's head and then took off her black chador. Her face might be suitably scrubbed and free of all Western make-up, but her pale skin and gleaming blonde hair would leave the mullahs in no doubt as to her European origin. Again firmly gripped by the pageboys, she nervously looked around before dutifully lowering her eyes. Who, she wondered, were these strange men whom the Prince was treating so respectfully?

'As you can see,' said the Prince with pride, 'she is respectful and humble in the presence of men and carefully supervised by my white eunuchs. Moreover, although it is not practical here in England to prevent her from seeing other men, at least she cannot, thanks to her shroud, arouse them by flaunting her beauty before them.'

The mullahs approvingly took in the shapeless black shroud that still covered her body below the neck, her thick, ugly boots and her thick leather gloves.

'It is clear, my brother,' said the older mullah, 'that you have not slipped into the wicked Western ways. Let the girl be covered again.'

The pageboys replaced Emma's chador and covered her head again with the all-enveloping shroud.

'But that is not all!' exclaimed the Prince. 'I would not

want you to think that I allow my Christian women to please themselves as they wish, even here in England. I think you would approve of the precautions that have been taken instead.'

He gave an order, and Emma was made to stand right in front of the two seated mullahs. Then, whilst one pageboy held Emma's hands behind her back, the other knelt down in front of her and began to unbutton the front of the long shroud. He pulled the sides of the shroud aside. Emma gave a little wriggle of protest as first her calves and then her thighs were displayed to the mullahs. Then she gave a horrified gasp as the pageboy gripping her hands whispered, 'Legs wide apart, bend knees!'

Oh, the shame! But she did not dare to disobey or to say a word. The pageboys had whipped her that very morning for answering them back. Perhaps they had wanted to get her into an obedient frame of mind for this. Well, they had certainly succeeded!

Slowly, almost tantalisingly slowly, the drapes of her shroud were pulled further apart. Was this why the pageboys had told her not to put anything on under the shroud? Suddenly she felt cold air on her naked belly. Glancing down she saw the two mullahs lean forward.

'Head up! Look straight ahead!' How many times had she heard the same order? But she obeyed it instantly.

Facing her was a large mirror. Horrified, she saw that her beauty lips were well displayed. Was it in anticipation of this that the pageboys had depilated her so carefully the evening before? Was she being displayed as part of some carefully worked out plan? But why?

Again she wondered who these strange, turbaned men were and why the Prince, who normally took precautions against even her face being seen by other men, was now happily having the most intimate part of her body shown off to these strangers.

She saw that the position she had been forced to assume was keeping her beauty lips erotically stretched – and yet they were still held tightly closed by the bar. She also saw that the little padlock hanging down between her legs was now well displayed too.

'Feel her,' invited the Prince. 'Satisfy yourself that she is kept pure – until the pageboys unlock the padlock when she crawls to the foot of my bed. Satisfy yourselves that here is no brazen Western hussy, but rather a frustrated young woman kept under strict control.'

Emma could hardly keep still as she felt the men's hands explore up and down the lines of rings, trying in vain to force even a little finger past the bar.

The two mullahs looked again at each other and nodded.

The kneeling pageboy let the skirts of Emma's shroud fall and refastened the buttons. Then she was led out of the room.

The mullahs embraced the Prince.

'My son,' said the older one, 'we shall report that you are indeed a true believer, a true follower of our Islamic revival, a worthy Prince, and a strict controller even of despised Christian women.'

'You are too kind, my brothers,' said the Prince, greatly relieved, his tongue still firmly in his cheek.

18

Henry!

Emma looked around at the other guests as she walked into the huge Slete Engineering box at Newmarket Races. It was the Prince's last day before he had to return to Arabia and her last day masquerading as his concubine.

Her pale blue suède suit was entirely hidden by the shroud, and under the chador her face registered astonishment as she recognised Henrietta, the wife of Henry, her longtime on-and-off lover.

Henrietta was gazing through small binoculars down along the right of the course to where the three-year-old fillies were being led into the starting stalls. There were over fifty other guests in the box, and the Prince was leaning over the balcony beside Henry's elegant wife, telling her about his Dancing Slave. The filly stood a fair chance of winning before retiring to stud to have her foal.

Emma edged her way to stand beside Henrietta and heard her say that her own filly, Mary of Scots, was very fit and what an exciting finish it would be if they fought it out for the first and second places. Emma knew she must not say a word or even give any indication that she understood what was being said.

'Yes indeed,' replied the Prince insincerely, as his jockey had been instructed to ride a hard race and to keep his filly out in front from the start.

Emma felt her inside lurch with lust and pride at the sound of her Prince's voice.

Then there was a disturbance as the large figure of

Henry came pushing his way over to Henrietta's side. Emma felt her heart turn over. Henry did not seem particularly interested in his wife's horse and, looking around at the other ladies present, he caught Emma's eye. She opened them both wide. Henry looked at the shapeless figure in black. He noticed that her eyes, all that could be seen of her, were remarkably blue.

'Shush,' he heard a familiar voice whisper from under the chador. 'It's me, Emma!' She was thankful that that day the pageboys had not sealed her mouth with sticking plaster!

With her blue eyes she indicated the exit, then turned to head out of the box.

The announcer was just calling out, 'They are all in the stalls – and they're off!' as an astonished Henry followed Emma into the corridor.

'What the hell are you doing in this get-up, and with that Barbarosa of a man? For the love of heaven, Emma, what entanglement have you got yourself into this time?'

Emma giggled. She could hear the pounding of hooves and realised that time was very short. But before she could speak, Henry continued, 'Look, if you can get rid of your oil millionaire Prince, how about coming with us on a trip to Paris? Henrietta's been advised to have regular massages and you could easily learn what to do, and you could help with her hair and nails – which seem to take up so many hours of her days.'

'I'll see if I can,' whispered Emma, suddenly thrilled out of her life. 'I'm due back home again shortly, after the Prince leaves for Arabia.'

Quickly, she returned to the box to see the Prince looking animated with delight, his hand being shaken as the announcer called out, 'First, Dancing Slave. Second, Mary of Scots. Third . . .'

Emma found herself looking straight into the eyes of Henrietta. Henry's wife was surprised and annoyed to find her husband returning to the box beside some Arab woman instead of being with her as her filly fought an exciting finish and, to her mixed disappointment and delight, came second.

Henry put his hand on hers in a token gesture of sympathy. 'Sorry, my dear, but I have something amazing to tell you on the way home. It's a bit too delicate to mention here.'

The Prince was elated with his win and, with a degree of superstition, related the filly's success to the successful performance of his other winning filly, Irish Slave.

19

A Fond Farewell – and the Key Disappears!

It was the night before the Prince left for Arabia. They dined alone. For once the pageboys had to wait outside.

Emma was dressed as his houri. As usual her wide trousers were cut away in front to display the golden bar interlocking the lines of golden rings. The Prince was wearing a lavish, gold-embroidered caftan and was at his most charming. He also seemed curiously grateful.

'You have,' he said with a teasing smile, 'pleased me greatly in agreeing so happily to play the role of my concubine whilst I am here in England, and I am very fond of you.'

Emma felt her heart melting at the handsome Prince's words. All the humiliations, the strict control that the pageboys had imposed on her, and even her shameful mating and the dreadful time in the stables as a pony girl, seemed to fade away.

The Prince might be her Arab Master, cruel and selfish, but now she was being wined and dined alone with her handsome and very virile Arab lover! And he had actually said that he was fond of her! Oh the sheer delight! Who cared about female lovers when you could have a real man like this one! Even the memory of her recent exciting meeting with Henry was brushed aside.

'But,' went on the Prince more seriously, 'finding this girl Renata, about whom I told you, is extremely important. I want you to take whatever steps are necessary, at whatever cost, to trace her. Let me know immediately if you do – I promise I'll ask no questions about how you did it! Remember we believe she's back in the power of a woman. I won't be back in England for a couple of months, and so you'll be free to look for her.'

The Prince's hand reached across the table and stroked her cheek. Then it slipped down over her neck and shoulder and drew aside the silk gauze over her breasts. She could feel them swell. Already they were jutting upward and out, pushed by the tight and cunningly shaped, purple velvet waistcoat. Now her rouged nipples invited his fingers and lips.

He felt his manhood pulse. 'Come here, my dear,' he whispered turning his chair around. 'Come and be my jockey and ride a fighting finish.'

Emma sat astride his knees, facing him. He leant back, waving the key to her padlock tantalisingly. 'Stand up, for a moment,' he murmured, gently putting his hand down between her legs. With a muted click, the padlock, already well lubricated by Emma's desire, slipped into his hand, and was followed by the golden bar.

Then, when he had carefully repositioned her, his manhood pushed its way past the now freed beauty lips and deep into her. She gasped with pleasure.

Emma rocked back and forth, feeling the hard manhood rubbing ecstatically inside her. It was a new feeling. The G spot, she thought, as she changed to rising up and down, clenching her muscles. Or the one making the whole alphabet, I shouldn't wonder!

Using a circular movement, she suddenly pressed down hard on to the Prince, who surprisingly kissed her with real passion, his tongue deep in her mouth.

'Little Emma,' he murmured, 'little Emma, you really have been the best!'

The best! What praise! And that from a man who kept over a dozen beautiful young European women locked up in his harem, all of whom were jealously devoted to him and spent their days thinking up new ways of pleasing their Master – her Master, too.

His words and his surging emotion brought Emma to a sudden shuddering climax, her inside muscles contracting around his manhood as he too came in a wave of wonderful sensations.

'Master! Oh, Master!' she cried out aloud.

Emma returned to her chair in a daze and swallowed a glass of wine. The Prince's expression abruptly altered and became detached and severe.

'Come here,' he ordered, and back went the bar and click went the padlock. He rang a bell and in came the pageboys. He waved her away.

She felt slightly deflated as the pageboys took her back upstairs to her bedroom. The Prince's words 'You really have been the best!' returned to her mind. Did they sound rather final?

Alone in her room again, Emma stepped out of her pointed Turkish slippers. Kicking them aside, she undid the loops of the tight velvet bolero. She heard something fall on to the pile of the cream-coloured carpet. She checked that it wasn't an earring and then groped around her feet.

'My God, it's the key,' she breathed and there in her fingers was the little gold key to the padlock. It must have got caught in the ankle band of her voluminous gauze trousers as she had ridden out her fight to the finish astride the Prince. It had slipped past her foot and now lay tantalisingly in her palm.

Her mind raced — the Prince must not know she had it! But his servants must already be searching everywhere. Indeed, at that very moment the door flew open, and the two pageboys, ashen faced, ran in.

'Have you the key?' one of them demanded.

Emma shook her head. 'What key?' she asked with feigned innocence, panic making her tummy lurch. One pageboy picked up her bolero and shook it, while the other went to check her golden slippers and felt down to their upturned points. Unobserved, Emma slipped the key under her tongue.

The pageboys then gave her clothes a complete search,

leaving her naked with the aftermath of the Prince's lovemaking glistening on the insides of her thighs. One of the pageboys noticed it and gave her as thorough an internal examination as he could with the golden bar locked in place. Then she wrapped herself in her black negligée and waited while they examined every inch of the room. But they did not find the key.

'Whew!' breathed Emma as they closed the door behind them. She heard the bolts of the electronic lock slipping into place, and quickly cut a small slit in her powder compact and slipped the precious key inside it.

20

Masseuse!

Henrietta was, in fact, delighted that her filly had come second, as she had exaggerated its chances to the Prince.

As she and Henry drove the short distance to their trainer's Georgian house, they discussed the other guests in the box. Then she remembered. 'Who was that blue-eyed woman in that ghastly Arab shroud? Rather an amazing coincidence, surely, that you and she returned to the box together. Had you come across her before?'

Henry thought hard. He hadn't realised that Henrietta had noticed Emma, let alone that she would probably recognise her in future.

'And what was it that you were going to tell me about?' she continued. Henry always seemed to know the most intriguing details about people. 'Was it about her?'

Henry dismissed the very idea. 'Oh no, darling' he improvised, 'whoever she was, she only asked me for my card. No,' he went on deftly producing another story, 'what I was going to tell you was that they say the Prince is discreetly asking people about the mistress of his cousin, the late Crown Prince.'

'Oh!' laughed Henrietta. 'But who was she?'

'Do you remember how annoyed you were when that beautiful Polish girl, the one we met at that party, told us she was unable to accept your invitation to dinner? You were rather put out at losing such a suitable guest to seat next to that old lecher friend of yours, the Italian diplomat.'

'Oh, yes!'

'Well, in fact she was the Crown Prince's mistress, and as he had promised her the earth, she didn't want to lose him. The story is that he originally got her from a rich lesbian.'

'Oh! But what happened?'

'Well, the Crown Prince was recently killed in a car accident back in Arabia and she has disappeared into the blue. I suppose they want to find her because they're frightened she might sell her story to the media.'

'Or does Prince Faisal just want her for himself?' laughed Henrietta.

'Well, they do say that she's got some wonderful lovemaking techniques that whistle up the enthusiasm of even the most jaded palate.'

Henrietta looked intrigued. 'Rather like a certain lady of yesteryear who learnt her games in a Chinese brothel?'

'More likely from her lesbian former Mistress,' said Henry, 'but, for one reason or another, Faisal certainly wants to find her.'

'Perhaps just as insurance against his flagging powers?' queried Henrietta.

'Well, his reputation on that score is rather obscure,' replied Henry, thinking of Emma. 'He's been very discreet and hitherto no one knows if he goes outside his harem.'

They turned into the trainer's drive and Henrietta pressed Henry's knee. 'Let's have an early night, darling.'

In bed, after an excellent dinner, Henry slid across the sheets and undid the top button of his wife's satin pyjamas. She raised herself up and he eased out her large breasts. He put his face between them and breathed in her scent. Then he took a nipple in his mouth and sucked it deeply.

She leant across him so that her breasts hung down, and he sucked first one and then the other while she squeezed his nipples. But Henry's thoughts were far away as he fantasised about taking Emma to Paris with them.

He would ring Emma in a couple of days' time when she was home again and give her background instructions.

Then he would provide a plausible story for Henrietta's benefit, one that would intrigue her.

His imagination now pictured Henrietta's delight at the awakening of the sensual side to her cool nature. A young woman to do her bidding! And Emma? She would be the docile masseuse who knew she might be caned at the least provocation. And himself? Henry's mind began to overflow with ideas for his role ...

Three days later, Henry rang Emma. She answered in her social voice. 'Hullo, Emma speaking'.

'You can forget that tone,' Henry bellowed. 'I want to speak to my slave.'

'Oh yes, beloved Master, what can I do for you?'

Mollified, Henry continued, 'You will come to my house in Wilton Place at eleven in the morning on Tuesday. You will be yourself. We had not met before the Newmarket races. You will tell my wife that you were dressed up like that because the Prince had asked you to find a particular girl and you imagined she might perhaps be at the races in the entourage of one of the Prince's Arab friends. You had heard at the races that she might be with another rich Arab who lived in Paris and so you wanted me to provide you with a cover story for going there.'

Goodness, how clever, thought Emma. But what was this about a missing girl? Did he really know she was supposed to be looking for a girl? Or was it just his own imagination – a story made up to provide a reason for her accompanying them to Paris?

'You will say that before you were married, you were a qualified masseuse and beautician, and that you would like to accompany her on her proposed trip to Paris as her masseuse. The Prince is employing you, so no remuneration will be required – all you want is the chance to meet some of our friends. Got it all? Good!'

Henry rang off before Emma could tell him about all the fantastic things that had happened to her. But this exciting life had stopped for the moment and so, she mused, it might be rather fun to play the undercover agent, as Henrietta's lady's maid.

Henrietta, she thought, seemed rather nice, if a bit too much of a 'grande dame' to be easy to relax with. However, being her masseuse might be fun. Emma was curious about Henry's married life – and women always chatted freely when their bodies and hair were being beautified. Yes, she decided, I'll go along with this – and Henry, as always, pulls the strings.

The very thought of Henry made her feel sexy. She lay back and positioned her handmirror so that she could admire the gold rings. The bar, the padlock and, of course, the key were all safely in her bedside drawer. Emma ran her fingers up over the rings and they vibrated with a sensual tingle. She put a finger between her beauty lips and felt the honey, as Paddy called it, wet and inviting.

Then, gently stroking the now moist finger along the length of her beauty bud, she watched the soft nub enlarge and turn pink. The tip was too tender to touch, so she ran her finger up and down the tiny shaft.

'God, what a fabulous feeling,' she murmured to herself, and put the mirror down. The first shivers indicated her approaching climax. Her finger quickened as the sensations increased, then with a shudder and an internal spasm, she felt the wonderful glow and release of her orgasm.

Emma relaxed as the internal throbs faded. Then she restimulated her beauty bud and – Oh! Oh, the bliss of coming again.

She could not wait to feel Henry inside her, and the heights of ecstasy that she knew he could induce in her.

21

Henrietta Discovers Some New Delights

Henrietta lay on her front on the day bed in the Paris Hotel, while Emma massaged her neck and shoulders with tangerine-scented oil.

'What absolute heaven,' Henrietta said dreamily. 'You certainly have a wonderful touch, Emma.'

They had lunched on the balcony, and shared a bottle of cool white wine. Henrietta had taken off her bikini top and had told Emma she could do the same. Emma had come to feel emotionally attached to Henrietta, in much the same way as she had once developed a crush on a college lecturer with something of the same presence. She admired Henrietta's firm body, with its large high breasts and retracted nipples, and also her smooth creamy skin.

When Henrietta had asked for a massage, Emma had asked her if she would like to take off her bikini bottoms. This Henrietta had done, before lying down on the large white towel.

Henrietta now asked Emma to bring the telephone over and to put it on the floor. She dialled a number, and said, 'Is that my naughty Graf?'

Emma stopped massaging her in amazement.

'Go on!' said Henrietta to her in an authoritative tone. 'Don't take any notice of my call. You're making me feel very sensual, so I'm ringing an old friend who used to be my lover.'

The Graf was obviously delighted at getting the telephone call, and his deep voice could occasionally be overheard.

'So, you've just come in from playing tennis?' Henrietta said. 'Are you wearing a gown? Good! Now this is what you must do.' Henrietta's voice had become low and sexy. 'Now, sit on the bed and imagine that I am kneeling in front of you, and ... that I am opening your bath robe ... Oh, good, you're beginning to get excited! ... Oh, yes, that is a marvellous sight! Now lean back and let my fingers tickle under your balls ... You'd rather I used my tongue? ... Yes ... that does feel good – and is that a little drop of moisture I see?'

By this time Emma's amazement at this conversation had begun to arouse her and, subconsciously, her fingers were moving down over Henrietta's sides, gently stroking her thighs and moving up to her breasts. Henrietta raised herself slightly, and Emma cupped the firm breasts and gently massaged them.

The Graf was now silent, and Emma imagined him running his encircling fingers up and down his manhood. Then she heard a groan and Henrietta's response. 'I'm bringing my head down. I have very red shiny lipstick on my lips, and they are slowly parting so that I can take you in my mouth ... Yes, deep into my mouth ... and my breasts are on either side and rubbing against your balls. I'm licking you, sucking you ... You are very hard. What a man!'

The groans were very deep and coming one after another. Then the Graf gave a muffled shout and Emma appreciated that he had reached a climax.

'Goodbye, my darling Graf,' said Henrietta. 'Until we speak again.'

She replaced the receiver. Then she laughed aloud. 'Silly old goat,' she remarked to Emma. 'He's been impotent for years! But this reminds him of how much we enjoyed being lovers.'

She rolled on to her back, with her eyes closed. 'Put a scarf over my face, please. I may go to sleep and the light bothers me.'

Emma was very aroused, and concerned lest Henrietta wanted to be left alone. She wanted to continue massaging and stroking Henrietta, and to be able to touch herself, too. Thank heavens the gold bar was off!

Emma dipped her finger into the jar of tangerine oil, then gently slid it into her bikini bottoms and down between the gold rings, to touch the sensitive underside of her beauty bud. Then she put more oil on her palms and smoothed it over Henrietta's breasts. She longed to suck the nipples into prominence and, as she looked down at Henrietta's thighs, she could just discern the forward-placed bud between them.

Henrietta gave a dreamy sigh and her legs moved slightly.

'Yes,' breathed Emma, 'a little apart.'

She must have done it on purpose, Emma thought hopefully. Emma's hands passed around the nipples, which slowly hardened and came out. Emma was unable to resist fingering them and then, on an impulse, she lowered her head to kiss first one, and then the other. No reaction from Henrietta! Then came a murmured 'How delicious! Don't stop ...'

Emma, by now completely transported by admiration for the elegance of this stately woman, bent her head to kiss Henrietta between her legs. She ran her tongue up the insides of Henrietta's thighs and reached the top. She felt the firm beauty bud. She took it between her lips and licked its tip. Her fingers were round Henrietta's nipples, kneading and gently pulling. She could feel her own arousal turning her liquid.

She did not turn when she heard the door open, although she knew it must be Henry. Her lips were on Henrietta, and now she sucked hard, then alternated by putting her tongue inside this wonderful woman, before going back to licking her. All the time, she was fondling the firm breasts and pulling the large nipples.

She was aware of Henry watching this erotic scene. Then, as she bent over Henrietta, she felt her bikini bottoms being pulled down. Henry's large hard manhood was prodding its way through her beauty lips to her rear orifice. She felt a sharp spasm of new sensual desire as she realised that Henry was going to make love to her in the only way that gave her the maximum sensation.

In he slid, and she found the rhythm of his action was now controlling the rhythm of her tongue. As he withdrew his manhood slightly, so she too withdrew her tongue, and as he again thrust deep into her, so too she thrust her tongue deep into Henrietta, wriggling it as she did so. Her cries of delight as she felt him thrust were muted by Henrietta's beauty lips, and so, to Henry's surprise, it was his wife's cries which responded to his every thrust.

Henrietta smiled to herself. She had been right! There was more to all this than mere massage and looking for the missing girl for the Prince! What an amazing man her husband was. She was not a lesbian – she had had many male lovers, as well as two marriages – but this was her first experience of being touched up by another woman to the full sensual extent.

These thoughts chased her orgasm away from her senses, though she was thoroughly enjoying the sensations of Emma's lust. She had no feeling of resentment at Henry's action. No feeling of jealousy. She was totally included. In fact, he had probably connived at it for her. She waited while Henry's movement became feverish as he reached his climax.

Emma was apparently on another planet, overwhelmed by sensation as, with her tongue now lapping deep in Henrietta, she shuddered into her orgasm.

Henrietta took the scarf from her eyes and looked up at the two apprehensive faces, both glowing with sweat and satiation. 'I enjoyed that,' she said. 'Let's open a bottle of champagne.'

'Tell me about yourself, Emma,' said Henrietta as they sipped their champagne. Henry was showering, and they could hear splashing and operatic arias coming from the luxurious bathroom.

Emma was so overwhelmed by Henrietta's sophisticated

attitude that she told her her story – John's absences, the Prince, Ursula, and diplomatically abbreviated versions of how Henry had helped her out of some of her previous scrapes. She added that she had not meant to deceive Henrietta, but travelling with them was an ideal cover as she tried to find out about the missing girl.

'Then you had better come to the *soirée* tonight,' remarked Henrietta. 'Our host is a well-known homosexual and many of his guests will be from Paris' *demi-monde*. Henry will know some of them, but you and I can make a few discreet enquiries, as I won't know a soul.'

'Heavens, I do hope Ursula won't be there,' said Emma. 'They sound like just her sort of people.'

Henrietta's entry made heads turn. She was elegant in a black *couturier* dress, cut on the bias so that it accentuated her stately figure. Emma followed her in a charming pink taffeta suit, shorter than Henrietta's, and with her blonde hair worn loose.

There were some meaningful looks from one or two masculine-looking women.

'What a baby doll!' said a fat and rather swarthy Italian looking woman with cruel eyes. 'Is she for real? . . . Or for sale?'

'Oh, really, Francesca!' laughed another woman. 'Anyway, I rather fancy the Mistress.' Then, as Henry followed them into the room she added, 'Oh, how mundane! It's only a *ménage à trois*.'

The first woman spoke out again. 'I'm not so sure. She looks very much our friend Ursula's type and I think she's vaguely familiar. I'll ask Ursula when I return to London next week. My little Brigetta needs a companion, and this one looks like a definite possibility. They'd look so sweet together. Sweet and helpless! Let's go and find some supper and I'll discreetly find out this girl's name.'

Henry introduced his wife and Emma to their host and then left the two women chatting. Emma was vaguely aware that the eyes of the swarthy fat woman were on her, but decided that she was too unattractive for her to bother to go and speak to her.

Neither was Henry particularly interested in any of the other guests, and his mind was already wandering to dinner and a return to the hotel suite. 'Let's go,' he said before long, taking Henrietta's arm.

'Find out anything of interest?' she asked.

'Just one or two bits of gossip for you, which I'll tell you over dinner,' he said, as he manoeuvred them into a taxi, ignoring the idea of a nightclub and any delay in reaching their suite. 'But no news of your missing girl, I'm afraid,' he added to Emma.

Meanwhile the fat woman was chortling to her friend. 'Our host's just told me her name. It's Emma. I'm sure Ursula will know her! I want her!'

22

Ursula's Little Present

Emma was alone in her little office, thinking of the exciting weekend she had spent in Paris with Henry and Henrietta.

She felt happy and free. Yes, free, she thought, putting her hands down over her dress. She could feel the two rows of little rings, but now there was no curved bar to hold them frustratingly together. Yes, she was free! Free as a bird!

But what about the Eastern European girl for whom the Prince had asked her to keep an eye out? Was she still a free girl? What could have happened to her? Emma remembered that many of Ursula's girls, and those of her lesbian friends were from Eastern Europe.

She remembered that strange telephone conversation she had overheard when she had been staying with Ursula. Could they have been talking about this same girl?

Despite the exciting adventures she had enjoyed in the schoolroom, Emma was still a little hesitant about getting too involved with Ursula again. But Ursula was the only possible lead she had so far, in her quest to find the missing girl. And, after all, the Prince had promised to give her a handsome reward if she found Renata!

But enough of her, Emma thought. She was more interested in celebrating her own new-found freedom!

She slipped her hand up under her dress and up between the loosely cut legs of her silken panties – the ones with the crest of the Prince beautifully embroidered on them. How furious he would be if he knew that the little bar was not firmly locked in place. She gave a little tremble of fear. He must never know!

She laughed as she thought how easy it would be, simply to thread the bar through the rings again and then to snap the padlock closed, just before the Prince arrived back in England – doubtless with a duplicate key. She'd snap it back into place and, provided that neither the Prince, nor those inquisitive young pageboys, ever found the key amongst her things, he'd never know it had been off. And meanwhile she could experience the joy of once again being in charge of her own body.

Anyway she was free, she thought, as she gently began to play with her hot little beauty bud. Once again she gave a little laugh as she imagined the Prince's rage if he only knew what she was now doing. He would regard it as being on a par with being unfaithful, for he demanded complete purity from his girls, except when they were in his bed. Oh, how exciting it was to play with herself in this completely forbidden way! She began to think of the Prince and of his commanding ways . . .

Moments later, her arousal was well advanced. She could feel the climax approaching. Oh! Oh!

Suddenly the phone rang.

Oh no, she thought, not now! She would let it ring! But might it be Henry asking her to meet him for a weekend? Or perhaps even the Prince ringing from Arabia to ask after her? Damn!

Hastily and with a guilty look, like a little girl caught putting her hand into a jar of sweets, she took her hand away and straightened her dress. The Prince must never know!

Trying to get her breathing back to normal, she picked up the phone.

'And how's my little Emma?' came a familiar and hypnotic voice. It was Ursula!

'Oh, Madam!' gasped Emma, still breathing heavily.

'You sound as though you've been playing with yourself, Emma!'

'Oh no, I was just . . . running up the stairs to answer the phone.'

'I don't think so, Emma. I can always tell from your voice when you're lying. I think you've been playing with yourself. Have you? Have you found a way of unlocking that little curved bar? Have you, Emma? Have you?'

Her voice was more hypnotic than ever. Emma sat silently, not knowing what to say, her mind racing. How had Ursula guessed? She always seemed to guess everything.

'Is the bar off now, Emma? Were you playing with yourself? I think you were. Were you? Tell your Mistress!'

'Yes, Madam, yes,' Emma heard herself whisper.

'So the bar's no longer in place?'

'Yes – I mean no,' stammered Emma.

'And the little gold rings? Are they still in place?'

'Yes!'

'Hmm . . .' There was a pause as if Ursula was weighing up the effect the rings might have on some plan of hers. 'Well, all right then! I've been thinking of perhaps asking you to a special house party I'm throwing shortly in Ireland. I think you'd be very popular with my guests – and, without that bar, available!'

Available! And at one of Ursula's special house parties! Oh, how tantalising! And a chance, perhaps, to hear something more about that missing girl!

'Are you planning something special?' whispered Emma.

'Ah, yes, something very special. A big surprise! Something you'll never guess! Something very erotic!'

A big surprise! Oh, how exciting!

'Tell me! Tell me!' cried Emma eagerly.

'Oh no, that wouldn't do at all! Little Emma will have to wait and see,' laughed Ursula. 'But I will tell you that one particular guest has been asking whether you will be there. She said she had seen you recently and was particularly taken by you.

'Oh, how exciting.' said Emma, wondering who on earth this guest could be. 'Will I get to meet her?'

'Oh yes,' laughed Ursula. 'She thought you might make a very suitable little companion for her present girl.'

'Oh!' cried Emma, remembering what fun she had had

in the past with other girls serving the same Mistress – behind the Mistress' back of course, and provided there was no awful overseer supervising them.

Ursula laughed to herself. The girl was taking the bait very well! Now it was time to strike, for this time, it would be vital that the bar was not locked back in place when she arrived. She would have to take certain steps to ensure that it wasn't – and it would be amusing to keep the girl totally pure, and frustrated, until then.

'All right then, you can come – but only if you agree to do whatever I tell you.'

'Yes, Madam, of course!' cried Emma, frightened now of not being invited.

'Very well, then – and I think meanwhile I'll give you a little present. Yes, a special little present for little Emma – to remind her of her Mistress.

'A present!' cried Emma, as excited as a little girl who had been promised a treat by her favourite aunt. 'Oh, how lovely! What is it?'

'Ah, my little girl will have to wait and see!' laughed Ursula tantalisingly. 'You'll love it – and it will make you think of me and long more than ever to see me again soon.'

'Oh, how exciting,' squeaked Emma. Ursula, she knew, could be very generous when she felt like it. Might it be a new party dress? Or earrings? Or . . .?

'Oh, when can I see it?' she cried

'This afternoon!'

'This afternoon!' echoed Emma, astonished and delighted.

'Yes. If you're a good girl, we'll deliver it to your office this afternoon. It's only a few hours' drive from where I am. So make certain you're in your office at four o'clock this afternoon – alone, do you understand?'

Alone? Did that mean Ursula was coming herself? Oh, how thrilling. How mind-boggling!

'Oh, Madam, I'm just out of my mind with excitement!'

Emma heard a sardonic little laugh and then the telephone was put down.

* * *

For the rest of the day Emma's mind was in turmoil. She found it quite impossible to concentrate on any work. She rushed out to have her hair done and her face beautifully made up. She painted her nails and, knowing how fastidious Ursula was, even her toenails. She even painted her nipples, and powdered her prettily ringed beauty lips. Then she ran her little electric razor over her mound and powdered it carefully.

Finally, she ensured that the key to her little office was to hand, so that when Ursula arrived, she would be able to lock the door from the inside and ensure that they would not be disturbed. Oh, the anticipation of it all!

Standing on tiptoe and peering out of her top floor window, Emma saw a large car pull up opposite the small office building at four o'clock sharp. Was it Ursula's? Oh, the excitement!

But instead of the tall slim figure of Ursula, a large black man slowly and ponderously got out of the driving seat. He seemed huge and powerful. He was dressed as a chauffeur in a black peaked cap, a black double-breasted coat buttoned up to the neck, black breeches and black leather boots.

He took off his cap disclosing a shiny shaven head. He was clean-shaven but under the line of his chin was a strange, sharply outlined beard which gave him a menacing aspect. He looked, thought Emma with a shudder, rather imposing.

He looked up towards Emma's office and, with a shriek of terror, Emma realised she recognised him.

It was Sabhu!

Sabhu! That huge and terrifying Haitian with his broken English and dreadfully cruel ways, who now seemed larger and more powerful than ever. Sabhu, the monster whom Ursula had employed to supervise her girls. Supervise? He was more like an old-fashioned overseer in charge of the young female slaves in the old slave plantations of his native Haiti.

Was Sabhu now back, working again for Ursula? All the

terrible memories of the dreadful and degrading humiliations that she had suffered at the hands of this former circus animal trainer flowed back through her mind. Oh God!

She shivered as she remembered how this awful man had kept her both half-starved and well exercised. She remembered her embarrassed humiliation as he had stood over her as she performed, to his order, her natural functions, and how he had insisted on instant obedience to his commands.

She remembered his natural cunning in outwitting the girls under his control as they sought to find ways of escaping the sexual frustration he imposed on them. Nothing seemed to escape those bloodshot eyes. He seemed instinctively to know the secret thoughts and desires of Ursula's young women. Emma remembered only too well how terrified and embarrassed she and the other girls had been when he had accused them of playing with themselves without permission. She remembered how he would force her to confess to her impurity even though she knew that it would earn her ten strokes of his whip.

She remembered how he had kept her caged and had trained her to please lesbian women. She remembered how he had sometimes taken her out of her cage on a lead, and displayed her naked, in front of the other girls who would still be gripping the bars of the line of cages, to Ursula and her lesbian clients.

She remembered how, crawling on all fours like a dog, she had then eagerly looked up to the little viewing gallery, desperately hoping that she would avoid a thrashing from Sabhu by catching the eye of some fat and ugly woman, and so earn Ursula a large fee and Sabhu his tip.

At other times he had taken her down on a lead to Ursula's drawing room and there used his whip to make her prance around in front of a client, raising her knees high in the air. In either case he would then, whip in hand, put her through her well-practised tricks like a performing animal.

She remembered how he would pocket a handsome tip

if she pleased the client, and how he would thrash her if the client was not fully satisfied.

She also remembered how he would pander to the sadistic lust of the clients, and to their longing for power over a girl, by encouraging them to 'sponsor' their favourite girl. This entailed them paying large sums to Ursula for the girl to be tattooed on the belly with the client's crest, or on the buttocks with her initials, or for her to have her head shaved, or be brought into milk by Doctor Anna and her mysterious pills, or even worse to be ...

Thank heavens, Emma thought, that she herself was a married woman. Even if her husband was abroad for such long periods, the fact that he would eventually return had always acted as a brake on Ursula allowing her clients to sponsor Emma to have something awful done to her by Sabhu or Doctor Anna.

But nevertheless, even when she was allowed to live at her own home in the country, she remembered how Sabhu had maintained his complete mental ascendancy over her by making her report by telephone every day her intimate physical state, and even, at times, seek his permission before going to the loo.

Whenever Ursula summoned her to London, Sabhu would weigh her naked on arrival and thrash her if she had put on even one pound, or if he suspected that she had been playing with herself.

Oh, how she had hated him! Oh, how she had feared him! Oh, how she still feared him now!

Emma saw him go to open the rear door. Her heart was in her mouth. Ursula was about to step out! Ursula, the woman who had had such a dramatic effect on her life. The woman with whom she had been, and obviously still was, so obsessed. The woman she had adored – and hated. The woman she had tried to forget, but who had never really been far from her thoughts. The woman with whom she had only recently spent a thrilling ten days in Ireland.

But all that happened was that Sabhu lifted out a large suitcase. There was no sign of Ursula. Oh well, never mind, her present must be in the case. It must be rather big. Oh, how exciting! She could hardly wait to open it.

Then she saw that tucked under his arm was what looked like a sort of walking stick. How extraordinary, she thought, for such an active man as Sabhu to carry a walking stick.

Moments later there was the sound of heavy footsteps on the stairs outside and then a knock on the door.

'Just a moment,' said Emma. She had suddenly realised that she was wearing panties. With a gasp she remembered Sabhu's rage if he ever found one of Ursula's girls wearing anything under her skirt except a petticoat. But why did she worry? She wasn't one of Ursula's girls now. Sabhu no longer had any authority over her! She would just treat him curtly, thank him for bringing the present, and send him on his way.

Nevertheless, she found herself hastily tearing off her panties, and hiding them away in a drawer of her desk.

And what about her body hair? Sabhu had always been very strict about that. The sight of just one little hair nestling between a girl's beauty lips would drive him mad. Thank heavens, she thought, that she'd quickly run her electric razor over her mound earlier – she just hoped she'd made a sufficiently thorough job of it. But anyway, why she should she worry? Sabhu had no right now to inspect her intimately!

Hastily she looked in the mirror and smoothed her hair, then, trying hard to stop trembling and to put on a self-confident smile, she opened the door.

23

The Belt

'You put on weight, girl!' was Sabhu's unpleasant opening remark in his broken English, as he locked the door behind him. His remark completely took the wind out of poor Emma's sails. She had been planning to stand up to him firmly but now found herself stammering and blushing.

'Oh! I – Have I really? Oh dear . . .'

'I soon get that off you, eh? Well, girl, won't I?' He lifted his walking stick and prodded her tummy with the tip of it, as if to drive home his point about her weight. Emma jumped slightly, but then looked him straight in the eye, a defiant expression on her face. Sabhu responded to this by prodding her once again with the tip of his stick, forcing her to keep her distance from him, and then brandishing it threateningly. Then he drew it back, as though he were going to prod her with it again, and this time he saw her flinch – and when she glanced up at him again he saw fear rather than defiance in her eyes. 'Well, girl?' he barked. 'Won't I soon get all that excess fat off you?'

Emma nodded dumbly.

Sabhu lowered the walking stick and put it down on the table. Emma simply could not take her eyes off it.

'So you're going to do as you're told?' He put his hand down towards the stick again.

'Y – yes,' Emma stammered.

She watched him as he opened his case and gasped as she saw, lying on top of its other contents, a dressage whip with a red tassel. Sabhu's whip! The whip that he had so often used to force her into humiliating herself and into pleasing Ursula and her friends and clients. The whip that brought back so many dreadful memories.

Slowly he put the whip down on the table next to his stick. Emma could not take her eyes off them.

'I can see you've recognised your old friend,' he laughed sarcastically, 'and he seems to have brought back a few rather painful recollections doesn't he?'

Like a rabbit hypnotised by a stoat, she found herself nodding. 'Yes,' she croaked.

Suddenly she remembered she had not called Sabhu 'Sir' and that his standard punishment for any girl who forgot this was six strokes of that terrifying whip. Horrified, she saw him reach forward towards it.

'Yes, Sir!' she screamed. 'Yes, Mr Sabhu, Sir!'

Sabhu nodded, pleased that she had remembered.

'Good! But I think he would like to reacquaint himself with you properly, just to make sure. So hold out your hand – your right hand – out straight.'

Obediently, Emma held out her hand.

Sabhu slowly picked up the whip and raised it above his head. Then he brought it down hard across the palm of Emma's hand.

She screamed and clutched her hand to her breast. Her palm felt as if it was on fire.

Sabhu smiled. Yes, he felt, he had reasserted his physical dominance over Emma. She was once again clearly terrified of him. Now he would reassert his mental dominance over her as well. Perhaps a little humiliation, rather than pain, was now called for.

'Now give your little friend a nice kiss and thank him very much!'

'Oh, oh, I – I don't know what you mean,' stammered Emma.

'I think you do!' laughed Sabhu. He reached for the whip again. 'Perhaps the other hand might remind you! Hold it out!'

'No, please, Sir!' cried Emma. She fell to her knees and, lowering her head, passionately kissed the red tip of the whip. 'Oh, thank you so much for beating me,' she cried, the old words coming back to her fast. She felt foolish and utterly humiliated.

'Good little girl!' smiled Sabhu cruelly and put the whip down again. Yes, his mental dominance over the girl had been well and truly reasserted.

Emma, her eyes again out on stalks, now watched as Sabhu delved into the case and took out something that was wrapped up in tissue paper. Her present! But she could not see what it was.

'Well, girl, now it's time I gave you the Mistress' present.'

'Oh, thank you, Sir,' cried Emma eyeing all the tissue paper.

'Well, are you going to cooperate whilst I put it on you, or . . .?'

Put it on? Emma's heart gave a little jump of excitement. What could it be?

Sabhu glanced towards the dressage whip with its red silk tassel. It was extraordinary how such a pretty little thing could reduce a grown woman to a desperately obedient snivelling slave.

Oh yes, Sir – I'll do whatever you say, Sir!' she cried. She was longing to see what it was. Something that had to be put on her! Jewellery? How exciting!

'Lift up dress,' Emma heard him order mysteriously. 'Right up! Over your head!'

Mystified, Emma did as she was told. Could it be body jewellery?

'Very pretty,' she heard him say as he ran his fingers down the two lines of little gold rings. How embarrassing! In her excitement about the present she had forgotten all about them. 'And no bar to keep rings closed?'

'No, Sir,' said Emma. 'I've unlocked it and taken it off.'

'Mistress want make certain bar not locked back in place when you come for party. She want to keep you nice and open.'

What did he mean? Emma wondered. She heard a

rustling noise as if Sabhu was unwrapping whatever it was in the case. She tried to see what it was, but with her dress raised over her head she could not see anything.

Moments later, she felt something being put around her waist. It was stiff and wide, and yet felt somehow flexible. What sort of body jewellery could it be?

She could feel Sabhu pulling the two ends of it tightly together over her navel. He seemed to be pushing a flange on one end through a slot in the other. Whatever it was, it was now fastened tightly around her waist. What a strange present! And something else seemed to be hanging down behind her.

'Legs apart!'

Emma blushed. But she found herself obeying the order.

'Wider!'

Oh, the humiliation! But worse was to follow.

'Now, bend knees!'

Oh, the shame! And in her own office! With people going up and down the stairs just outside! What would that nice couple in the next door office say if they had any idea of what was going on in hers? It was all too awful! She tried to wriggle free, but the burly Sabhu held her tight.

'You keep still!'

She bent her head forward trying to catch a glimpse of what he was doing.

'Head up!' shouted Sabhu. 'You look down and you get whip!'

Terrified, she raised her head again. She felt Sabhu reach down between her widely parted legs and pull up, between them, whatever it was that had been hanging down behind her.

'Thrust belly forward!'

As she nervously obeyed yet another humiliating order, she felt something stiff and strong, a sort of pad, encasing her beauty lips. Then, horror of horrors, she felt Sabhu pull her beauty lips forward by the tiny rings, and then ease them, one at a time, through what felt like some sort of narrow slit. Her lips now felt tightly compressed but with the tips of the actual ringed lips themselves free. How odd!

Then Sabhu seemed to be pulling an extension of the pad upward and again fitting a slot over the flange over her navel. As he did so, she felt something pressing tightly against her little rear orifice. Oh, how awful!

She heard a click as if a padlock was being closed and Sabhu stood back. He looked down at her belly and nodded approvingly.

'Now you look down,' he said. 'Bar cannot now be replaced.'

Keeping her dress raised, Emma did so. She saw that around her waist was a flat black rubber belt. It seemed to be made of strongly reinforced vulcanised rubber, like that of a tyre but thinner. Both ends of the belt met over her navel where a little closed padlock was hanging from a metal flange embedded in one end of the belt.

Two metal slots, also embedded in the rubber, had been slipped over the flange and were kept in place by the padlock. One slot was at the other end of the belt to the flange and kept the belt firmly fastened around her slim waist. The other slot was at the end of a short length of similarly tough vulcanised rubber and kept the whole part that came up between her legs tightly in place.

Except for being made of rubber, Emma realised, the apparatus was rather familiar. It was a chastity belt!

To make sure that the gold bar was not locked back in place, Ursula had sent Sabhu here to lock Emma into some new type of chastity belt. Emma had again lost control of her body. This, then, was the present that Ursula had promised to give her! Oh, what a bitch she was!

But why had Ursula done it? Emma knew the answer only too well – to establish her power over her! Ursula would derive great pleasure from thinking about poor Emma, her slave, being driven almost out of her mind with frustration before that special house party in Ireland! And the girl would also be wondering what plans Ursula had for her that made it so essential that she could not replace the bar.

The belt was, Emma realised, a little like the metal chastity belts which Ursula had, in the past, sometimes made her wear. But this one, being made of rubber, fitted more closely and more comfortably. It was wider around the waist and less likely to rub or chafe the skin. Moreover, she realised, being mainly made of rubber it would not set off the metal detectors through which passengers had to walk at airports.

Looking further down, she saw that the piece of rubber which ran down over her belly from the padlock was attached, with strong-looking staples, to a triangular-shaped and cleverly curved rubber pad with reinforced edges. It was this which she had felt encasing her beauty lips so entirely.

The pad was also, rather mysteriously, fitted at the top with another little metal flange, much like the larger one on one end of the belt. What caught Emma's eye, however, was the slit in the centre of the pad through which she had felt her ringed beauty lips being pulled. They were now beautifully on show, with the rings looking rather like a set of wedding rings in a jeweller's display case.

'Very pretty,' murmured Sabhu as he ran his hand up over them, adding with a laugh, 'and nicely displayed for my inspection.'

Blushing, Emma felt his fingers trying in vain to penetrate between her proffered beauty lips.

'And now you not able to touch little beauty bud,' he laughed cruelly. 'And no little games with a cucumber or a dildo!'

Cucumbers! What sort of a girl did he think she was! Again he ran his hand up and down her beauty lips.

'But I not want you playing with vibrator on exposed beauty lips!' Again he laughed cruelly, and then stood back. 'You hold position,' he warned Emma.

He went back to the case he had carried up from the car, and picked up a small, stiff white plastic grille, peppered with tiny holes. At one end were two little hooks and at the other a little slot.

Turning back to Emma he clicked the little hooks at the bottom of the grille into place at the bottom of the rubber pad, down between her legs. Then he brought the white grille up over her still proffered beauty lips and slipped the slot at its top end over the flange at the top of the rubber pad. He clicked a small padlock closed and the stiff little grille, with its numerous tiny holes, was locked into place.

'There, that's better,' he grunted.

There was now no sign of the pouting beauty lips. They lay hidden beneath the grille.

Emma looked down at the white plastic grille with dismay. It was clearly designed to prevent a girl from even touching her beauty lips, never mind exciting them with a vibrator. The little holes, however, would allow the flow of her liquids out – and the passage of cleansing fluids in. There were even tiny rings to enable a girl to attach, when required, an absorbent pad.

By unlocking the little padlock, Emma realised, and lifting off the plastic shield, her beauty lips could be inspected without the whole belt having to be removed. Moreover, she realised, with the plastic shield removed, she could be made to use the exposed tips of her beauty lips to give highly erotic pleasure to another woman, whilst receiving almost none herself.

'You try touch yourself,' Sabhu ordered with a smile. Nervously, Emma put a hand down. She could feel a steel wire running down the edge of the pad inside the rubber. There was no way that she could get even a little finger under the pad.

But how, she wondered, would she ever be able to perform her main natural function while locked into this monstrously efficient belt? She could still feel something thick and rubbery running up between the cheeks of her backside.

As if reading her mind, Sabhu pointed to the floor. 'Get down! Squat!' he ordered contemptuously, pushing her down by her shoulders. 'Now, girl, with left hand,' he continued, 'you reach back and pull rubber thong to left and with right hand you pull right cheek of bottom to right. Get it?'

Then the blushing Emma was made to practise the procedure, straining with her left hand to hold the strong rubber thong aside whilst making sure, with her other hand, that her rear orifice was clear. Oh, how shame-making!

Finally satisfied, Sabhu pulled out a mobile phone. He dialled a number.

'Mission accomplished,' Emma heard him report. 'She now all locked up!'

Was he speaking to Ursula? She longed to grab the phone, to beg Ursula to have her released – or to tell her what she thought of her cruel deception about the present. But, still squatting, with the whip visible on the table in front of her, she did not dare to move.

Then she saw Sabhu pick up and close his case and unlock the door. Without a word he left, shutting the door behind him, and leaving a shattered Emma, her mind in a whirl, groping her way around her office and finally collapsing into her chair.

She was vaguely aware of hearing the Mercedes start up and drive away. She put her hand down over her dress. No, it wasn't all a bad dream. The strange belt was, as Sabhu had reported on his phone, locked in place – and firmly. Very firmly.

It would, she realised, allow her to move about and, being made of rubber, would move with her body. But she would be aware of it all the time. She laughed ruefully as she remembered what Ursula had said about the present reminding her of her Mistress. It would do that all right, the whole time, making her feel like Ursula's slave, her property with which she could do as she wished.

Emma was no longer free – oh, it was all so unfair! Scarcely had she got free of the Prince's little locked bar than Ursula had had her locked into this newfangled chastity belt. It just wasn't fair. It just wasn't, she sobbed, putting her head in her hands and starting to cry. And just when she had been expecting a lovely present. No, it wasn't fair.

Then she saw the note on her desk. It must have been placed there by Sabhu. It was in Ursula's handwriting. Brushing aside her tears, she read it eagerly.

Be at the information desk at Luton Airport at noon sharp on Tuesday 28th. You'll be joining a big house party and I want you to be looking your best. Bring your prettiest long off-the-shoulder evening dress – and your sexiest nightdress! You won't need anything else! I don't now have to bother to warn you to be a good girl in the meantime. The belt will ensure that you are – and make sure that the bar can't be locked back into place!

Emma gasped. At first she felt resentment, and then excitement, and finally thrilling anticipation. So it was going to be a real house party! Dressing up in long off-the-shoulder dresses! And she was to bring her sexiest nightdress! Oh! And who was going to be there to see them? And she was not to replace the bar so that she would be readily available. But available for what? And to whom? Oh, the anticipation!

But what did Ursula mean about her not needing to bring any other clothes? What did her Mistress expect her to wear the rest of the time? Had she secretly got some lovely Irish tweeds in store for her? Naked under a tweed suit! Oh, how exciting! Another present, a real one this time! Oh, she simply could not wait!

But damn this wretched new belt!

She looked again at the date. Oh no! The party was not for three weeks. Three weeks locked into this damned belt. Three whole weeks of thinking of nothing else but of when it was going to be taken off.

But it was also rather exciting being left locked up in this new type of belt. Oh, how cruel Ursula was – and yet, Emma had to admit, how clever!

24

Emma Meets her Little Companions

Wearing slacks over the stiff rubber chastity belt Emma arrived at the hotel near the airport which was to be the meeting place. At the reception desk she asked for Ursula and was taken upstairs to a large suite.

She saw that Ursula was standing by a window, a glass of champagne in her hand. She was talking animatedly in a mixture of German and English to two other women. One looked to be in her forties and was tall and slim, with short fair hair. The other seemed older and was short, dumpy and dark-haired.

At first Emma was ignored and left standing awkwardly by the door with her suitcase.

'So, then, to the success of our house party,' Emma heard Ursula say in English, as she raised her glass. The other two women smilingly raised theirs too.

'And we are agreed, then,' Ursula added, 'I take a twenty per cent commission on any goods sold – as I'm sure they will be.'

Goods sold! What did she mean? Emma wondered. Ursula was always selling her pictures, but what about the other two women? Were they artists too?

'Or hired out,' said the fat woman. 'I like to get mine back again – to be retrained and offered for hire again.'

'Yes, I expect I will be hiring out one of mine.'

Oh, thought Emma, naively, I wonder who she means?

'Provided,' Ursula went on in a businesslike voice, 'that the girls have signed the contracts of service that I sent you, we can always negotiate a deal. The whole point of the contracts was that they said in the small print that the period of service was indefinite and that they could be transferred to another person at any time. My other two had no idea what they were signing – they just thought it was a joke.'

'Mine too,' laughed the fat German woman.

'And mine,' added the tall one. 'They may be in for a bit of a shock!'

'Indeed,' said Ursula with a smile. Then she turned to the bemused Emma. 'Now, Emma, go next door and meet your little companions.'

She pointed to a closed door and pressed a bell. The door opened and there stood the dreaded figure of Sabhu. He was dressed in black like a butler. He was holding something behind his back with one hand. With the other, he beckoned to Emma. Nervously, she drew back.

Then Sabhu took a step towards her and raised his other hand. To her horror she saw that he was holding his dressage whip. Rooted to the spot, she saw him point the whip towards her. She almost jumped out of her skin when he gave it an experimental swish. Again he silently raised one finger and beckoned her. Then he pointed to the open door.

'Yes, Mr Sabhu, Sir!' she heard herself scream, as she ran towards the door. 'I'm coming, Sir! At once, Sir!'

She heard Ursula and her friends laugh. She saw Sabhu give a little bow, evidently pleased with this demonstration of his power over the girls in his charge. Then the door closed behind her.

She saw that she was in a large bedroom, and her eye was immediately caught by four blonde foreign-looking girls sitting silently on a row of upright chairs, each with a large suitcase on the floor in front of her. Two of them looked like sisters. How extraordinary, Emma thought. Then she remembered that Ursula's lesbian friends were particularly keen on having and dominating pairs of girls; close friends, sisters, twins, or even mothers and daughters

– or aunts and nieces, she thought, remembering Norah and Ingrid.

Sabhu brandished his whip at the girls. They all sat back nervously, their eyes fixed on the little red silk tassel at its end. Obviously, Emma thought, they, like herself, had all been introduced to this terrifying implement.

She saw that they were all dressed in identical grey schoolgirl capes over old-fashioned black gymslips, grey felt school hats, white socks and flat-heeled shoes – identical, Emma realised, to the uniform she had been made to wear the last time she had stayed at Ursula's house in Ireland. Were these girls new recruits, destined to join Ingrid and Norah in the schoolroom? Was that what the house party was all about? Oh no! Or were the girls just dressed like this for the journey as a little preliminary brainwashing for something else? Gosh!

'Passport!' said Sabhu.

Dumbly Emma groped in her handbag and then handed the passport to him. She saw him put it with four other strange-looking ones. Then he took her bag as well, leaving her with no money, no credit cards, no cheque book, and without her address and telephone book, or even a pen. Clearly Sabhu had been put in charge of all the girls.

She saw that in the middle of the row of chairs was an empty one. Hers! Silently Sabhu pointed to it with his whip. She saw that folded up on the empty chair was a set of the schoolgirl clothes. Obediently she ran towards it.

'Everything off!' ordered Sabhu in his thick half-French, half-Caribbean accent. 'And put present clothes into suitcase.'

Hastily Emma unbuttoned her silk blouse and slipped it off. Leaving on her lacy bra, she reached for the white cotton schoolgirl blouse.

'I said everything!' shouted Sabhu, angrily raising his whip. She saw that on top of the pile of clothes was a simple cotton bra. Nervously eyeing the walking stick, she slipped off her own bra and put on the cotton one. Then she put on the white cotton blouse.

She looked at the black cotton knickers on the chair and

thought of how embarrassing it would be to undress in front of Sabhu and these girls – especially as she was locked into the rubber chastity belt.

She looked around and saw, through an open door, a bathroom. She picked up the knickers and the gymslip and started to walk towards it.

'No!' came Sabhu's voice. 'You undress here!'

With a little sob of despair, Emma pulled down her trousers and, leaving the panties she had on half-hiding her belt, reached for the black knickers.

'No! I said everything off!' roared Sabhu

As she slipped down her satin panties, Emma saw that the girls' eyes were wide with astonishment as they saw the black vulcanised rubber chastity belt with its white plastic grille. Then, quickly, she put on the knickers.

Moments later, the transformation was complete. Her own clothes had been neatly packed into her suitcase and there were now five schoolgirls, dressed in school uniform, sitting silently on the row of chairs.

Sabhu walked down the line, raising each girl's chin in turn and inspecting her. When he reached Emma he smacked her face.

'Too much make-up for school,' he said harshly. 'Schoolgirls only allowed lipstick and powder – and brush hair down straight.'

Almost as bad as having to show a scrubbed face in a chador, thought Emma, as she washed off her rouge and eyeshadow in the bathroom.

'Now pay attention, you girls,' said Sabhu, speaking very slowly. Clearly the other girls' grasp of English was rudimentary. 'You not spend penny on aeroplane. You spend penny now!'

One by one, each girl was called forward, taken into the bathroom and made to take down her knickers. Then, blushing with shame, each had to relieve herself whilst Sabhu stood over her, his dressage whip raised.

Soon it was time to go. Ursula and the two women, who, Emma realised, must each be the Mistress of two of the girls, left in a smart car. The girls and Sabhu followed behind in a minibus. The other girls smiled shyly at Emma, but they were all far too scared of Sabhu's whip to dare to say a word.

At the airport they silently queued up at the counter with their luggage whilst Sabhu handed in their tickets. He also ensured that they would all be seated in one row, so that they would have no opportunity to talk to anyone else. It was much the same at the immigration desk in Ireland with Sabhu handing in their passports. Emma's heart was in her mouth as she went through the metal detector, but all was well and neither her rubber chastity belt nor its plastic grille triggered off the alarm.

Sabhu handed out girls' comics as they all sat in a row of seats waiting for their flight to be called. To the casual observer they were just a party of schoolgirls going back to school, and watched over by a nice friendly black man.

On board the plane, whilst Ursula and her friends enjoyed more champagne in the first class section, the girls sat in the back in economy class. Sabhu sat in one of the aisle seats, making sure that no one got up to walk up and down the plane and that they were only given orange juice to drink. Oh, how jealous Emma felt when he ordered a gin and tonic for himself.

25

Strange Preparations – But For What?

Emma gasped as the door to the big bathroom closed behind her. She and the other girls had rushed into the room, terrified of being lashed by the dressage whip that Sabhu now held in his hand.

The room seemed to have changed a lot since she had last seen it three months earlier. The bath in the middle of the big room was much larger and instead of one loo and a bidet, there was now a line of three of each. None of the loos had seats. Had all these alterations been made in preparation for the influx of girls for this strange house party?

There was a line of make-up tables and mirrors, like in a theatre dressing room. There was also what seemed to be a proper hairdresser's armchair, facing a basin and a mirror – a proper hairdresser's armchair, thought Emma, except that there were leather straps on the arms and front legs. She wondered why.

But what really caught Emma's eye was the sight of Ingrid and Norah silently standing to attention on a little platform that ran down one side of the large room. It was separated from the wall by a few feet and on the back of the platform was a raised railing.

She was also surprised to see that high up behind the platform was a line of glass jars, each with a rubber tube hanging down from it. Each had its own tap. Other tubes, also with taps, ran down to the jars from two plastic tanks.

Emma then gasped as she saw that standing in front of Norah and Ingrid was the dreaded plump figure of Ursula's sinister lady doctor, Doctor Anna, her black doctor's bag resting on a table.

But why was she here? Emma looked around the room for Miss Peabody but there was no sign of her. But surely, as a governess, she played a key role in Ursula's schoolgirl fantasy? How strange! Were they not to play at being back in the schoolroom after all?

Emma took a closer look at the aunt and her niece, along with whom she had been so humiliatingly treated as a mere schoolgirl. She saw that they seemed to have lost their schoolgirl look. Instead, they seemed more like two almost identical adult women, beautiful and sophisticated. They were dressed alike in long, cream-coloured silken tunics fastened over the shoulder. Their faces, eyes and eyelids were heavily made up. They looked more like grown-up twin sisters than an aunt and her niece being made to pretend that they were still schoolgirls.

On each woman's forehead was a large black circle, like a tattoo but evidently just a transfer. Inside the circle on Ingrid's forehead was the figure '1' and on Norah's the figure '2'. Was this to help the house party guests to identify them? Emma wondered, nervously. Was she too going to be numbered – like an animal?

The two women's strikingly beautiful and identically tinted honey-coloured hair also caught Emma's attention. Instead of weaving it down her back in schoolgirl pigtails as she had done in the schoolroom, each woman now had her hair beautifully waved down over her shoulders in a long, fashionable style.

It was, thought Emma, as she watched them proudly tossing their silky hair back, as if, unbeknownst to them, their beautiful long blonde locks had been prepared for some strange sacrifice. But what?

Had, Emma wondered, Ursula tired of playing at schoolgirls with them? Were they instead now destined, as an aunt and her niece, to play a new role in the strange house party for which she and the other girls had been brought here?

She remembered Ursula saying that neither Norah nor her niece now had any family or business ties that might require their return to Norway. Did that mean that Ursula felt that she could do what she liked with them? How awful! Emma knew only too well from her days in Ursula's cages how, in an intensely emotional lesbian atmosphere, a girl could be brainwashed into willingly accepting the most terrible things and then begging for more.

She looked again at Ingrid and Norah and saw that they were standing to attention with their wrists strapped, wide apart, to the shiny metal railing behind them. They were quite helpless. Goodness!

Meanwhile Sabhu had gone over to Doctor Anna who was warmly shaking him by the hand.

'Nice to have you back,' Emma heard the lady doctor say in her strong German accent, adding with a laugh, 'and I see you've brought some pretty young things with you. Is there anything about them that might be of interest to me – professionally, of course?'

Sabhu pointed to the sisters. 'You could almost say that they were twins,' he said.

'Ah,' said Doctor Anna, with a knowing look. 'Sisters and twins always make more interesting subjects.' Doctor Anna laughed mysteriously. Interesting subjects for what? Emma wondered nervously, but the Doctor changed the subject. 'And, as you can see, I've got two little lambs nice and ready for you!'

'Ah!' replied Sabhu rubbing his hands with anticipation. 'The little lambs ready for the sacrifice – ready to be shorn!'

Lambs ready for sacrifice, mused Emma. Ready to be shorn. Were her earlier suspicions about to be confirmed?

'Oh yes,' she heard Doctor Anna reply, 'but I also have another little surprise for you as well!'

'You mean,' exclaimed Sabhu, pointing at Norah who was standing tethered on the platform next to her niece, 'that she's now . . .?'

'See for yourself! But we don't want to frighten the other girls. Not yet!'

Sabhu laughed and then, turning to the girls he had brought, raised his whip menacingly and barked in his broken English, 'Form line! Facing wall! Tallest on right, shortest on left. Stand to attention! Heads up, hands straight down your sides. No talking! And no turning around!'

Emma found herself in the middle of the line of nervous young women, all of whom were looking straight at the wall. However, she could not help surreptitiously glancing back. Out of the corner of her eye she saw Doctor Anna reach up and quickly unfasten the bows, on Norah and Ingrid's shoulders, which held up their tunics.

Proudly, she began to slip the tunics down over their breasts. 'Heads up, girls!' she admonished in her strong German accent. 'Shoulders back!'

Then, turning to Sabhu, she asked, 'Well, what do you think of them?'

Emma was surprised at how much bigger and firmer both women's breasts now seemed to be, and how they were now also lined with prominent blue veins. Then she gasped as Doctor Anna let the tunics fall to their waists, exposing to view little pointed silver filigree cones over each of Ingrid's and Norah's nipples.

She saw that at the back of each little cone was a silver ring that gripped the base of each nipple, forcing the nipple itself out into the cone. But that was not all, for at the pointed end of each of the filigree cones, and resting against it, was a silver barbell with a small round knob on each end, to which were attached the two ends of a pretty little semicircular silver ring. Was this the work of Doctor Anna?

There was a little circular hole at the end of each filigree cone. Was it, Emma wondered, for the tip of the nipple? But, she thought, no nipple would naturally be long enough to reach the end of the cone – or if, momentarily, it did so, it certainly would not remain protruding from it!

Then her eyes widened when she saw that the tip of each nipple did indeed jut out from the end of the cone, and that it was held in place there by one of the little barbells, which actually went through the tip of each nipple, stretching the whole nipple unnaturally. It must, she thought, be terribly painful to have one's nipples extended in this way.

Or had Doctor Anna perhaps gradually fitted longer and longer cones to each girl, slowly stretching and elongating Norah and Ingrid's nipples? Had Ursula perhaps made them jealous of each other by giving a little prize to whichever of them had the longer nipples at the end of each month? Oh, how shocking and yet ...

Suddenly, through her thin knickers, Emma felt a lash of Sabhu's whip fall on her buttocks.

'Emma!' came his angry voice. 'Eyes to wall!'

Hastily Emma fixed her eyes straight ahead. Oh, what a fool she had been to think that she could get away with trying to take a peek at what Sabhu and Doctor Anna were doing!

But her mind was racing. Shocked, she remembered that Ingrid had spoken of Doctor Anna's strange injections and pills, and of how, to her own astonishment, she had shown signs of coming into milk. My God, thought Emma, Ursula has now allowed Doctor Anna to really go to town on both of them.

But, she wondered, had Úrsula had this done merely for her own amusement, or rather in readiness for this house party? Anyway, the two women had seemed very proud of their swollen breasts and elongated nipples.

Grinning, Sabhu went over to the helpless women. With one clearly experienced hand he unscrewed the knobs on the ends of the barbells and then, very delicately, withdrew each barbell from the nipple which it had pierced.

'You will not need these any longer,' he laughed as he slipped the filigree cones off each girl's nipples. The nipples remained strangely elongated with an almost animal-like quality. 'Ah, Doctor, you have succeeded in stretching them very well. Congratulations!'

Then he began alternately to squeeze and pull one of Norah's nipples and, with the other hand, to do the same to one of Ingrid's.

'Like milking young cows,' Emma heard him say.

The two women were soon sighing and writhing, tugging in vain at their hands which were still fastened to the bar behind them. Emma did not dare to look around, and was able only to imagine the erotic sight of the two women's faces and necks reddening – as well as their breasts. Emma found that she could not help beginning to wish that her nipples too were being squeezed and rubbed, and milked, even if it was by the terrifying overseer Sabhu.

'Congratulations!' Emma heard Sabhu say again to the smirking Doctor Anna.

'Yes,' she replied. 'Very nice and responsive. We get a good flow now!'

'Yes,' Sabhu laughed. 'I think guests will pay very well for these two. Are you planning to give them the next stage of your treatment?'

'If a guest is willing to pay!' said the lady doctor, with a hideous grin, as she rubbed her hands together. 'Meanwhile they can have your treatment!'

Sabhu laughed. 'Yes, that'll make them look even more animal-like!'

Doctor Anna now pulled the women's silken tunics down over their hips. They slid to the floor.

The women were now stark naked. Sabhu grunted in approval as he saw that on each of the women's flat bellies was a slightly larger version of the tattoo-like transfer of the black ring and a number. Once again, he was struck by how alike, below the numbers, the two women's hairless mounds and beauty lips looked, and also their slim hips and long legs. They made a perfect matched pair.

'Miss de Vere has now got these two working together very well as a team in her bed, despite their jealousy of one another,' said Doctor Anna.

'Jealousy makes young women more eager to please,' said Sabhu knowingly.

'Especially,' agreed the doctor with a cruel laugh, 'an aunt and a niece. But we mustn't gossip. You've got to get your girls secured next to mine on the platform before the ladies arrive to see the little lambs being shorn.'

Another mention of lambs being shorn, thought Emma. What exactly did they mean? But her thoughts were interrupted by Sabhu.

'Now, my little girls,' said Sabhu walking up and down behind the line of now trembling young women like a sergeant major, his terrifying whip tucked under his arm. 'So now we strip, yes? – Hands on blouse buttons!'

Suddenly Emma yelped and almost jumped out of her skin as again he laid a sharp lash on her buttocks.

'You obey orders quickly, or you get another lash!' cried Sabhu, now taking his whip away again from Emma's bottom. 'Hands on blouse buttons!'

This time Emma rushed to obey.

'Blouses and bras off! Hold in right hand.'

Moments later the five young women were standing to attention in front of him, still facing the wall, but now topless and blushing.

'Drop blouses and bras on floor! You not need them here!' There was a rustle as they fell to the ground. 'Now, keeping heads up and not looking down, off with shoes and stockings . . . and now gymslips!'

Again there was a sudden cry, this time from another girl who had been slow to obey.

'Now off with black knickers!'

Sabhu grunted his approval at the sight of the five soft girlish bottoms lined up in front of him, as their owners continued to stare fixedly at the wall in front of them.

'Oh,' Emma heard Doctor Anna laugh, 'I see one of them is wearing the new type of chastity belt – the heavy rubber type.'

'Yes, it very good,' she heard Sabhu say. 'Keep girl pure. I think soon ladies all put their girls into these.'

Emma blushed again as she realised that the doctor was referring to her.

'Clasp hands behind neck!' she heard Sabhu order from behind them, his whip raised. 'Now turn around!'

The five naked young women turned around to face the long platform. Emma blushed again as her chastity belt was disclosed. She could see Ingrid and Norah looking open mouthed at the white plastic grille locked over her beauty lips.

'Heads up! Keep still!' ordered Sabhu. Then he came down the line and put a transfer of a black ring containing a number on each girl's forehead. Emma saw that her number was '5'. The girls had to stand there until Sabhu was satisfied that the transfers had taken. Then, one by one, they were ordered to the platform.

'Number Five! On to platform!'

Quickly Emma's wrists were secured to the rail behind her.

'Next!' Sabhu called out.

Soon Emma found herself standing in the middle of a line comprising all seven young women, all secured to the rail and all, except for Emma with her chastity belt, stark naked. The two pretty sisters, now marked Numbers Six and Seven, were on her right, and her other two travelling companions, marked Numbers Three and Four, were on her left.

Sabhu now came back to her with Doctor Anna. He reached forward towards her and picked up the little padlock that kept the white grille in place. He unlocked it, and lifted off the grille, disclosing to Doctor Anna the line of Emma's gold-ringed beauty lips – squeezed through the slit in the rubber pad below. Then he put the white grille back down. 'This to prevent girl from using vibrator on beauty lips,' he explained to Doctor Anna, 'whilst allowing girl to spend penny through grille.'

The lady doctor nodded and ran her hands up and down the now exposed tips of Emma's beauty lips, pleased to find that they were held tightly compressed, and admiring the tips of the gold rings.

'Very pretty,' she said. 'It will make her more sought after by guests.'

Sought after? Goodness, thought Emma.

Sabhu now unlocked the main padlock hanging on the front of Emma's stomach. He lifted the slots in the rubber and the belt fell away to the floor. Doctor Anna parted Emma's now fully exposed beauty lips and felt up inside her.

'She is nice and ready,' she said, to Emma's alarm. 'She would make an excellent subject. Such a pity that Ursula never let me use her.'

Satisfied, she stood back and nodded to Sabhu.

'Thrust bellies forward!' he ordered. He picked up his dressage whip. Terrified, the girls all hastily obeyed. 'More!' he ordered.

Emma found herself thrusting her tummy forward until she resembled a girl well advanced into expecting a happy event. Now that she was standing up on the platform her belly was almost level with Sabhu's face. How embarrassing!

'That better,' said Sabhu. 'Now stay like that!'

He came down the line of women and, as and when necessary, stuck a larger transfer, again with a black ring with the girl's number inside it, on each of their bellies. All seven young women were now neatly and prominently numbered on their foreheads and bellies.

'Now you learn your numbers,' said Sabhu. 'From now on you have no names, just numbers. When I call 'Number!' you call out numbers in turn starting with 'Number One' – understand? Right – Number!'

'Number One!' came Ingrid's voice from the right hand end of the line.

'Number Two!' Emma heard Norah call out. Soon it was her turn to call out 'Number Five!'

26

Shorn and Cleaned Out

Doctor Anna handed Sabhu a pot of some strange green ointment. He nodded. 'Heads up. You not look down!' he ordered.

Then he went behind the line of silent young women, his whip raised. The women were trembling with fear and anticipation. Now what was going to happen? Why had they been made to stand up on this platform with their hands tied to the rail behind them?

'Legs wide apart and knees bent,' he ordered. There was a little cry from one girl as the whip touched her between the thighs. It was enough to make them all obediently assume the humiliating position.

He came around to the front again.

'Lean back!'

He raised his whip. The women all leant back against the rail behind them. Sabhu went down the line of silent women, checking that the beauty lips of each one were now nicely thrust forward – proffered for what was now to happen.

Suddenly there was the sound of footsteps outside.

Emma did not dare to turn her head, but she was aware of the door opening and of Ursula coming in with the two women who had travelled with her on the plane.

'What an erotic sight!' she heard the tall German woman say, as she surveyed the line of women, all leaning back with their legs apart and their knees bent.

'Sabhu disciplines them very well,' added the fat one. 'How clever of you to find him!'

'Yes, he's a treasure!' agreed Ursula. 'He was training performing animals in a circus and I thought he'd make an excellent girl trainer – and he certainly has!'

The two German women laughed.

'And this is Doctor Anna,' said Ursula to her guests. 'She's also a treasure. There's nothing she can't do with a girl – or rather with her body!'

They all shook hands in the formal German way and then started an animated conversation in German – which Emma could not understand – laughing and pointing at the various girls and at Ingrid and Norah in particular.

'This is my prize matched pair – an aunt and her niece, and very alike. As you'll see, Doctor Anna has got them nicely ready for this houseparty – and much improved their market value!'

The two German women laughed and, reaching up, carefully weighed their breasts and squeezed their strangely long nipples.

'You could get a lot of money for these two,' said the tall woman admiringly, again speaking in German so that Ingrid and Norah would not understand. 'Have you a particular client in mind?'

'Yes, an Egyptian multi-millionaire. But you haven't yet seen half of what we are going to do to them to attract his attention – and his cheque book!'

'Ah!' laughed the two women in unison.

'But what about your other one?' asked the tall woman, pointing at Emma.

'Oh, I've got some very special plans for her, too!' replied Ursula with an enigmatic smile.

Ursula motioned for them to stand back and Sabhu now opened the mysterious pot and again went down the line of naked young women, each of whom was straining to hold her embarrassing position. He rubbed the ointment into their mounds, and then over their proffered beauty lips.

Emma blushed as she felt the big Haitian rub the ointment all around each of her golden rings. But she did not dare to look down.

Then the burning sensation hit her. Indeed, all the girls were soon writhing and crying out with the pain of the strong depilatory as each one tried desperately to free her hands from the bar behind her and rub the burning ointment off her intimacies.

'Keep heads up!' ordered Sabhu to the wriggling and now sobbing girls, waving his whip menacingly. 'Look ahead!'

It was indeed a good demonstration of the power he had established over them all, Norah and Ingrid included, that none of the crying girls dared to look down to see what had been done to her, not even when he came down the line again to apply more of the burning ointment, this time actually between each woman's beauty lips, even though he must have known that no hair grew there.

Soon the room was full of even more little cries as the women writhed helplessly up on the platform, unable to free their hands to wipe the burning cream away.

At last the burning sensation began to ease and Emma saw that Ursula was again talking to her two companions, again in German. The fat woman came over to Ingrid and Norah and stroked their long silky blonde hair.'

'Such a pity,' she murmured.

'Yes, I know,' replied Ursula, but you wait and see the final effect. Sabhu is an artist at doing it.'

'Ah!' laughed the fat woman cruelly. 'And are the girls terribly ashamed?'

'Only at first. Then they soon learn to be rather proud of their unusual appearance,' replied Ursula. 'It makes them so different from their owners' other girls.'

'And how much more exciting they'll look without it – just two little animals!' laughed the tall, slim, one. She pointed to their breasts. 'And very interesting little animals, too.'

'Yes, that's the whole point. I understand that the Egyptian keeps a little private zoo, and is always on the lookout for exotic creatures to put into it!'

The two German women laughed and continued down the line, evidently pleased with the way in which their own girls had been so thoroughly depilated and fascinated by the sight of Emma's golden rings.

'This'll make her popular with the clients,' said the fat German lady.

'And they'll still show, even when she's wearing her costume,' said Ursula with an approving laugh, making Emma feel more confused than ever as to what was going to happen to them.

'Begin with Number One,' ordered Ursula.

Sabhu now unfastened Norah's hands from the rail. Before she could even think of running away, he gripped her by the arm and led her to the strange hairdresser's chair. Then, almost before she had realised what was happening, her hands were once again pinioned – this time by straps tying them to the arms of the chair. Then Sabhu strapped her ankles to the front legs of the chair. Once again, she was helpless.

Ingrid and the other young women now watched openmouthed as Sabhu picked up a pair of long scissors. Taking the lovely soft honey-coloured, tresses growing on one side of Norah's head in one hand, he began, with the other, to cut them off. Looking in the mirror at the awful one-sided effect, Norah screamed in horror.

Strapped into the chair, she writhed and wriggled, still screaming. Sabhu smiled and stood waiting for the tantrums to subside. Then he moved over to the other side of her and repeated the process. Norah's hair was now just an inch or so long. She was weeping.

Imperturbably, Sabhu picked up a pair of electric clippers and ran them in a line back from her forehead to the nape of her neck.

'Oh, let me take of a photograph of her like this!' cried the big German woman. Soon her flash camera was busy recording for posterity Norah's utter humiliation.

But there was worse to come, for Sabhu started to run the electric clippers all over her head. Norah wept inconsolably as, through the short stubble, the shape of her skull became evident, giving her a strange and subhuman appearance. Then, holding her head still with one hand, Sabhu deftly ran the clippers over her eyebrows, the lack of which gave her an even more bizarre aspect.

But, Emma saw, even now he had not finished. He picked up a multi-headed electric razor and, pulling the skin of her scalp taut, he began to shave her head all over, going around and around with the buzzing razor, until her scalp was beautifully smooth and shiny all over – and free of all stubble. It gave her a strange inhuman and animal-like appearance.

'And now to complete the effect,' laughed Ursula, 'we eliminate the eyebrows.'

Sabhu ran his electric razor over Norah's eyebrows, removing all trace of them and leaving her indeed looking even more animal-like.

'Oh yes, very good,' cried the fat woman enthusiastically. With those nipples, and her head and now her eyebrows shaved, she certainly looks a very suitably erotic creature for your client's zoo.'

Doctor Anna then slipped a strange looking metal helmet over Norah's now bald scalp. She inserted a plug into a socket and then switched it on. There was a humming noise from the helmet.

'This,' explained Doctor Anna, 'stops the roots. Stops hair growing back for a while.'

Emma gasped. Poor Norah! But the doctor's next words frightened her even more.

'I now working on similar instrument to stop body hair from growing back too. I make fortune in Middle East.'

Indeed, thought Emma, thinking of all those white women in the Prince's harem whom it took the black eunuchs so much time to keep hairless. But, she knew, such an instrument would also be highly popular amongst Ursula's lesbian friends, for they too could not abide any hair on their girls.

Finally, Doctor Anna lifted the helmet off the sobbing Norah. Her scalp seemed more shiny and smooth than ever. Sabhu untied her from the chair, led her back to her position on the platform and refastened her wrist straps.

Sabhu then stood back and, pretending to be undecided, pointed his long whip at each horrified girl in turn. No, thought Emma, no! Not me, no! But she was too scared of the whip to open her mouth

Then the whip finally stopped moving. It was pointing at Ingrid.

'No! No!' she screamed aloud. 'Please! Please!'

The merest flick on the nipple from the tip of Sabhu's dressage whip reduced her to sudden silence. Dumbly, like a lamb being led to the slaughter, she let Sabhu untie her wrists and lead her over to the chair.

'I want to keep these two a fine and unusual matched pair of animals,' Emma was horrified to hear Ursula say to the two German women. 'I think the effect when our guests first see them is going to be electric. They'll be fighting to get them! I think it will put up their value considerably.'

'And so the Egyptian will pay all the more to get them!' laughed the fat woman.

'Yes! The effect is quite wonderful!' laughed the tall German woman.

'Well, you can always have your girls done too, at some point,' said Ursula with a cruel smile.

It was just before Ursula and the two German women left that Emma learnt the purpose of the strange long rubber tubes hanging down from the two tanks behind the platform. Two tubes fitted with taps, one tube from each tank, led down into a line of glass jars, from each of which a long tube, also fitted with a tap, hung down towards the platform.

'Mr Sabhu,' said Doctor Anna, pointing at the tubes and handing him a pot of petroleum jelly, 'it's important that before we go any further we wash these girls out properly. My pills always work better on an empty stomach.'

'Pills?' queried the tall woman, echoing Emma's own thoughts. 'Does she mean . . .? Or . . .?'

'Both,' laughed Ursula, 'depending on what the client wants!'

'Ha ha!' laughed the German woman knowingly, but Emma was left wondering what Ursula had meant.

Meanwhile Sabhu had nodded to Doctor Anna and had gone behind the platform.

'Heads up and eyes straight ahead! No looking around and no looking down!' Emma heard him call out behind her. Not again, she thought.

'Bend over! Legs apart!' came the next embarrassing orders, followed by a strange one: 'Tongues out!'

The frightened girls, including the now bald and strangely dehumanised Norah and Ingrid – Numbers One and Two – quickly obeyed. But Emma could not help feeling a real fool as she bent over, her hands fastened to the rail behind her and her head up and her tongue out. Why did they all have to put their tongues out? she wondered. Was it just to silence them, or to make them feel even more subservient?

'Oh, don't these little bottoms look sweet,' she heard the fat German woman say, as Ursula led her and the tall German woman behind the platform. Were they going there to have a better look at whatever it was that was about to happen? Certainly the sight of the line of naked women, all dutifully bent over as they were, must make for an erotic sight, she realised.

Then she heard Norah, who was at one end of the line, give a little muffled cry. It was followed moments later by one from Ingrid, and so on up the line.

Emma wanted to look back to see what was to be done to her, but before she could do so she was stopped in her tracks by a menacing warning from Sabhu behind her. 'Keep eyes fixed ahead.'

Suddenly she felt her rear orifice being greased, and moments later she too gave a little muffled cry as she felt something long and hard being inserted up her backside. Was this one of Doctor Anna's suppositories? she wondered anxiously. Still keeping her eyes obediently fixed ahead, she tried to eject it with her muscles. But it was too long!

She heard the watching women give a cruel little laugh as they saw her buttocks twitching. Embarrassed by this, she then heard Sabhu laugh too. Then he thrust the well-greased tube even deeper into her.

Moments later she heard the girl on her other side, Number Six, give a little cry and then Number Seven at the other end of the line.

Sabhu now came down the front of the line. He smiled as he saw the seven pretty young women all standing in a line. All were still neatly bent over, with their heads up and their tongues out – and, unbeknownst to them, leading up from each of their backsides was a rubber tube.

Doctor Anna nodded to him. 'Just a little at first please, Mr Sabhu. Half a litre each from the right-hand tank will do nicely as a start.'

Sabhu went back behind the women and, unseen by them, turned on one of the taps above the glass jars. A blue soapy liquid ran from the right-hand tank into the glass jars and when the measuring scale on the side of each glass jar showed half a litre, he closed the tap.

When all seven glass jars held exactly the specified amount, Sabhu looked quizzically at Doctor Anna. She nodded. 'One at a time, please, Mr Sabhu.'

'Keep eyes to front and tongues out,' warned Sabhu again. Then out of the corner of her eye, Emma saw him turn the tap below the glass container high up behind Norah. Immediately she heard Norah give another little cry. What is being done to her? Emma wondered. She saw Doctor Anna go up to Norah and look at her tongue. She heard Norah catch her breath several times as if something rather drawn-out was happening to her.

'Next, please, Mr Sabhu,' Doctor Anna called out and turned her attention to Ingrid, who also, suddenly gave a little cry.

And so it went on until the doctor stood in front of Emma, looking at her tongue. Why? she wondered.

'Next one, please, Mr Sabhu,' Emma heard her call out.

Then suddenly she felt a gush of liquid pouring into her. She too found herself giving a little muffled cry. She wanted to call out, to demand to know what was being done to her, and to insist they pull out whatever it was that had been inserted up inside her. She was, though, too scared of Sabhu's whip not to put out her tongue, and her hands were too tightly fastened, wide apart, to the bar behind her to allow her to get at her rear orifice.

She just had to stand there whilst the liquid continued to gush into her from the glass jar high above her. As it did so, she felt Sabhu's hand come around from behind her to cup her now swelling belly. Soon it was joined by that of Doctor Anna. She now realised what was being done to her – and simultaneously to the other girls too. But how much more could her little tummy take?

At last she felt the gushing stop. Oh, the relief. But then she heard Doctor Anna, who was finishing with the girl at the end of the line, call out, 'Please switch to the other tank now. I always use it first time. Completes the process very well – gives a good clean out. Another half-litre this time, too.'

Sabhu closed the taps leading out of the glass jars and opened those leading down from the other tank. Instantly the jars started to fill – this time with a strange bright red liquid.

Moments later the whole process was repeated as the jars emptied themselves into the line of straining and wriggling young women, whose bellies were now beginning to show even more distinct signs of swelling. And whereas before the blue liquid had just given Emma a nasty uncomfortable feeling, this one seemed to cause a burning sensation.

Emma was wondering how much more of this she could take. She was fearful of disgracing herself, but the long nozzle was acting as an effective stopper.

'I think, ladies,' said Ursula pointing to the line of loos and making for the door, 'that it's time we left nature to take its course – or rather for Sabhu to ensure that each girl in turn properly empties herself and is then washed, and of course dressed, for her new role!

What new role? What did Ursula mean? Emma wondered, as she, too, writhed under the new flow into her tummy. Dressed as what? Schoolgirls again? Were they all to go into Miss Peabody's schoolroom? But if so, why were they all being so humiliatingly cleaned out? And where was Miss Peabody?

27

'Oh, What Pretty Little Bitches!'

Half an hour later, Emma was sitting in the huge bath, laughing and giggling like a little girl, with all the other girls, the now bald Norah and Ingrid included. The latter two kept looking in the various mirrors around the room, not sure whether to be horrified at what they saw, or to be rather intrigued.

Sabhu, his coat off and his short sleeves rolled up displaying his muscular arms stood back, contentedly watching his charges. He liked to see grown-up women reduced to the level of young girls, innocently splashing and teasing each other.

Earlier he had made each of them in turn stand up and, parting their legs, had washed them all over. He looked at his watch. It was time for the next stage.

He went to a cupboard and took out a studded black leather dog collar and an elasticised dog suit. It was covered in short hairs and was spotted like the skin of a Dalmatian dog. It was designed to look very, very realistic.

Above the black muzzle and just over the eyeholes was the number '5' inside a black ring. The same number and black ring were also marked on the skin's left hindquarter.

Sabhu clapped his hands. There was a sudden silence.

'Number Five! Out!'

Nervously Emma stepped out of the bath and, after picking up a towel, dried herself. Sabhu beckoned her to stand up on a little stool in front of him. Blushing with embarrassment, Emma did so.

Sabhu picked up first one of her legs, and then the other, and thrust them into the hind legs of the dog suit. Then he pushed her arms into the front paws and zipped the suit up the back to her neck. He nodded with satisfaction as he saw that it clung to Emma's body like a second skin.

He made her turn around and saw that the gold rings in her beauty lips were gleaming through the little slit cut in the suit between the legs. He checked that the slit came far enough up behind to leave her rear orifice bare. Yes, the bitch would be able to perform her natural functions – to order! He saw, too, that her nipples protruded through two little cutaway circles over her breasts. Otherwise, her body was completely covered, completely hidden, by the dogskin.

Gripping her hair with one hand, he used his other to pull the headpiece of the suit on over her head, pulling it down over her eyes and mouth and then fastening it at the neck. Two little eyes peeked out at him through the small eyeholes.

Then, before the girl could say a word, he closed the zip over the mouthpiece, effectively muzzling and silencing her. The girl was now breathing through the two small holes in the very lifelike plastic dog's muzzle that now fitted over her own nose. It was shiny, black and pointed like that of a real Dalmatian. Two ears, again shaped like those of a real Dalmatian, stood up over her own concealed ears, to which they had been cleverly secured.

He smiled as he saw that the girl's hands were now immobilised in mitt-like paws. She would not now be able to hold anything, nor to undo the zip down her back, nor to pull off the headpiece.

He fastened the heavy dog collar around the girl's neck by means of a tiny padlock at the back of her neck. Then he snapped a dog lead on to the ring at the front of the collar. Finally he picked up his long whip.

'Down, Bitch Number Five!' he ordered. 'Down on all fours – and remember you always now crawl. You only stand up if ordered. Pads on knees and on paws make crawling easier. And remember, your dogskin not protect you from my whip. See!'

Emma gave a sudden jump as he struck her on her hindquarters. She tried to scream, 'Yes, Mr Sabhu, Sir!', but nothing more articulate than a series of realistic little barks came out past her tightly muzzled mouth. Astonished, she realised that her mouthpiece automatically broke into little wuff-like barks, whenever she breathed heavily or tried to speak.

It was a demonstration of Sabhu's continuing power which was not lost on the other girls as, still sitting in the bath, they watched, silent and open-mouthed, what was being done to Emma. They were shocked by the way in which she had been transformed into a dog, capable only of giving little barks. But, like Emma herself, each was also silently resolving that she would instantly obey any future orders from Sabhu – anything to avoid that terrifying whip!

As she knelt on the tiled bathroom floor, Emma felt the thick pads on her knees and under her paw-like fists, which would indeed make it easier for her to crawl and gambol on all fours like a real dog.

Sabhu put down his whip and stood back to take a better look at Emma. Yes, helplessly fastened inside the dogskin, she made a very pretty little Dalmatian bitch – and a realistic one, too, except that she had only two nipples!

But, he knew, he must now get on and put the other girls into similar dog suits, and start their training. He tied Emma's lead to a ring on the wall then turned back to the bath.

'Number One out!' he ordered.

Obediently but nervously, Norah stepped out of the bath.

Meanwhile Emma was looking into a mirror. She gave a little gasp of horror behind her zipped-up mouthpiece as she saw how she, a beautiful young woman, had been turned into a very fair imitation of a dog – a dog with the number '5' apparently branded on to its hairy forehead and hindquarters.

She gasped again as she saw that, except for her two

little protruding nipples, there was no sign that inside the dog suit was a pretty girl. She had lost her identity, just as she had done when she had been heavily veiled and robed by the Prince's pageboys. She was now just Bitch Number Five!

It was two hours later. Two hours in which Sabhu, aided by his terrifying whip, had been busy training his seven Dalmatian bitches to move and behave, in their realistic dogskins and headpieces, like real dogs.

So it was that he was now leading a little pack of cavorting and eagerly barking young Dalmatian bitches out on to the lawn in front of the terrace on which Ursula and her two friends were having tea. They had, Emma saw as she peered up through her little eyeholes, been joined by several foreign-looking men and women. The houseparty must have arrived!

As usual, Sabhu held his whip in one hand, but in the other he now held seven leads, each fastened to a studded black leather collar around each of the Dalmatians' necks. He was using his whip to encourage the bitches to gambol about like young puppies, in a way that he must have made them practise, barking happily at each other as they did so.

'Oh, what pretty little bitches!' Emma heard a man say in a strong foreign accent. She saw that the voice came from a short, rather gross-looking man wearing sunglasses. He was dressed in an expensive-looking blue suit. He might, she thought, be Middle Eastern, perhaps Egyptian to judge from his suit. He put down his cup of tea to take a better look.

'But those two ...' He was pointing at Ingrid and Norah. 'Look at their teats. They seem very long for a woman. Well! How very interesting!' He gave a cruel laugh. 'But of course, I like collecting unusual creatures.'

Emma saw that Doctor Anna was now handing around some papers. It was, in fact, an attractively printed programme for the houseparty, and Doctor Anna was pointing out the different numbered bitches and their description in the programme.

Emma would have been shocked if she had seen her own description:

Number Five. Irish. Well educated. A very attractive thirty-year-old blonde bitch of good potential who has not yet had a litter. Well trained. Obedient and affectionate. Would make a good serving girl for a lady of taste and refinement. Available only for hire for a limited period.

'I want to see more of Number Five – she sounds just what I am looking for,' said a large fat woman, speaking in a loud voice with a strong Italian accent. On hearing her, Emma once again turned her dog's head in the direction of the terrace.

Goodness, thought Emma, wasn't that the fat woman she had seen looking at her at that party in Paris? And might she be the guest whom Ursula had said had already shown some interest in Emma? Oh no! Not that fat slob of a woman, she thought. She remembered that Ursula had said that the woman in question was interested in her being a companion for her present girl. Poor girl! Fancy having a Mistress like that one!

'Ah, Francesca! You haven't seen anything yet!' she heard Ursula laugh. Francesca! Wasn't that the name of the woman she had overheard ringing Ursula, during her previous visit to Ursula's Irish house? The one who had been talking, it seemed, about a baby girl? No, she decided, it can't be the same one. This fat slob hardly looked sophisticated enough.

Suddenly Emma saw that Ursula was pointing down to the other end of the lawn.

She caught her breath under her dog muzzle as she saw, coming around the corner, a tall, thickset woman dressed in breeches and boots. It was Miss Peabody! No longer dressed as a governess but as a kennel maid!

She was holding a short whip, and in her free hand she held the leads of four other Dalmatian dogs. Two were real ones, and the other two were humans fastened into realistic dogskins, just like Emma's.

Emma gasped as she saw that these human dogs were no

larger than the real ones. They were tiny! How extraordinary! They must be dwarves!

Emma again caught her breath as she remembered that Doctor Anna had always been keen to use dwarves and pygmies in her experiments. Had she produced these two for this strange houseparty? Goodness!

At the sight of the bitches, both the real dogs and the human ones made little barking noises and strained at their leads.

Peering through her little eyeholes, Emma watched in astonishment as Miss Peabody let herself be dragged by her group of straining dogs up towards Sabhu's group.

As they got closer she saw that hanging down between the legs of the real Dalmatians were little furry testicles. They were dogs, not bitches! Then she gasped as she saw, similarly, that hanging down between the legs of the two human dogs – the only part of their body which could be seen, were two sets of very human-looking testicles. My God, she thought, they must be male dwarves!

She also noticed that the skin of these human testicles was black. Could they indeed be pygmies? Pygmies specially brought here by Ursula for this strange weekend?

She saw that like the dogskins of the human bitches, those of the two human dogs were marked on the forehead and on the hindquarters, one with the figure '1' and the other '2'.

The male dogs were now cavorting and dancing around the bitches, pulling at their leads. Emma suddenly felt a wet muzzle – that of one of the human dogs – probing and sniffing between her hind legs. She screamed a protest, but all that came out was a little welcoming bark that made the women on the terrace burst out laughing.

'Well, there's one little bitch who's keen to meet the stallion dogs,' laughed the gross, Levantine-looking man.

'Shush!' laughed a tall, hard-faced woman on his right, speaking in an American accent. 'It's all supposed to be a surprise for them!' She studied the printed programme in her hand and then said in a whisper, so that the dogs on the lawn would not hear, 'I see she's been earmarked for Dog Number Two.'

A woman sitting next to her laughed and turned over the page of the programme. 'Yes, and he does seem to have been used as a stallion hound by a surprisingly large number of people for such a young ... dog!'

'It's not the number of times that a dog is used that's important,' objected a stout woman dressed in tweeds, 'but how the progeny turns out. Look at page three, where the progeny of my two dogs, real ones, is listed. See how many winners at Crufts they've sired. That's why when Ursula asked me to bring over two of my prize dogs from my breeding kennels, I also brought over a couple of brood bitches, with their litters of pups – sired, of course, by my dogs. I expect we'll see them later.'

'What I always like to see,' interrupted a tall, austere-looking man with grey hair, who spoke with a slight German accent, 'is how the various bitches move in comparison to the dogs.'

'Right!' said Ursula who had overheard this remark. 'You can compare them all!'

A few minutes later Sabhu was tossing a hard rubber ball up and down in his hand. Emma, Ingrid and the dog marked '2' were all excitedly jumping up and down as they eyed it. The zips over their mouths had been pulled back, disclosing their white teeth.

Suddenly Sabhu threw the ball across the lawn. 'Fetch!' he cried.

The two bitches and the dog bounded after it on all fours. Emma was longing to get up and run, but did not dare to do so. She knew that with her hands immobilised by the paw-like mittens, the only way she would be able to pick up the ball and bring it back to Sabhu would be by carrying it in her mouth. With her Mistress looking on, she was determined not to be beaten by her old rival Ingrid, or by the dog. She was going to be the first to get to the ball and pick it up with her teeth.

Emma did indeed get to the ball first, only to have it snatched right out of her mouth by Dog Number Two. He raced off with it back to Sabhu, hotly pursued by Bitch Number One and a furious Bitch Number Five.

There was a burst of applause from the spectators up on the terrace. Emma was thrilled when, after the zip over her mouth had been closed again, her Mistress actually came over and gave her a little consolatory pat on her hindquarters.

'Clever little bitch,' she said. 'You tried hard to win, I know.'

Then it was the turn of the two sisters and Dog Number One to chase after the ball, and then of the remaining three girls and, this time, both dogs.

'Very interesting,' was the comment of the dog breeding woman in tweeds.

'Come and have a closer look at them at the kennels before dinner this evening,' Ursula invited the guests. Of course, the bitches will not be performing until tomorrow, but it'll still be an interesting sight.'

28

The Kennels

Miss Peabody now led the stallion dogs off to a large barn-like building. They disappeared into it. Then Sabhu led the bitches over to it.

Emma was astonished to see, as she crawled through the barn door, two semicircles of dog cages, each consisting of a central cage, and four or five smaller surrounding ones. The two semicircles faced each other.

Each cage had a little cemented run in front of a small wooden kennel and was separated from its neighbours by the cages' iron bars. More iron bars provided a roof over each cage, some three feet above the floor of the run.

There would, Emma saw, be no question of her climbing out of her cage or even of her standing up in it. But Sabhu's whip or walking stick could easily be thrust between the bars to give a girl a flick or a sharp prod, and he himself could easily reach down into the cages.

There was no sign of Miss Peabody, nor of the human stallion dogs, but in the two dog cages in the centre of each semicircle were the real dogs, each watching proudly as, one by one, the human bitches were put into the small cages that surrounded their own one.

It made Emma think of a harem.

She was astonished to see that, in each of the semicircles of cages, there was a cage containing a real Dalmatian bitch, each with a litter of half a dozen young puppies. She also saw that the human bitches marked '1' and '2', Ingrid and Norah, were both put into cages next to the real bitches with the litters. She wondered why.

Soon Sabhu thrust Emma into one of the little cages. She saw that, as with the other cages, a ring was set in the the cement floor in front of her small kennel. Through it ran a chain. Sabhu fastened her thick leather collar to one end of the chain. She saw that the other end of the chain led out into the passageway, so that, if it was pulled, then she in turn would be pulled right down to the ring and held completely helpless.

Without any more ado Sabhu now left her run, closing the gate behind him.

Bitch Number One, Norah, was already in one of the cages next to hers. She could not help noticing how Norah's elongated nipples, still the only part of her body, apart from her beauty lips, that was visible, hung down prominently and realistically, just like the teats of her neighbour, the real brood bitch.

Emma was then surprised to see Sabhu thrust both Bitches Numbers Six and Seven, the sisters, into a cage on the other side of her own one – both in the same kennel. Two bitches in one kennel! She saw him fasten both their collars to one end of the same chain. If the other end was pulled from the passageway, then both of the bitches would be dragged down by their collars to the ring. How odd!

She also saw that at the bottom of the bars which separated all the cages, including those of the brood bitches, were small remotely controlled slots. Looking at them, she realised that when lifted, they would allow access between one cage and another.

How odd she thought, naïvely.

But she was more alarmed when she realised that the gates might also allow the stallion dogs to enter any bitch's cage within their semicircle. Indeed, each stud dog was already running up and down his small cage, and looking to be in a heightened state of excitement.

Emma looked at the dog on her side and saw the little red tip of his manhood thrust out from its hairy protective pouch. My God! The brood bitches must be exciting him – come to think of it, she recalled Miss Peabody spraying them with something or other. She had assumed it was something to calm them down – evidently it was having the opposite effect on the stud dogs!

Now she saw that Bitches Numbers Six and Seven, on the other side of the stud's cage, had also crawled up to the bars that separated them from the dog, and were also looking at him through their little eyeholes. Again, she thought, it was as if all of them, the real brood bitch included, were in his 'harem'. She suddenly realised that she was feeling strangely jealous of the other bitches. Goodness, she thought, how bizarre!

Looking across the passageway to the other semicircle of cages, Emma saw that two of the other bitches were in cages on either side of the dog's cage, and that the remaining two bitches, including the real brood bitch, were out on the wings of the semicircle. Ingrid was in the cage next to that of the brood bitch.

Like her own group, they were all in the dog's 'harem'!

Then suddenly Miss Peabody appeared, leading her two human dogs. Emma watched in astonishment as Sabhu now removed the two real dogs from the centre cages and replaced them with the human ones.

But these two human ones also seemed to be interested in their 'harems', peering at the human bitches through their own little eyeholes. Indeed, Emma now saw, as she looked at 'her' stallion dog, that whereas with the real dog in the cage next to hers, a short stubby red manhood had begun to protrude from the dog's hairy belly, now a longer, equally aroused and very obviously human, manhood protruding from the dogskin that covered whichever small man was inside it.

Having noticed earlier that the creature's testicles were black, she was not surprised to see that the manhood was also black, with the typical dark purple tip of the manhood of a black man – or rather, in this case, of a black dwarf! She could see that it was true that whilst dwarves might have tiny bodies, their manhoods were, incongruously, man sized!

Emma found, to her shame, that she could scarcely take her eyes off the purple manhood of Dog Number Two. She could feel her beauty lips glistening with arousal between her legs. Nor she saw, looking across at the cage of Norah, was the Norwegian girl any less aroused.

Emma saw that the straw-strewn kennel in her cage was open to view from the passageway. Clearly there was to be no privacy here, she thought ruefully. Moreover she would be spending most of her time in the cage crawling up and down the small cemented exercise area in front of the actual kennel.

She saw several dog biscuits and a tiny scrap of meat in a trough-like bowl outside her kennel and, having eaten almost nothing since leaving home that morning – and then, of course, having been washed out – she felt very hungry. But until the zip over her mouth was pulled back, she would just have to remain hungry. However, she found she could suck up a little water through the zip fastener from a small water trough in her cage.

Later, Ursula brought her guests over to the kennels for the evening rounds.

They were greeted at the door of the barn by Sabhu, now happily back in his old circus role of being in charge of performing animals. He was dressed in tight-fitting white breeches, black leather riding boots, a black belt through which was thrust a short dog whip, and a peaked cap. His large, oiled, muscular torso was bare, and glistening like that of a heavyweight boxer. He looked a frightening figure to the little bitches chained up in their runs, as they nervously peered up at him through their little eyeholes.

Minutes before, he had hosed down each cage kennel. The kennels were now immaculate.

The guests walked up and down, admiring both the arrangements for kennelling the human bitches, and the realism of their dogskins.

'Before we allow the little bitches to enjoy a light evening feed,' Emma heard Ursula announce, 'they must have their pills. If you look at your programmes, you can see the regime that Doctor Anna has devised for each bitch, so as to get her ready for her particular fate. Note also the colour of the corresponding pills.'

Emma gave a little shiver. Different regimes for the different bitches? What regimes? And to get them ready for what? She saw Sabhu holding three little bottles of pills – one green, one blue and one red.

'Now, as you will see from your programmes, Bitch Number One is on red pills. You and I know what effect they will have, but of course she has no idea!'

The watching guests laughed cruelly.

Effect? What effect? wondered Emma, as she saw Sabhu reach down through the bars of the roof of Norah's cage, unzip her mouthpiece, and thrust two red pills into her mouth, stroking her throat to make certain she swallowed them. Were they contraceptive pills? Or ones to keep her in milk? Goodness!

'And for our two little sister bitches, Numbers Six and Seven,' she heard Ursula say, it's the green pills.'

There was a pause as the two bitches were made to swallow their green pills.

'And of course, for Bitch Number Five –' Emma jumped as she heard Ursula mention her number '– it will be the blue pills.'

Moments later, Sabhu pulled back Emma's zip fastener and thrust three little blue pills into her mouth. Blue pills! What were they? she wondered anxiously. If the red ones were contraceptives, then might these blue ones be – her mind raced – fertility drugs! Or was it the other way around? Goodness!'

Desperately, she tried to spit them out, but Sabhu's hand was now over her mouth. She tried to hide them at the side of her mouth so that she could spit them out later, but Sabhu was too experienced to be taken in by that. He stroked her throat, just like a vet stroking the throat of a dog to make it swallow its pills. She found herself swallowing them. Satisfied, Sabhu closed the zip over her mouth and stood up, leaving Emma feeling humbled and confused. What was being done to her by the awful Doctor Anna?

Then a thought occurred to her. Supposing the red pills were to keep Norah in milk, then might the blue ones be to bring her into milk? Oh my God! And what then would the green ones be for? Then she remembered the way in which Doctor Anna had used pills to control, or alter, a girl's monthly cycle. But why?

Oh, how she longed to call out to Ursula, to beg her to tell her what her pills were for. But, of course, even if she could have spoken, she knew that Ursula would not have told her. Her Mistress did not, as Emma knew so well, like curiosity in a girl!

Meanwhile Sabhu had finished giving the bitches their pills.

'Ladies and gentlemen,' Emma heard him say. 'With your agreement, before we allow our little bitches to eat, I think we should give priority to the next generation.'

The guests were mystified by what he meant until he pulled the ends of the bitches' collar-chains, forcing each girl's head to the ring in the centre of the cement floor of her cage.

'Kneel up on all fours!' he then commanded, emphasising his order with a rattle of his whip on the open bars of the roof of the bitches' cages.

Emma was now on all fours with her body raised, her bare nipples hanging down below her, her head held down to the floor and, she realised, her intimacies on display to the guests through the cutaway in the dogskin between her legs. But why on earth did Sabhu want them in this humiliating position? Was it simply to show off his power over the bitches to the guests?

Suddenly her question was answered – but in a totally unexpected way. Just as the real stallion dogs had been removed from their cages to make way for the human ones, so the brood bitches were now led away. Their little puppies ran after them, frolicking with each other as they went. Oh, how adorable they were! Emma longed to pet and cuddle them.

She had watched earlier as one of the bitches had fed its young, and had felt a deep, sympathetic ache in her breasts as she had seen the tiny creatures pulling on their mother's teats. One glance at the other girls had told her that this charming sight had affected them in the same way.

Then she saw Sabhu and Miss Peabody striding back towards the cages with what seemed to be more human Dalmatians in tow. Emma counted seven and, as they got closer, she noticed that they seemed to be just a little smaller than the stallion dogs, and that their suits were slightly different, too. The muzzles were shorter and less pointed – just like the puppies' muzzles had been. They must be human puppies!

As these puppies – one for each girl, Emma realised – were put into the cages previously occupied by the brood bitches and their real puppies, she noticed something else. The hindquarters of their suits were cut away in much the same way as her own was, and in each case a pair of dark-skinned beauty lips peeped out. The puppies were pygmy women, which accounted for their slightly smaller size.

Now Sabhu pulled a lever, and the gates between the cages slid open. Almost immediately, the little human puppies started to explore the neighbouring cages, yelping a greeting to the bitches within them.

Emma felt a puppy nuzzle her, then reach up to suck at her exposed nipples. The feeling, both on a physical and on a mental level, was extraordinary. Instead of angrily brushing the little creature away, she found herself remaining quite still, kneeling on all fours and longing to be able to feed it.

But the watching guests were fascinated to see that the puppies were soon bickering over the much more prominent and more rewarding nipples of Norah, and, across the passageway, of Ingrid.

Indeed, seeing the way the guests were riveted by this sight, Emma wondered whether this was why Ursula had had both women's breasts enlarged, had had them both brought into milk and had had their nipples so strangely elongated. Had she carefully planned it all to provide a little extra erotic entertainment for the guests at her house-party? Or were they really paying guests – rich men and women who had come to see young women being subjected – to what exactly? she wondered.

And if they had been astonished by this, what would they say when they saw the two young women's shiny bald heads? Or, come to that, the two lines of golden rings in her own beauty lips? Was she too part of the human circus that Ursula had devised to entertain her clients?

Not until the puppies had taken their fill, and returned to their mothers' cages, did Sabhu again unfasten the zips over the bitches' mouths, and this time leave them open.

Suddenly finding her mouth free, Emma was tempted for a moment to spoil the impression of well-disciplined womanhood, and of well-trained little performing dogs, by calling out a protest. But the sight of the tip of Sabhu's whip pointing menacingly through the bars at her breasts reduced her to instant silence.

Similarly, although she was by now almost dying of hunger, she and the other bitches had all previously been warned by Sabhu that they must not take even a crumb of their food until he gave them the order – and then they were to gobble it all up like ravenous dogs.

Here again, she had been tempted to ignore his warning and to bury her head in her trough. But one glance at his whip had been sufficient to halt her in her tracks. Now, like all the other bitches, she knew that before being allowed to eat she would, on the order 'Beg!', have to sit up on her haunches with her front paws raised in front of her, just like a dog begging for a biscuit.

Now kneeling, like the other bitches, on all fours in front of her feeding bowl, she was longing to hear this order, as she knew it would be followed by the order 'Gobble!' – her cue to drop back on to all fours again and thrust her mouth into her trough.

'Beg!' came the order, and the bitches all squatted up on their heels, their eyes on Sabhu and their front paws held up in front of them. Again there was a little round of applause from the watching guests.

Then came the order 'Gobble!'

The watching guests could scarcely believe the degree to which these human bitches were behaving like real ones. It was indeed an erotically arousing sight.

'That's all, ladies and gentlemen,' called out Ursula. 'We must leave these little bitches, or anyway some of them, to get their strength up for tomorrow!'

What does she mean? Emma wondered. What's happening tomorrow?

'And a delicious supper awaits us,' added Ursula. 'It's only informal tonight, so that, like the bitches, everyone can recover from their journey and get their strength up for tomorrow's fun and games!'

Fun and games, mused Emma as she eyed the hard floor of her kennel, her immobilised paw-like hands and the chain fastened to her collar. And now they were going off to a delicious dinner, leaving her with the remnants of her dog biscuits and scraps of meat. And to think that Ursula had told her to bring her prettiest long off-the-shoulder evening dress!

'But, of course, tomorrow it's a black tie dinner – then dancing,' added Ursula.

'A fat lot of use all that'll be to me,' Emma said bitterly to herself. 'I shall just be stuck here, zipped into this damned dogskin and locked into a kennel! And to think that Ursula told me to bring my sexiest nightdress!'

29

Entertaining the Houseparty

All night Emma tossed and turned on the little pile of straw in her small kennel. Being designed for real dogs, there was no room in it for her to stretch out. She had to lie curled up – just like, she realised, a real dog. Her collar chain clanked with her every movement and little woofs came from her clever headpiece every time she coughed or cleared her throat. But at least the elasticised dogskin kept her warm.

As she lay wondering what Ursula had in store for her and the other bitches, she kept hearing the clanking of the other bitches' chains and their unintended little woofs.

But was she being cleverly brainwashed into feeling like a bitch? Certainly, what seemed to be dominating her thoughts was the presence, only a few feet away from her, of human Dog Number Two. Peering through the bars of her cage she could see him as he lay in his kennel. She could also see him when he came out of the kennel to stretch or to cock his leg against the bars of her cage, his black manhood emerging from the dogskin as he did so.

He, similarly, would see her, she realised, when she came out of her kennel to spend a penny, shyly, on to the sloping cement floor of her cage. She found herself, more and more, thinking of him not as a small black man in a dogskin, but as a real, fierce dog, surrounded by the cages of his bitches.

She also kept thinking of the little human puppies in the cage next door. She would look at them curled up in a heap on the floor, just as the real puppies had curled up against their mother. But the little gates at the bottom of their cages had been left open and now she could see that two of them were curled up against Norah, occasionally helping themselves to her milk.

Oh, how she longed to feel a little human puppy curling up for warmth against her, too. But no puppies bothered to come into her cage. They had learnt that there was no milk for them there. It made her feel very jealous of Norah.

She remembered the excitement of feeling a puppy sucking, hopefully, at her exposed nipples. How lovely it must be for Norah. Her jealousy redoubled. She remembered those strange pills that she had been given. Might she soon be able to feed the puppies after all?

Next morning nothing very much happened. Sabhu came and again hosed down the cement floored cages, and allowed each bitch to eat a couple of biscuits. Then he left them alone, each one eyeing her pygmy dog Master and wondering what was going on. Emma could not help thinking of what Ursula had said about the bitches 'performing' today.

Then suddenly Sabhu came back and placed some chairs in the centre of the two semicircles of cages. Some seemed to be facing towards the other semicircle, some directly towards hers.

The guests came in. Through the slits over her eyes, Emma recognised the fat, cruel-looking Egyptian-looking man and the fat woman with the Italian accent. Then she shuddered as she saw that both Doctor Anna and Miss Peabody were with them.

'Do have a look around,' she heard Ursula say, as if she were inviting them to inspect her pictures in a gallery. Then moments later she heard her say, 'Right, well if you're all ready, let's get on with this morning's programme. You will see that this evening we have a gala double performance, but now, as a little introductory item to get us into the right mood, I should like to present Bitch Number Five and Dog Number Two.'

She nodded to Sabhu, who was again dressed in his circus lion-tamer's outfit. He came over to the cage in which Emma was cowering. He raised his long whip above the bars over her cage. She trembled with fear as she watched him drop a plastic bolster through the bars and then, reaching down, place it near the ring through which ran the chain to her collar.

Then he stepped back and pulled the other end of the chain, dragging her nearer and nearer to the ring. Finally, her neck was hard up against the ring.

'On your back!' he ordered, raising his whip to enforce his commands. 'Hips on the bolster. Legs apart. Front paws behind your head!'

Scared stiff, Emma found herself lying on her back with her hips raised up on the plastic bolster, as if proffering herself. Horrified, she watched Miss Peabody go to the next-door cage, the one containing Dog Number Two. She saw that the dog – or was it a pygmy? – was now eagerly running up and down his little exercise area. She saw Miss Peabody raise the lever which in turn raised the barred gate between the two cages. Instantly the dog bounded into her cage.

With a cry, she tried to get up and run into the kennel itself, but of course her collar chain held her fast. She saw Sabhu thrust his whip down towards her through the bars of her cage. She froze in horror, her hips still raised by the plastic bolster.

'Legs well apart!' warned Sabhu.

The human dog now came over to her. She could see his purple manhood thrusting out proudly from the dogskin and his heavy little testicles hanging down between his legs. She tried to scream, but her cries were cleverly transposed into little welcoming barks by her mouthpiece.

How tiny he is, thought Emma.

Then he moved in between her legs. His head reached up only to her exposed nipples. She lay quite still, mesmerised by the sight of Sabhu leering down at her through the bars of the cage, his whip ready in his hand.

The human dog, the pygmy, started to suck at first one

of her nipples and then the other. Oh, the excitement! But oh, the shame, as she felt herself becoming aroused. She heard the spectators laugh, but she could not stop herself from becoming wet between her legs. Oh, how humiliating!

She saw Doctor Anna make a sign and then Miss Peabody reached down and gripped the human dog's collar.

'Down, Pedro! Down!' she ordered.

The dog slipped down Emma's body slightly and, as she lay there too terrified to move, she felt his manhood probing between her beauty lips. Seconds later, she was penetrated.

She raised her head slightly and looked down towards where the tiny human dog was lying on her belly like a little doll, thrusting in and out.

Then suddenly, before she could reach her own climax, it was all over and she felt herself being drenched by the seed of ... what? As she felt the seed slipping deeper into her, she remembered the coloured pills. Please, God, don't make the blue ones fertility pills, she prayed.

She was aware that the human dog had now been put back in his cage. She tried to get up, so that she could make some attempt to wash the seed out, but she was still held on her back by her collar. Terrified, she felt, for the next half-hour, the seed slipping deeper and deeper into her whilst the spectators laughed at her muted little moans.

Meanwhile she was aware that the audience had turned their chairs around and were now watching Dog Number One mount Bitch Number Three, in the same way as she herself had just been so shamefully mounted.

But there was a difference. After the audience had departed for cocktails and a good lunch, Doctor Anna had Bitch Number Three taken out of her cage by Sabhu and put into a little alcove. The door was not properly shut and Emma saw that the bitch was lying on her back on some sort of couch. Then she saw Doctor Anna scrub her hands, put on a white operating gown and cap, and pull on some rubber gloves.

She thought she could make out Doctor Anna

apparently bending over the bitch and stroking her, just like a vet might do to soothe a real dog. The bitch, who had been rather agitated, seemed to relax and Emma saw Doctor Anna raise her ankles one at a time and put them into what seemed like a pair of widely spaced cups.

She was then horrified to see Doctor Anna fill a syringe from a medical vacuum flask which she seemed to have taken from a refrigerator. Just then Sabhu went into the alcove, closing the door behind him. What on earth were they doing? she wondered.

A little later the bitch, now very much herself again, was put back into her cage and the Doctor left to join the guests at lunch.

There was now silence in the cages. Still shocked at what she had seen, Emma wondered what was going to happen next. What was going to happen at the 'gala double performance' that evening?

30

A Gala Performance and a Gala Dinner

Emma took a back seat at the gala performance, which took place early that evening. She had heard that pygmies were highly potent and were quickly able to perform again, but even so she was surprised at the performance she now witnessed.

First the two sisters, Bitches Numbers Six and Seven, were made by Sabhu to lie side by side, their hips raised high by the same plastic bolster and their necks held tightly to the same ring in the floor of their cage. To Emma's acute jealousy, and accompanied by the applause of the audience, both were then mounted in turn by Dog Number Two – Emma's own Master.

Secondly Norah, Bitch Number Two, was taken out of her cage and put into that of her niece Ingrid. Watched closely by the fat Egyptian they, too, were both mounted – this time by human Dog Number One.

Emma saw the Egyptian go up to Ursula and whisper something in her ear. She saw Ursula smile delightedly and then shake her head and her finger, as if to say that she needed more. The Egyptian walked off angrily, shrugging his shoulders.

Then, as the audience left, she heard Ursula call out to Doctor Anna, 'You'd better make certain about these two. I don't want them sent back by a dissatisfied client demanding his money back!'

Doctor Anna then had them both taken into the alcove and once again Emma saw her put on a white gown and rubber gloves. She saw her produce several flasks, again apparently from the refrigerator, each marked with several letters and numbers. She saw her appear to be loading several syringes.

Then the door was shut and Emma was left wondering what was going on, and what Ursula had meant. Was Doctor Anna simply making sure that they remained, or perhaps stopped being in milk, or was something more sinister being done to them?

A quarter of an hour later, Doctor Anna opened the door, wiping her hands as if very satisfied at a job well done.

Sabhu now put the two bitches back into their cages. Norah's eyes, half hidden by her dogskin, seemed to be glistening – though whether with pride or with tears, Emma could not be certain.

An hour later Sabhu, now mysteriously dressed again in black like a butler, returned. To Emma's astonishment he led all the bitches not just out of their cages, but back up to the house and up into the same bathroom that they had previously used.

Here he took off their dogskins and headpieces, leaving them naked except for their black leather dog collars. The sight of Ingrid's and Norah's still shiny bald heads was astonishing. They themselves took one look in the mirror and burst into tears.

Then he ordered them all into the large bath. The girls were all longing to talk to each other about their extraordinary experiences, but Sabhu, his whip in his hand, allowed not even a whisper.

After he had checked that they were all thoroughly washed, and that their black ringed numbered transfers were still properly fixed on to their foreheads and bellies, he pointed to the line of dressing tables and mirrors and told them to use the selection of creams, rouges, lipsticks and scents provided to make themselves both look and smell beautiful.

If only, thought Emma, that awful black ring with the number 5 wasn't still stuck on my forehead! Nor that studded leather collar around my neck. But they were rather exciting!

Suddenly Sabhu opened a wardrobe. In it was a line of gorgeous silk and satin evening dresses of every hue – and matching high-heeled shoes. Emma recognised the one she had brought – her favourite – and slipped into it. The other girls were doing the same, their shame at what had been done to them in the kennels forgotten as they preened themselves in the mirror – and, except for poor Ingrid and Norah, adjusted a lock of hair here or a curl there.

Sabhu clapped his hands and made the girls line up for inspection, making one go back to touch up her eyeshadow and another to put on larger earrings. Then he briefed them carefully on what they were to do. 'Remember, I watching you all evening!' he warned them ominously, pointing once again to his whip. 'And remember too, you not allowed any champagne or wine – only orange juice. Doctor Anna not want her pills' effect spoilt by alcohol!'

He laughed cruelly and Emma was again left wondering what would be the effect of her pills.

Having put Ingrid and Norah together at the end of the line, he led them all downstairs and made them wait outside the drawing room door whilst he went in. Emma heard him announce, 'The young ladies are ready for your inspection!'

Then, one by one, he called them forward into the room. Emma was nervously biting her lips as she waited. Was her hair all right? Had she chosen the right colour lipstick and eyeshadow? Would Ursula approve? It would be too shame-making to be told to go back and scrub it all off and start again, but that, she knew, was just the sort of thing that Ursula might do if she thought she was getting too big for her boots.

Her reverie was suddenly interrupted. 'Number Five!' she heard Sabhu call.

Taking a deep breath, she stepped through the door.

It was an elegant and sophisticated scene that greeted

her. A little catwalk had been arranged along one long wall of the large room. Sitting facing it on little golden chairs, were Ursula, her two German friends and half a dozen clients. Emma caught her breath in astonishment as she saw that they were all – men, women, and even the fat, swarthy woman – wearing black dinner jackets and bow ties! Goodness!

She caught her breath, for she knew that Ursula's lesbian friends and clients enjoyed dressing up as men in the evening, especially if girls were going to be present. It was a way of showing off their dominance.

The girls whom Sabhu had called forward before her were still, rather shyly, walking up and down the catwalk on their high heels, like models at a fashion show, whilst the clients, pencils in hand, were making notes on their programmes.

Blushing delightfully, Emma too started to walk up and down. From under her lowered lashes, she saw that the horrible Francesca could hardly take her eyes off her. Ugh!

Then suddenly Sabhu announced, 'Numbers One and Two. A matched pair. An aunt and her niece!'

There was a gasp as Ingrid and Norah, their bald and well-polished scalps gleaming and making them look more alike than ever, stepped up on to the catwalk. Obviously Ursula had deliberately kept them back until last.

The Egyptian's eyes were out on stalks. 'They'd look wonderful in my zoo,' he murmured to Ursula. 'I offer you another ten thousand – each.'

'Make it another fifty thousand and they're yours,' laughed Ursula.

Just then Ingrid and Norah turned, their low-cut dresses showing off their blue-veined and much enlarged breasts. Their prominent and stretched nipples were clearly visible, thrusting against the thin silken material. They made a highly erotic sight.

'Ah!' cried the Egyptian enthusiastically. 'All right, another twenty thousand. They would be perfect in my zoo.'

'But worth even more if they're also perfect in your bed,' laughed Ursula. 'Try them out to tonight – unless someone else buys them in the auction.'

'Auction? Someone else?' The Egyptian was looking furious. 'You mean . . .?'

'Wait and see,' laughed Ursula, signalling to the guests to get up and giving Sabhu a nod.

The girls were now allowed down off the catwalk and taken around by Ursula to meet her guests, whilst Sabhu served champagne and, for the girls, orange juice.

It was an extraordinary and exciting feeling, thought Emma, flirting and gossiping with these sophisticated people as if she were a free woman, when only a few hours earlier they had enjoyed watching her being made to perform with a pygmy in a dogskin. She still, however, had a degrading dog collar around her neck, and a number emblazoned in black on her forehead!

The fact that all the female clients were wearing dinner jackets like those of the men, and were flirting with the girls in competition with the men, made it all the more extraordinary. And were the girls all really up for sale? Goodness! Was she?

At dinner each girl was placed between a male and a female client. The bare shoulders and low-cut dresses of the girls contrasted delightfully with the tailored evening dress of their neighbours. The conversation was light and amusing. Except for the numbered transfer on each girl's forehead, it might have been a typical country dinner party.

The man on Emma's right, a charming German, and the woman on her left, an intelligent American, made no reference to the day's events, as they talked politics and of the theatre. Emma almost began to wonder if it had all been a bad dream.

The dinner was delicious, and beautifully served by an obsequious Sabhu. Indeed, Emma was soon so relaxed that she almost poured herself a glass of wine. A sharp cough from Sabhu, and an equally sharp look, brought her back to reality and made her quickly put the wine decanter down untouched. Damn Doctor Anna and her pills!

Halfway through dinner Ursula invited the men, and 'the ladies so charmingly dressed as men', to move around two places. To Emma's horror the fat, swarthy Italian woman now sat herself down next to her. Oh, what a cruel-looking woman she was, whether dressed as a woman or a man.

'And now, child,' she began, putting a hand on Emma's thigh under the table, 'how would you like to serve me?'

She squeezed Emma's thigh.

Serve her? Ugh! Greatly daring, Emma picked up Francesca's hand and firmly put it back on the table. Francesca's eyes gleamed with rage. Who did this chit of a girl think she was?

'Don't you play the innocent with me, my girl,' she exclaimed angrily. 'One day you'll be begging me to touch your thighs – and elsewhere.'

Emma saw Ursula look up from across the table, her attention caught by Francesca's angry tone. She had to do something quickly to correct the situation, or she'd be in dead trouble.

'Oh no, Madam,' she said with a smile, putting the woman's hand back on her thigh, and thinking quickly, 'I just thought for a moment that I was still in that dogskin and I didn't want you to spoil your hands.'

It sounded weak, but it was all that she could think of at the time.

'Hm!' grunted Francesca, not knowing whether to believe the girl or not. 'All right! Now, give me your hand.' With that she placed Emma's hand on her tummy. Under the trousers, Emma felt something hard and erect. A manhood! But she was a woman, surely? Was she wearing a dildo strapped on to her crotch under her trousers?

'Play with it, girl,' the fat woman said. 'Go on! Or I'll tell Sabhu.'

Emma caught her breath and, gripping the manhood, started to rub it up and down. The woman turned her back on Emma and started a long conversation with her other neighbour, but Emma could see that her eyes were glistening with pleasure.

Still talking to her neighbour, the woman put her hand down under the table and discreetly unzipped her trousers.

Emma's hand was now on the realistic rubber dildo. She got the feeling that it was a double one, which meant that by gently rubbing it up and down she was giving real pleasure to this horrible woman. Ugh!

After dinner there was dancing. The music was slow and romantic. The lights were very low.

Emma longed to be in the arms of her Mistress, but it was the olive-skinned Egyptian who claimed her first. He hardly bothered to say a word as they danced, but took advantage of the darkness to put his hand into her décolletage and feel her breasts and nipples. Was he disappointed that they did not compare with those of Ingrid and Norah? she wondered.

'No, I do not see you in my zoo,' he said as the music stopped.

Thank God for that, thought Emma.

Then it was a by now rather drunken, fat Italian woman who led her on to the floor. She kept running her hands up and down Emma's back in a horrible way, pressing her against the dildo under her trousers. She was a little shorter than Emma and Emma, to her horror, felt herself beginning to react as the artificial manhood pressed against her beauty lips.

'Oh, yes, you'd make a lovely companion for my little baby girl,' the woman murmured drunkenly.

Suddenly Ursula clapped her hands and Sabhu made all the girls go out of the room and back up to the bathroom.

There, under Sabhu's watchful eye, they all had to take off their evening dresses, spend a penny, and – surprise! surprise! – put on their tight, black-and-white-spotted, dog suits again. This time, though, the headpieces and the immobilising gloves were left off, and instead they were told to touch up their make-up. But it was not only their faces that they were told to paint.

Looking in the mirror Emma saw a strange, slender dog with the head of a beautiful blonde woman and human hands. It was marked on its forehead with '5' in a black ring, and had a black dog collar, two bright scarlet nipples and gold ring jewellery in its scarlet-painted beauty lips. She looked, she thought proudly, irresistible!

Then Sabhu made them line up again and, to Emma's astonishment, he fastened manacles on to each girl's wrists, with a foot of heavy chain linking them. But that was not all, for in the middle of the connecting chain was a large link, from which hung another foot of chain. Sabhu now locked the end of this to the ring at the front of their collars, and Emma found that she could not lower her hands below her waist.

Now manacled and helpless, she found herself standing with the other girls outside the door of the drawing room. Their manacles clanked with their every movement. But this time they were, rather mysteriously, going to be called into the room in the reverse order to the last time. This time Ingrid and Norah, as Ursula's own prize matched pair, were to go in first.

'Ladies and gentlemen,' she heard Ursula call out through the half-open door. 'Now that you have seen our lovely bitches performing in their dogsuits, and met them socially over dinner, I'm sure you're longing to get to know them even better – and where better to do this than in your bed? So I'm going to auction their services for the night.'

There was a buzz of excitement.

'Of course,' Ursula went on, 'this will also give you a chance to try out the goods before you make your sealed bids – yes, sealed bids – tomorrow evening, after the further performances in the kennels.'

Another murmur of conversation greeted this announcement. Sealed bids!

'Alternatively,' Ursula said with a teasing laugh, 'if you have already made up your mind as to which of the bitches you want, then here is an opportunity to make sure that the goods are not sullied by your rivals before tomorrow's sealed bids!'

She paused to let the point sink in. Several of the keenest buyers, she thought, would pay a large sum to keep their desired bitches pure!

'I shall, of course, be auctioning together our prize

matched pair – the aunt and her niece.' Here Ursula paused. Seeking to arouse a little competition, she looked meaningfully at both the gross Egyptian man and the sophisticated-looking American woman. 'You may also be interested in bidding for our two very pretty sisters –' here she looked at the grey-haired German '– but they, like the rest of the remaining five bitches, will be auctioned individually.'

Emma heard some laughter. What about her, she wondered, anxiously, who was going to buy her for the night? A man or a woman? Gosh!

'Oh, one final point,' added Ursula. 'I'm afraid that we have had to manacle the bitches, for we don't want any of them escaping during the night. But I'm sure you'll appreciate them all the more that way.

Ursula's guests had assumed that the girls would reappear in their evening dresses, or perhaps in nightdresses. There was, therefore, a gasp of delighted surprise when, in response to Sabhu's call of 'Numbers One and Two', Ingrid and Norah crawled through the door on all fours and then crawled up on to the catwalk.

They were dressed in their dogsuits, but with their bald heads and made-up faces exposed. Their long nipples, which were now painted scarlet, hung down beneath them and their hairless beauty lips, which had been similarly painted, glistened between their legs.

They each made a fascinating cross between a beautiful woman and an attractive bitch as Sabhu led them, by their leads, crawling down the catwalk.

'Well, what am I bid for this lovely pair, specially trained to give pleasure in tandem?' asked Ursula. The bids came in fast, much to the rage of the fat Egyptian, who found himself beating off a whole series of determined bids – and not only from the American lady. As Ursula had intended, it was a carefully planned foretaste of the sum which would be required in order to secure them permanently at the next day's sealed bid auction.

Finally the Egyptian secured the pair of them, and Sabhu led them down from the catwalk to crawl up to where he was seated. Then Sabhu bowed and handed their leads to the Egyptian.

'Number Three!' called out Sabhu as he led a very pretty blonde girl up on to the catwalk. Disappointed at not securing Ingrid and Norah for the night, the other guests were soon bidding against each other for this lovely creature, who was eventually knocked down to the American lady.

'Number Four!' Emma's heart was in her mouth, and she was far too overwrought to listen to the bidding.

'Number Five!' Emma felt a sudden tug on her collar and she crawled along behind Sabhu. Reaching the catwalk she saw that Ingrid and Norah were now sitting on the outspread knees of the fat Egyptian, who was busy playing with their long nipples.

One of the blonde girls was kneeling at the feet of the American woman, licking her hand and gazing up at her with adoration – or perhaps with relief at not having been bought for the night by someone else. The other blonde girl was licking the shoes of a stern-looking woman.

'So, what am I bid for this little creature?' Emma heard Ursula say. 'You can read all about her in your programmes.' Once again the bids came in fast, and Emma was horrified to see that the fat Italian woman was bidding hard. Finally, Emma was knocked down to her. Oh no! But a little swat from Sabhu's whip quickly had her scuttling along behind him to the woman's feet.

'Well little bitch?' came a drunken voice. 'Are you going to be a good little girl?'

Too scared to say a word, Emma started to lick her new temporary Mistress' shoes.

31

Goodbye to the Kennels

Early next morning there was a sudden warning rattle at the door of Francesca's bedroom. It was, Emma knew, Sabhu going around the bedrooms reclaiming the girls.

She looked at the large fat body lying snoring in the bed. A rubber dildo stuck up obscenely from between the woman's thighs. Emma shivered with disgust as she remembered how the drunken woman had made her lie on her tummy and had then made her beg to receive the dildo up her behind.

She remembered how she had screamed out and tried to wriggle away, but had been held helpless under the woman's weight. With her hands manacled to her neck, she had been even more helpless – and, to her shame, aroused.

But then, suddenly, all the drink had caught up with the fat Italian woman and she had fallen fast asleep, with Emma pinned down beneath her, impaled on her dildo.

For hours Emma had lain there helpless. Then, anxious not to awaken the woman lest she started up again, she had managed first to slip off the dildo and then, very carefully, to slide out from under her. Still terrified that the woman might wake up, Emma had snatched a few hours sleep on the floor.

Never, she resolved, would she have anything more to do with this awful Italian woman.

There was another rattle at the door. It was, she knew, the signal for her to go and join the others.

She was still wearing her dogskin, and the manacles and

collar were still locked in place. Her dog lead still hung down from the ring at the front of her collar. Awkwardly, because of the manacles, she got up and ran on tiptoe to the door, and then, bending her knees so that she could reach down to the handle with her manacled hands, she opened it.

There stood Sabhu, dressed in his circus lion tamer's suit and holding the other girls by their leads. Several looked as though they had had a fairly exhausting night. He grabbed Emma's lead and shut the door behind her. Then, without saying a word, he set off down the corridor and up the stairs to their large bathroom, the girls running along behind him.

Once in the bathroom, he locked the door.

He unlocked the girls' manacles and let them stretch their arms for a moment.

'Take off dogskins,' he then ordered. Emma and the other girls put their hands up behind their necks and pulled down the zip fastener that kept the costume in place. Except for their collars they were, once again, stark naked in front of this terrifying man.

He picked up his long whip. The girls were all eyeing it nervously. He pointed with it to the long bench running down the room. 'Up!' he ordered.

Oh no, thought Emma, not that. Then she remembered that Doctor Anna had said that the pills always worked better on an empty stomach, and that Ursula had told the guests that there would be further performances in the kennels today. My God!

Once again Sabhu strapped each girl's wrists, wide apart, to the rail behind them. As before, they would not now be able to get at the tubes pushed up inside them. Emma saw him turn the taps which let the soapy blue liquid into the individual glass jars behind each girl. Please don't let him use the awful burning red liquid as well, she prayed, remembering that Doctor Anna had said she always used it for the first time.

Sabhu came around to the side of the bench, his whip raised. 'Position and tongues out!' he ordered. Emma remembered only too well what she had to do.

Sabhu nodded with pleasure as he saw all seven girls bend forward, their legs apart and their knees bent, their heads raised, their eyes fixed ahead, and their tongues and, of course, their hands held back. They made a nice sight. A picture of disciplined womanhood. A credit to his power of command. He was like a drill sergeant adjusting the alignment of a line of recruits. One small adjustment was needed to bring them into a perfect line.

'Number Five! Tighter!'

Hastily Emma bent her knees more and thrust up her buttocks.

Moments later she felt the well-greased long nozzle penetrate her, and then she heard a little series of moans coming up the line as one at a time, Sabhu turned on the taps below each jar.

Half an hour later the girls, dressed again in their dogskins, were back in their cages. Emma found herself eyeing her human dog neighbour – her Master!

Then suddenly Sabhu came back. He went straight up to her cage, unfastened her chain, snapped on a lead and took her out of the cage.

Through her little eyeholes, Emma peered around at the other cages, at the other girl-bitches crawling up and down their cages and at the two very virile human dogs. She had a premonition that she was being taken away from it all, that she would not see her companions again, that she would not find out what happened to them, and that she would never know just what Doctor Anna had been up to. Ursula was so secretive!

She felt sad. There had been some terrifying moments in the kennels, and in the bathroom, but also some very exciting ones.

She felt little tears running down her cheeks inside her headpiece as Sabhu led her crawling across the lawn, back to the house and into Ursula's private office.

32

An Offer has been Made for Emma

Ursula, wearing reading glasses and a business suit, was sitting at her desk looking at some papers. She said nothing as Emma, wearing her complete dog suit, was led up to her desk.

There, unexpectedly, Sabhu unzipped Emma's mouthpiece, but kept her kneeling on all fours in front of Ursula's desk. 'You no speak without permission,' he ordered harshly.

Although she was no longer muzzled, and though there were so many questions she longed to ask, she did not dare to say a word. Sabhu, still holding her lead, was standing right behind her, his whip in his hand.

Finally, Ursula took off her glasses.

'Well, little Emma, you're a lucky girl. You're going to earn your Mistress a lot of money. I've had a very interesting offer for your services this morning.'

Emma's heart was in her mouth. Not that awful Egyptian! And anyway what about her husband? He wouldn't be abroad for ever. And what about the Prince, who was expected back in a couple of months?

'Yes,' continued Ursula, as though she had picked up on Emma's worries. 'It'll only be for a month – but it'll be a very exciting month for you, and a very profitable one for me!'

What did Ursula mean? Emma wondered anxiously.

Was she going to be hired out to somebody? She knew that Ursula never shared the proceeds with any of her girls – they had been trained by Sabhu to do as they were told purely for love of their mistress. But to whom was she going to be hired out?

'Of course, I shall want you to sign a contract of service for that month, a legal contract stating that in consideration for your board and keep, and being given special training, you agree to serve your Mistress in whatever way she wishes.

A Mistress! She would have to serve a Mistress. It might be rather exciting and it was only for a month. Provided it wasn't that awful Italian woman!

'Yes,' went on Ursula, 'I've agreed to let my Italian friend Francesca have you for a month, so ...'

'No!' screamed Emma. In her anguish, she completely forgot that Francesca was also the name of the woman to whom she had overheard Ursula talking, about a girl who might be the late Crown Prince's missing concubine.

'Not her! I won't! I won't!'

Then she screamed in pain as a furious Sabhu laid a glancing but painful lash upon her buttocks. 'Silence!' he roared.

Shocked by the pain, Emma reverted to silence, while looking resentfully up at Ursula through the little eyeholes.

Angrily, Ursula got up from her desk. She looked down at the human bitch humbly kneeling in front of it.

'How dare you question my orders?' she said. Then she paused. 'Very well then, if you're not prepared to do as you're told for my friend Francesca, then you'll just have to learn what happens to girls who dare to disobey me!' She turned to Sabhu. 'Take this disobedient little slut next door and thrash her,' she ordered.

'No, no, please,' Emma sobbed, as she knelt contritely before Ursula; but then she felt Sabhu's hands grip her and pull her up on to her feet. She lowered her eyes.

'Twelve strokes!' she heard Ursula order coldly, in a clear, harsh voice.

'No! No!' she pleaded.

'And leave the door ajar.' Ursula reached for the house phone and dialled a number. 'I'll invite Francesca down so that she can hear the slut getting her come-uppance whilst we have breakfast together.'

Francesca, that ugly brute of a woman, was going to hear her being thrashed! Like Ursula, Francesca too stood no nonsense from a girl. She knew just what she wanted from Emma and was apparently prepared to pay Ursula a large sum to get it.

But how could Emma agree to serve her? She was, she kept telling herself, a married woman with a life of her own, the concubine of an Arab Prince, the ...

None of that mattered now as Sabhu unzipped the back of her dogskin, and slipped it down to her knees. He left the headpiece on her. 'Bend over chair!' Sabhu ordered Emma. 'And stop that snivelling!'

Emma knew better than to argue and bent over, offering her bare bottom for punishment. She saw Sabhu look down at her from behind, and she blushed scarlet at the thought that her carefully depilated beauty lips would now be on display to this frightening man.

Biting her lips, she watched him go to a cupboard and take out a long whippy cane, flexing it with both hands. It had a little silver tip at one end and a curved handle at the other.

She could now hear Ursula and Francesca laughing together in the room next door. She heard the rattle of cups and saucers, as Ursula offered her guest a scone. Oh, those swine, she had thought, they are both as bad as each other, the way they treat poor young women. But she had been wrong, she now knew. She feared and respected Ursula, but loathed Francesca.

'Keep your hands gripping the back of the chair,' ordered Sabhu, now standing right behind her and still flexing the cane menacingly between his hands. 'Head up! Keep your eyes on the wall! Arch your back! Now up on your toes and thrust back more with your bottom!'

Sabhu was getting her into the correct position for a beating. There was silence now from the room next door.

Emma could imagine the two women exchanging smiles. Oh, how she hated them!

Out of the corner of her eye, she saw Sabhu eyeing her bottom and taking aim with his cane. He turned sideways-on and rose up on his toes like a bullfighter about to administer the *coup de grâce*. Oh, the sheer horror, the sheer exciting horror of being beaten by this man!

'One!' she suddenly heard him say.

There was a sudden swishing sound and she bit her lips hard as her bottom seemed to have been struck by a line of fire. She gripped the back of the chair extra-hard to stop herself from putting her hand back to ease the terrible pain. She knew that to do so would have meant the stroke not counting. She had not, however, been able to prevent herself from giving a pathetic little cry which had been greeted by laughter from next door.

'Two! ... Three! ...' and so the beating went on. It was terrible but, Emma realised through her tears and cries, Sabhu was not using his full strength. She shuddered to think how much pain she would have felt had he been doing so.

... 'Six!'

Then there was a pause.

'Bring her back in here,' she heard Ursula call out. 'Let's have a look at her!'

Sabhu closed the zip fastener across the mouth of her realistic headpiece. Then, still leaving the headpiece in place, he made her step out of the dogskin. Emma glanced in the mirror. She saw a beautiful young woman, but with the head of a dog – and a muzzled one at that.

Making her get down on all fours, and again holding her by the lead attached to her heavy studded leather collar, Sabhu led her back into Ursula's private office. Only a close observer would have seen that her eyes, visible through the small eyeholes, were still weeping.

He led her up to the sofa on which the two women were now sitting and made her turn around and show them the marks of the first six strokes.

'An excellent beginning, don't you agree, my dear?'

Ursula said to the laughing Francesca, who, stimulated by the beating, seemed to have recovered from her heavy drinking the night before.

'When you have given her the remaining six strokes,' Ursula said to Sabhu in a cold voice, 'put her belt back on her, take her to the airport and put her on the next plane for England – she can rot there in her belt until she comes to her senses. I'll delay the morning's performance until you get back.'

Then, turning to Francesca, she said with a cruel laugh, 'She doesn't yet know that her husband is unexpectedly flying back for a quick weekend in England before returning to the Pacific for a couple of months. He was unable to reach her at their home and, knowing that she often works for me as a sales assistant at the exhibitions of my paintings, he left a message at my gallery.'

'So?' laughed Francesca.

'So, now she'll have to think up a good story to tell her husband to stop him finding the belt that we're going to lock on to her!'

Appalled, and with her bottom still smarting, Emma had wanted to protest, but before she had been able to say a word, the two laughing women had risen and left the room.

Sabhu had then marched her back to the next room. For a brief moment she thought she might persuade him to forego the rest of her thrashing now that his audience had left. But it was a vain hope and the remaining six strokes had been just as painful as the first six. It had been terrible.

Then he made her stand up straight and step out of her dogskin. He unfastened her headpiece and unlocked her collar. Except for the rings in her beauty lips, she was now as naked as the day she was born.

'You keep still,' he ordered. Emma blushed. 'Now hold your breath and look straight ahead!'

Then he again fastened around her waist the flat rubber belt, the same German-designed belt which had proved such an effective chastity belt before she had come to this house party. She remembered that, being made of rubber, it had not triggered off the security checks at the airport on her way here.

Emma did not dare to look down, but she could feel Sabhu putting the belt on her in the same way as he had done before. Then, when it was in position, he checked again that her beauty lips were tightly compressed between the two edges of the slit in the rubber pad between her legs. It was the tightness of this slit that made it quite impossible for a girl to get at her little pleasure bud behind her Mistress' back – or use a dildo to excite herself.

Emma, still looking straight ahead, could feel him pulling her beauty lips through the slit so that they would be held pouting in the correct innocent position. Oh it was all so awful having this done by a man, even if he was her beloved Mistress' loyal manservant.

Satisfied with her now tightly pouting beauty lips, Sabhu then dropped down over them the plastic grille. This grille would, Emma knew, prevent her from so much as touching her beauty lips, and would certainly stop her, in her desperation to obtain relief, from trying to excite them with a vibrator.

Yes, she thought bitterly, it was all very clever and cunning, but not so funny if it was your beauty lips that were being kept out of sight behind the grille, or your hot little beauty bud that was being kept totally inaccessible, and totally frustrated, beneath the stiff rubber pad.

Emma gave a little gasp of despair as she heard the click that denoted that the shield was now held locked into place.

'Turn around and bend your knees!' Sabhu had then ordered. Now seated behind her, he had checked the tension in the rubber thong which covered her rear orifice. He had to ensure that it would stay firmly in position, but that she would also be able to pull it to one side when she needed to relieve herself.

'Thrust bottom back!' he then ordered. 'Head up! Shoulders back!'

Emma blushed as she assumed the required position and

felt Sabhu check, once again, the tension in the rubber thong.

Satisfied that all was in order, Sabhu made Emma turn around again. He now snapped a strong little padlock through the flange holding the slotted ends of the belt in place above the girl's navel. There would be no way now that she could get out of the chastity belt unless either he or Ursula unlocked the padlock.

Emma gave a gasp of despair. She knew that the design of the belt allowed it, at least in theory, to be worn almost indefinitely without any physical damage being done to its wearer. She also knew, however, that any unfortunate woman who, like herself, was locked into such a belt would constantly be aware of it, both physically and mentally.

33

Emma has to Decide

It was late in the evening and Emma was sitting alone in her little office in the market town.

She was holding her head in her hands in despair and desperation as she waited for the phone to ring, trying to decide what she should say – yes or no.

The very thought of entering the service of Francesca repelled her. She simply could not bring herself to do it. What did Francesca want her for? She remembered how the woman had drunkenly driven her dildo up her little bottom. Ugh!

On the other hand, being locked into the awful rubber chastity belt was having a terrible effect on her. She simply could not stand it any longer. It was driving her mad, not only from physical frustration, but also from mental shame – and from fear.

What would happen, for God's sake, when the Prince came back and found it?

And what about her husband? It had been difficult enough booming off poor John that first weekend after she had returned from Ireland, when he had unexpectedly returned to England for a couple of days. Supposing the belt was still on when he next came back? She could not go on booming him off indefinitely – and yet Ursula was apparently quite happy to leave it on 'until she came to her senses' and agreed to enter Francesca's service.

As Emma well knew, it was keeping a married woman locked up in a chastity belt, in her own home, under the unsuspecting eye of her husband, which gave Ursula a particularly thrilling feeling of power.

Emma had been so repelled by Francesca that she had completely forgotten an important point – that the woman whom she had overheard telling Ursula about a girl she had bought back from a rich Arab had also been called Francesca. Now, like a bolt from the blue, it struck her that they might be the same person. So, what was she doing sitting here when she could, perhaps, be finding the Prince's missing girl?

The Prince had told her to take whatever steps were necessary, at whatever cost, to trace the girl. But was this too great a cost? Especially as she was not completely sure that she was on to the right Francesca. Oh, if only Ursula was not so secretive! If only she did not have a hang-up about her girls being inquisitive!

She moved uncomfortably in her chair – that damned belt! She was constantly aware of its degrading and humiliating presence.

She thought back to the terrifying and yet exciting time she had spent in the kennels. For the umpteenth time, she could feel herself becoming wet and aroused under the belt. Oh, how she longed to touch herself, to give herself relief. She was so damned frustrated!

How much longer could she continue to refuse to do what Ursula wanted, when one word on the telephone would bring her release?

Who was going to ring? Probably Francesca, but it might be Ursula. She wasn't sure. All she knew was that, whilst she had been out at lunch, Sabhu had left a message on her answering machine warning her to expect an important call in her office after six that evening, and ordering her to wait there for it.

There was no way she could ring Ursula, even if she could pluck up enough courage to do so – for Ursula did not like being rung up by her girls. Emma did not even know her number and Ursula had been careful to ensure that she did not learn the name of the large house in Ireland to which she had twice been taken. Indeed, Ursula might well now be on her way to England and she did not know Francesca's number either.

So, all she could do was to sit and wait. She did not dare to go home. Keeping her waiting like this was, she realised, all part of the power game that Ursula liked to play with her – like a game of cat and mouse.

Desperately she tried to make up her mind what to say when the phone did ring. She was still besotted with Ursula and hated being in disgrace. She was also consumed with jealousy over Ursula's other girls. Had she really disposed of Ingrid and Norah? Had she already replaced them? How disappointing that Ursula, in turn, did not seem to be in the least bit jealous of Francesca. Had Ursula planned it all right from the beginning as a convenient way of getting rid of her? Or was she really just hiring her out temporarily in exchange for the large fee that she had been offered by that ghastly Francesca? Oh, she felt so helpless.

Outwardly, of course, she was still her charming, vivacious and well-dressed self. No one would ever have guessed that under her smart office suit, an ingenious modern chastity belt was locked around her waist and pressing tightly against her beauty lips.

Nor would anyone have guessed that the only keys to this tight and very effective chastity belt were held not by a man, but by a woman – Ursula, who was apparently still in Ireland.

The humiliation of being kept locked in her chastity belt, like the pain in her bottom, was something that never left her thoughts as she waited on tenterhooks for the phone to ring.

Suddenly the phone did ring. With a shaking hand she picked it up. She still didn't know what to say.

It was Henry! Henry cheerfully talking away to her as if she didn't have a care in the world.

'Oh darling!' she sobbed. 'Oh darling!'

'You sound pretty fraught,' laughed Henry, 'what's the trouble? Don't say she's put the belt back on you again!'

Apart from Paddy, Henry had always been the only

person to whom she could really talk. He was the only person who knew all about her, even about the rings and the belt, and even about Ursula, whom he jovially regarded as a rather inferior rival. Suddenly she found herself pouring it all out – about the Prince, about the missing girl, about the houseparty, about Francesca, once again, about the belt.

'Well, as I always say, first things first. I've heard about that girl your Prince wants to find. She might well be in the hands of your repulsive Francesca – or rather back in her hands. The only way you're going to find out is to go and see. And the only way you're going to get to do that is to go and work for her for a month. A month isn't long. But another month in that belt and you're going to end up in the loony bin!'

'So?' queried Emma. Oh, how she admired Henry's quick and decisive way of getting to the root of a matter.

'So, off you go, and then come and have dinner with me in a month's time and tell me all about it – unless that Prince of yours has turned up again.'

Then he put down the phone.

Immediately it rang again. Ursula!

'Well? Has the little girl come to her senses yet – or do I leave the belt on for another month?'

'No!' cried Emma. 'No, Madam, for God's sake, no!'

'So,' Ursula's voice was harsh and firm, 'are you now willing to sign a binding contract of service with Francesca, and willing for her to take any steps she feels necessary to enforce it?'

Emma's heart was in her mouth, but Henry had cleared her mind.

'Yes, Madam, yes.'

'Very well, then. Catch the late evening flight today. I've booked a seat for you and your ticket will be waiting for you at the airport. Sabhu will meet you. You needn't bring any clothes. But, if you're not on the plane then you'll stay in the belt for another month. And no talking to strangers on the plane!'

With that, she too put down the phone.

34

Cash On Delivery

Emma was now in a mad rush to get to the airport in time. All she could think of was the threat of another month in that dreadful belt.

All went well. The ticket was waiting for her at the airport. She caught the plane. Sabhu was waiting for her on arrival. She saw that he still carried his whip. He said nothing as they drove through the darkness to Ursula's house. She still could not make out exactly where it was.

There was no sign either of Ingrid or of Norah as Emma, still wearing her office suit, waited outside Ursula's office, but Emma thought she heard some girlish laughter coming from the schoolroom in the nursery wing. My God, she thought, is Ursula training up a replacement team, another matched pair?

Suddenly Sabhu ushered her into the office. Once again Ursula was sitting at her desk.

'Sign there!' was all she said.

Dumbly, Emma did as she was told. Ursula seemed in such a bad temper that she did not dare to take the time to read what the contract actually said.

'Give this copy to Francesca,' said Ursula to Sabhu. 'I'll keep the girl's copy.'

Then she turned to the frightened Emma. 'Now go with Sabhu. He'll hand you over to your new Mistress. Go!'

'But . . . but . . . the belt . . . isn't going to be taken off?' stammered Emma.

'Why? Did you think you were going to be able give

yourself a little relief?' replied Ursula with a cruel laugh. 'You'll be lucky – and I shouldn't try chancing your arm with Francesca either. If there's one thing she can't stand it's little girls playing with themselves.'

Emma blushed. 'Oh, no, Madam, I – I . . .

'No,' said Ursula firmly. 'The belt stays on until your new Mistress, or her agents, have signed for your receipt and Sabhu has been given a cheque, made out to me, in payment for the goods ordered. Cash on delivery is how I do my business, whether it's my pictures or my girls – and I'm not going to risk you trying to get out of your contract by running away before you're safely locked up by your new owner.'

Locked up, thought Emma. Goodness! How terrifying – or did she mean exciting! 'But where are we going?' she asked.

'That's none of your business,' was the reply. Again Ursula turned to Sabhu. 'Take her away – and don't forget to bring back the cheque!'

They caught the late night plane to London. Once again Sabhu said nothing. At the airport a chauffeur-driven hire car was waiting for them. They drove, in the darkness, through a bewildering maze of streets and finally stopped outside a house in what was obviously a well-to-do residential area.

Sabhu took Emma out of the car and rang the bell. The door was opened by a beefy-looking black woman dressed, to Emma's surprise, as a child's nurse. 'Is this the new young baby, then?' Emma was surprised to hear the woman enquire of Sabhu in a strong Caribbean accent, as she looked Emma up and down. Then she gripped Emma's arm. 'Come along with Nanny,' she said kindly, leading her into the house.

Nanny? How strange, thought Emma. Then she remembered that first conversation she had overheard and Ursula's remark about how clever the Francesca she had been talking to had been to find a 'suitable nanny'. Goodness, thought Emma, then this Francesca must indeed be the same one, which meant that perhaps she was hot on the trail!

Nanny reminded Emma of Scarlett O'Hara's childhood nanny in *Gone with the Wind* – big, black and reassuring. She warmed to her immediately. After all the harshness of Sabhu and the dog cages it was a lovely change to find a nice, kind, old-fashioned nanny.

As she was led through the hall she saw a large and very expensive-looking, old-fashioned black pram. She also caught a glimpse of a large, beautifully decorated drawing room. Then Nanny, as Emma was already mentally calling her, unlocked a door which led into a ground floor wing of the house.

'I think I'd better just lock the door again,' said Nanny ominously, 'you never know with them at first.'

'Yes,' said Sabhu, 'and I expect you'd like me to help get her properly ... dressed!'

'Oh, that would be kind of you, Mr Sabhu,' replied Nanny. 'It's very late and we don't want any trouble with her, do we? We don't want her getting worried and excited, and Mistress won't want to be disturbed at night by her baby crying,' replied the black woman mysteriously.

She led Emma into what appeared to be a bathroom, but to Emma's astonishment it was evidently a child's bathroom, with plastic ducks in the bath and children's pots, decorated with clowns and fairies, in the corner. On a white sideboard were several baby bottles, cans of baby talcum powder and a large box of rompers.

Goodness! Emma remembered that the Prince had said that the missing girl, Renata, might have been pregnant when she was returned to her former Mistress. She also remembered that she had heard Ursula had been talking to Francesca about a baby girl called Brigetta. Might this be Brigetta's bathroom? Might this big black woman be Brigetta's nurse? Emma's brain was in a whirl.

She heard Sabhu give a sardonic laugh behind her.

'This one's such a pretty little thing,' she heard Nanny say to Sabhu.

Emma looked around in vain, expecting to see a little baby girl. Surely they weren't talking about her?

'Now, come over and sit on Nanny's knee and give her a kiss,' said Nanny, holding out her arms to Emma as she sat down on a large upright chair. Emma ran over to her. Then, like a little girl, she sat on her knee and, reaching up, planted a kiss on her cheeks.

'What an affectionate little girl she is,' laughed Nanny. 'It's best if they're nice and gentle – they settle down much better to the routine. And I think she'll make another lovely little baby for Mistress. She does so love them!'

Settle down better to the routine? What routine? Another baby? Suddenly alarm bells began to ring in Emma's brain. She tried to get up, but Nanny held her firmly and she felt Sabhu's whip touch her arm threateningly. Terrified, she now kept quite still.

She wanted to cry out, to ask what was happening, but before she could say a word, Nanny had picked up a baby bottle and had thrust the teat into her mouth.

'You have a good little suck,' she said reassuringly, patting Emma's back as if she were a real baby. 'It's a lovely taste, isn't it?'

Held like a baby having its bottle, Emma soon found herself sucking eagerly at the rubber teat. She was thirsty after the journey.

She began to feel drowsy. She'd forgotten just how sleepy warm milk could make her feel.

'We'll start her on real milk tomorrow,' she heard Nanny say in a proud voice. 'It's so good for them, and breast feeding is natural for babies – once their little tummies have got used to it! And it gets them so nice and slim – just like Mistress likes them to be!'

Confused, Emma heard Sabhu laugh, but this time he sounded far away. Oh, how sleepy she felt! As Nanny lifted the now empty bottle away, Emma put her head on to Nanny's ample and reassuring bosom and closed her eyes. She felt so safe and warm. All her worries about coming here were suddenly forgotten.

'Now we must get baby ready for bed,' she heard Nanny say, stroking her hair. 'What a sleepy little girl.'

Emma was vaguely aware of her coat being undone and slipped off, and then her skirt. She was even more vaguely aware of Nanny laughing as she handed Sabhu a cheque and received the contract in exchange. Then there was a lovely feeling of relief as the belt was removed. She heard Nanny clapping her hands in delight and exclaiming, 'Oh, just look at these rings! Don't they make baby look pretty!'

Then, she felt something else being put on her, as though to replace the belt. She felt herself being lifted up by Sabhu, and then she finally fell asleep.

35

Found!

Emma slowly began to awake. She was aware of lying on a rubber sheet. How strange. Where was she? And she was sucking something. It was rubbery but tasted rather nice. But she didn't seem to be able to get rid of it. How odd!

She put up her hands to touch her face. There were pretty little knitted woolly gloves on her hands, but she couldn't flex her fingers, and she couldn't hold anything. Indeed, under the innocent-looking gloves, she could feel them being held closely clamped together as if she was making a fist.

Slowly she opened her eyes wider. She was lying curled up in a little child's cot. There were white-painted bars on one side – and more bars over the top! She stretched out a gloved hand and found that she couldn't move the bars. She was fastened into the cot.

She tried to cry out, but the rubber thing in her mouth silenced her. Fastened to the side of the bars was a little mirror. She looked in it and saw, staring back at her, the face of a little baby – a baby with a pretty little lace cap on her head that hid her hair completely and which fastened with a bow under her chin. There was a pink ribbon in the cap. Pink for a baby girl! In her mouth was a large rubber baby's comforter. No wonder she could not speak! It was tied, also with pink ribbon, behind her neck.

She seemed to be wearing a short lace baby's dress, and on her feet, she saw, were pretty little knitted socks that matched her gloves.

But there was something odd between her legs. She looked down and saw some transparent plastic rompers covering a thick white nappy that came up between her legs and was fastened with a large safety pin to the part that went around her waist. It was made of towelling.

She gasped. Not only had she been dressed like a baby, and given a baby's comforter to keep her quiet, and baby gloves to keep her helpless, but she had actually been put into nappies!

Thinking back, she realised she had a very vague recollection of it all being done, but so gently, so tenderly that she must have fallen asleep at some time during the process. It certainly hadn't occurred to her to protest at any time.

Ursula got a thrill from undermining her girls' perception of themselves as independent, sophisticated grown women, by dressing them up as much younger schoolgirls. Francesca seemed to be taking the same idea to the extreme.

She remembered the contract which she had signed for a month's service. Did her duties include allowing herself to be treated like a baby?

She heard a rustling noise from the side of her cot – the side which had no bars. Was there another cot there? Was there another little baby girl in it? She gave a little mooing noise from behind her comforter and back in reply came a similar little mooing noise. There was a girl there – and she was also sucking a comforter. Was she in nappies, too, Emma wondered?

Just then she heard a door being unlocked and in came Nanny – the big, kind, black nanny she had seen the previous night. The one who had given her a bottle.

She saw the strong-looking woman lean over and pick something up. It was a girl! She was carrying a grown-up girl! A girl dressed just like Emma was, as a baby with a little cap, funny-shaped knitted gloves, a comforter, rompers and a bulky nappy which emphasised how tiny her waist was.

She watched through the bars of her cot as Nanny put

the helpless girl down on her back on a couch, which was also covered in a rubber sheet. Then she saw Nanny bend over the girl.

'And has baby been good?' Nanny said as she unfastened the rompers and the nappy. 'Oh, good little girl!'

Then she saw Nanny pick up the girl again and sit her down on a little pot. She saw the girl, who seemed very pretty, look at her, blush and then smile behind her comforter. Emma smiled back. She had a friend, a little baby friend, a friend in adversity!

She watched as Nanny cleaned the girl with cotton wool, picked her up again and, sitting down on another tall-backed chair, put her on her knee. She saw the girl eyeing Nanny with anticipation.

'And is the little baby longing for her feed?' Nanny asked. Emma heard the girl nod avidly and give a little moan. Then, astonished, she saw Nanny unfasten her dress and lift out a large breast. The girl's eyes lit up and she put her gloved hands up to it.

Nanny laughed and untied the bow of the ribbon which held the comforter into the girl's mouth. Emma's heart missed a couple of beats. Might, perhaps, the girl now say something? But she just continued to make little gurgling noises. Was talking forbidden here? Did they have to behave like little babies all the time?

She saw Nanny hold her breast out to the girl who eagerly began to suck out her milk. Soon she had drunk the breast dry and turned as if begging for the other one.

'No, little baby, that's for your little friend,' laughed Nanny, tying the comforter back into the girl's mouth. Then she put her breast away in her dress. Was that all the girl was going to get for breakfast? Goodness! Was that why she was so slim?

Nanny picked the girl up again and laid her back down on the couch. Emma saw her take a clean nappy, put it on the girl, fasten it with the safety pin, and pull up the plastic rompers.

Then she lifted the girl and carried her to the playpen in the middle of the room. It too had a rubber sheet over the padding which covered the floor. Like Emma's cot it too had bars over the top.

Emma saw Nanny bend down and fasten an oversized baby harness over the girl's shoulders and around her tiny waist. She was now tethered in the playpen and forced to crawl around it on all fours, just like a real baby.

Then Nanny looked at Emma as she knelt on all fours in her cot.

'So, has the new baby seen our happy little routine?' she laughed. All that Emma could do was make a little mooing noise, as Nanny now lifted off the top of the cot and, reaching down, lifted Emma up in her strong arms. She too was carried over to the couch and her nappy was removed.

'Mistress will soon want you to start your potty training,' she said to the horrified but silent girl, as she put her into a fresh nappy, 'but not yet!'

Moments later, an astonished Emma found herself, in turn, sitting on the big woman's knee and sucking at her other large breast. The milk was strange-tasting but quite nice, though she hoped that she was also going to get something more substantial for breakfast.

'That's enough for now,' said Nanny putting away her breast and then replacing Emma's comforter. Emma gave a gasp of disappointment, and she gasped even more as the big woman continued, 'Baby'll have four feeds a day and nothing else for a week, then we'll have to see about the odd spoonful of baby food. But Mistress will first want to see this really slimmed down,' she said, patting Emma's little tummy.

Nanny now lifted Emma up and put her into the playpen with the other girl. She strapped a harness over Emma's shoulders which kept her down on all fours.

Nanny gave each of the girls a small teddy bear and a child's rattle to play with. Then she closed the top of the playpen with a catch and went out of the room, carefully locking the door behind her. Now that they were alone, the two girls, both effectively muzzled by their comforters, smiled happily at each other and gurgled away like real babies as, with their gloved hands, they tried to hold their teddy bears and rattles.

Letting her teddy bear drop to the rubber-covered floor of the playpen, Emma started to play with two rows of beads on the side of the playpen. Then, bored and full of remorse at having abandoned her teddy, she tried to hold the rattle in her helpless hands. There was nothing else to do. It did, after all, make a pretty noise, and her teddy did look so sweet and helpless – just like herself, she thought.

Then something suddenly caught her eye. There was something tattooed on the inside of her companion's left thigh. It was green – a green hawk!

Emma's heart beat fast as she remembered that the Prince had said the missing girlfriend of the Crown Prince could be recognised by his crest, a green hawk, which was tattooed on to her inner thigh! Here she was!

Clever Emma had found her! There could be absolutely no doubt, now, that this Francesca was indeed the very one to whom she had heard Ursula talking. Everything now fitted into place – Ursula congratulating her on getting the girl back, on keeping her in a playpen, on finding a Nanny – who was also a wet nurse – to look after her, and on giving her the pretty name of Brigetta!

It was all so obvious now! To keep Renata out of circulation and to stop her from running back to the Crown Prince, Francesca had amused herself by treating her like a baby. She was keeping her as helpless as a real baby, with a real nanny-cum-wet nurse to feed her and keep an eye on her – and, to mark the way the girl was now being treated, had even changed her name from Renata to Brigetta. Goodness!

And now, for the cruel Francesca's amusement, Emma was going to be treated as a baby girl too!

How could she let the Prince know that she had found Renata? Oh, how pleased he'd be! How pleased with her! All she had to do was ring him up and tell him the exciting news. He'd then come to England and do a deal with Francesca, the girl's Mistress, and both of them would be able to leave this place! Whoopee!

Then she came back down to earth. She had just signed a contract of service for a whole month to Francesca. The chances of her being able to escape from the playpen, or from Nanny, for long enough to make an overseas call must be pretty remote. And even if she did, the gloves on her fingers would stop her from dialling, and the comforter strapped into her mouth would stop her from saying an intelligible word!

No, she would just have to serve the whole month for which Francesca had paid Ursula. Not until her period of service was up would she be able to contact the Prince.

Oh well, she thought, better late than never. She'd just have to lump it for the next month. And anyway, it was rather exciting being treated like a baby girl by Nanny, even if the Mistress was rather unattractive.

She looked across at the other girl. Yes, she was very pretty, with lovely soft blue eyes. No wonder Francesca had wanted her back. No wonder she kept her here, out of sight, in this nursery. No wonder the Crown Prince had been so keen on her!

She had a suspicious thought. Would the Prince also be keen on her? Had he perhaps already seen her? Was that the real reason why he wanted her found? Was he simply using Emma to get another pretty girl for his harem? She remembered she had wondered about that when he had originally said he just wanted to have the girl disappear, out of harm's way, and away from the temptation to sell her story to the Press. And where better for her to disappear than into his harem of European women?

Goodness! Poor girl, did she have any idea of what was now in store for her? But at least she clearly wasn't pregnant. At least there'd be no little threat to the succession for the Prince's ruling family to worry about!

36

Francesca's Baby Girls

Suddenly the door opened and there was Nanny, obsequiously ushering the equally large Francesca into the nursery. It was early and she was still wearing a satin housecoat.

She looked at the two baby girls in the playpen and clapped her hands with joy. 'Oh, what pretty little babies!'

She came over to the playpen. Emma and Brigetta looked up at her helplessly, able only to make little moaning noises, and unable, like real babies, to grip anything.

'Oh, Nanny,' she said, 'don't they look sweet? What a lovely pair! I can't wait to show them off to my friends. They're going to be so jealous! We'll tell them all that they're twins. Little twin baby girls! And how is the younger twin settling down?'

'Oh, she's a sweet little baby. I gave her her first bottle last night and then this morning she had her first proper feed. Her little tummy took them very well, though I expect she's still feeling a little hungry. Her tummy will take a little time to contract and get used to her new diet, but her comforter will make her feel less hungry.'

'And what's your plan for her?'

'Oh, I think we'll keep her on mother's milk for a week, and then perhaps let her have the occasional bottle and then perhaps a little baby food.'

'Oh, don't start the baby food too soon,' cried Francesca, 'I want her to have a really tiny waist just like Brigetta's when I show her off at my ladies' tea parties.'

'Oh, don't worry, Madam, she'll soon be as slender as a reed!

Poor Emma was listening to all this with mounting concern. Never had she imagined, when Ursula had sold her to Francesca for a month, that she was going to be put into nappies and just fed on mother's milk.

'And, of course,' she heard Nanny continue, 'I like my babies to get plenty of sleep between their feeds. Little baby Emma slept very well after her bottle last night. She was asleep before she was even put into her cot!'

Francesca smiled. Emma shuddered.

'And I'll be starting her potty training today,' went on Nanny.

'Good! We don't want any nastiness when I show them off.'

'And I thought I'd take our little twins out for an airing in the park this morning.'

'It's just as well I had that special big pram made. I told them I wanted it to hold some big twins.'

'Oh, yes, Madam, it'll hold them very well.'

'Right then! I've got a busy morning and a lunch engagement, but perhaps they could join me when I get back? We'll have a little competition!'

It was an hour later when Nanny, wearing her smartest uniform, pushed the big pram out of a special side door and on to the pavement which led to the park.

All that could be seen of the occupants, under the big sun hood, were two little heads, each covered in a pretty baby's cap, and each sucking the rubber teat of a large comforter. The rest of their body was hidden by baby blankets, under which their wrists and ankles were strapped to the side of the strongly built pram.

They were thus held quite still and unable to move – and, thanks to their comforters, unable to call out.

Emma looked around her. How strange to be out in the open. She could not move or speak. Her tummy felt strangely empty, and she remembered the earlier humiliating potty training. She kept looking up at the smiling reassuring face of Nanny as she pushed the pram along.

She could not take her eyes off Nanny's large bosom. Oh, how she was longing for another feed – only the big rubber teat of the comforter stopped her from crying out for one.

Then she became aware of trees and grass and of other smartly dressed Nannies also pushing prams and exchanging confidences about their babies. One or two of the prams seemed to be rather large ones, pushed by big jolly Nannies, and holding rather large babies with big staring blue eyes and comforters in their mouths. How pretty they looked, Emma thought. Did she too look a pretty baby? Was she as pretty as Brigetta?

One or two of the Nannies came over and peered into the pram.

'Little twins!' she kept hearing. 'Oh, your Mistress must be very pleased.'

Then she fell asleep and when she awoke she was back in her cot, wearing a little harness to stop her trying to climb out.

Emma was sitting on Nanny's knee. Nanny was holding her with one hand and with the other was supporting a big black breast, on which Emma was eagerly sucking.

Brigetta was crawling in the playpen, trying to wave her rattle.

Finally, to Emma's disappointment, Nanny put away her breast. 'And, now, you little babies are going to be taken to crawl into Madam's bed. But you've both got to be very good little girls and please her,' she warned.

Nanny, big and strong, brought Emma and Brigetta into Francesca's bedroom strapped into a twin pushchair.

They were, of course, still wearing their nappies and baby clothes, but Nanny had made one change – she had tied a new type of comforter into their mouths. In their mouths was the usual big rubber teat to keep them quiet but, sticking out from it, in front of their mouths, was a small vibrator. It was controlled by a little switch beside their mouths.

Before leaving the nursery, Nanny had switched on the vibrators to make sure they worked properly. When she switched on the one strapped on to Emma's mouth, a strange tingling sensation had gone right through her head. Nanny had made her practice thrusting the vibrator to and fro.

Emma now saw that Francesca was lying on her back in the curtained four-poster bed with her knees apart under the bedclothes. Her hips were raised as if she were lying on a bolster.

Without a word, Nanny unstrapped Brigetta and carried her over to the foot of the bed. She untied her comforter, lifted up the bedclothes at the foot of the bed and pushed her in. Then she stood back, her powerful arms folded, and watched approvingly as a little hump moved up under the bedclothes towards the Mistress.

Emma saw Francesca put her hand down as if to adjust Brigetta's position. Then, satisfied, she made a further movement. A gentle humming noise came from under the bedclothes. Emma saw that the hump was moving slightly as if Brigetta was moving her head in the back and forth motion that Nanny had made her practise.

Little moans of delight were coming from Francesca.

'Let's have the other one, too,' she called out to Nanny.

Nanny started to unstrap Emma. 'The girl who gives the most pleasure will get a double feed next time,' she whispered, 'and the other will get nothing!'

Emma's eyes opened in horror. Miss her next feed? Completely? Oh no! She'd do anything rather than that. Her feeling of repulsion towards Francesca vanished under the threat of missing her next desperately needed feed.

It was with this thought running through her mind that she, too, was ushered up between the bedclothes at the bottom of the bed. Just as her head was thrust up under the bedclothes, Nanny switched on the vibrator she was gripping in her mouth.

Emma knew that she must crawl up to her Mistress, proffering the little vibrator held in her mouth.

In the darkness under the bedclothes, Emma felt Brigetta kneeling with her head down between Francesca's outstretched legs and raised hips. She was moving the vibrator attached to her mouth up and down.

Emma was still thinking of Nanny's whispered threat. Determined not to be seen off by Brigetta, she pushed her head down alongside hers. She could feel Francesca's horrible hair-covered beauty lips – not at all nice and smooth like her own. Gently, she too began to thrust her vibrator towards her Mistress.

Francesca lay back and smiled. Oh, the ecstasy! And the best part of it was that the two girls were not getting any fun themselves under their nappies – nor would they.

She lifted up the bedclothes to see the two pretty baby bonnets moving silently to and fro between her legs. Each girl was gripping her little vibrator tightly in her mouth, and trying desperately to give more pleasure than the other. Sometimes they would even try to push the other's vibrator away from their Mistress's pleasure bud. Two pairs of pretty, innocent blue eyes looked up at her, each silently begging for a sign that it was her vibrator which was giving more pleasure.

Francesca laughed at the little competition going on between her legs. She would, she decided, have things a little more organised. Leaving Brigetta's vibrator deliciously tickling her beauty bud, she pushed Emma's head further down so that her vibrator could reach up inside her.

Oh, the twin feeling of sheer delight! Twins! Yes they were a delicious pair of twins, each straining to outdo the other.

Her pleasure gradually built up and then reached a crescendo. Francesca was gasping with delight. She was not absolutely certain as to which vibrator was giving her more delight, but she knew that she must choose between them so that one would be punished and the other rewarded. Then, next time, both would try even harder.

Her whole body was shivering with thrills. Suddenly she exploded into a series of shattering climaxes, wriggling uncontrollably, as the two girls tried to keep their vibrators in place.

It was Emma who, an hour later, was happily sucking first one of Nanny's breasts dry and then the other, and it was Brigetta who was jealously and hungrily watching from the playpen.

Perhaps, Emma was thinking, this month wasn't going to be so awful after all.

Epilogue

Emma put the receiver back on the telephone and sat rigid on her bed, apprehension making her insides churn.

What could John mean? He had sounded most unlike his usual rather dithery self and not, as he had always been in the past, full of tender concern for her. His voice had sounded positive, rather clipped, as he had told her that he was winding up his oceanographic work and that, after visiting a distant cousin in Antibes, who was terminally ill, he would be returning home.

There was, he had said, something extremely important he had to tell her – something which, he regretted, would in some ways change her lifestyle. She had asked him to tell her immediately, but he had said he would prefer to tell her in person.

'My God! He's going to divorce me,' she cried aloud, and burst into tears. The last thing she wanted was for her marriage to end. She much enjoyed their lifestyle, the freedom it gave her, and the visits to John's eminent relatives on his periodical returns home. She really loved John, in her fashion, but her many adventures had also been huge fun. She had no regrets, but, alas, he must now have found out. Oh dear! But just what had he heard? There was so much! And about whom?

Anyway, had she not been left so continuously alone, there would have been no occasion for her to have looked outside their marriage for her fun. Her mind was in turmoil. What could she do to prove to John that she would now be faithful? Have children? It wasn't too late. Yes, that was it! She would become a stay-at-home wife and start a family. That would show him how much and how seriously she valued their marriage.

Henrietta had intimated that there would be no more Paris interludes. She had not been married long and wanted Henry to herself.

Ursula seemed to have tired of her, and, as for the Prince, he had now stopped her allowance. Delighted with Emma's news of the missing girl, he had lost no time in negotiating the release of Brigetta from Francesca, keeping her new name to disguise her former identity as Renata, the Crown Prince's girlfriend.

He had immediately sent her back to his harem to be properly trained and disciplined. But then, delighted with the result, he had brought Brigetta back to England to replace Emma as his companion here – half to Emma's chagrin, but also half to her relief.

So even the Prince does not need me any more, wept Emma. Everyone has always just used me for their own ends – and, whilst they were about it, used my own poor little end, too! And now John may not want me either.

I know what I'll do! I'll have a party! I'll invite them all, even pretty little Brigetta and the horrible Francesca, and they'll all be so wrapped up with their own affairs that John will believe me when I tell him that I couldn't possibly have done anything wrong with any of them.

Emma cheered up. She loved organising parties. We'll have a big dinner party and dancing,' she thought. 'It'll be a welcome home for John. I'll have it on his second night home, and not let him drop his bombshell beforehand.

A car scrunched up the gravel drive, and Emma quaked with trepidation at John's return, not least because she would have to find some way of explaining the gold rings – but thank heavens, she thought, at least there is now no golden bar and padlock to have to be explained away as well.

A few hours later they were sitting opposite each other

in the centre of the long dining room table. As yet, they had hardly said a word to each other. Emma was wearing her slinky black dress, and had realised that John did not approve. She was trying to be feminine and to flirt with her husband, but her efforts were falling on stony ground. Clearly his mind was elsewhere, and her panic grew.

'I don't want my life here to end,' she squeaked suddenly. 'I love you so much!'

John snapped out of his thought. 'Well, it will have to change,' he said sombrely, 'and we shall have to decide where we are going to live. The timing of your party has not been brilliant.'

Emma felt quite ill with anxiety. She came around to his side of the table and kissed the back of his neck.

'I thought we'd have coffee and a liqueur upstairs,' she said hopefully, and to her relief he smiled.

'Good idea,' he said.

Emma planned how she would quickly put the bar and padlock back in place and then, parting her negligée, would give him the key. It was, she would say, her way of showing how faithful she was – after all, this explanation had worked with Ursula, and she had a far more suspicious mind.

Then she would make passionate love to him.

But John had other ideas, and one glance at her in her negligée made him turn for the door. 'Emma. I'm totally bushed, and with your party on tomorrow I'd better catch up on my sleep in the dressing room.'

Emma cried herself to sleep. Everything was crashing down around her. Her husband didn't want her, her friends were all tied up with their own lovers. No one wanted her. She was totally alone. She began to feel very sorry for herself.

It was party time and Emma's guests were arriving and greeting each other with kisses and laughter. Champagne was being handed around in the large hall, and they then made their way into the drawing room where John and Emma waited.

He was wearing a double-breasted dinner jacket with a dark green cummerbund, and Emma was wearing a deep blue wild silk dress. Her eyes were made-up with blue eyeshadow and her blonde hair was wound up in a high chignon. She looked wonderful; everything was in order.

Thirty of their guests would dine with them, and be joined later by another forty who were dining in private houses. Nothing about her calm appearance indicated the effort she had put into the evening, for John, although she was extremely anxious about what he had to tell her. He had agreed to the information waiting until after the party, only commenting, 'Well, it's not conclusive yet ... I'd better go and look at the guest list, and see who I'm sitting next to.' This had been followed by, 'Oh good, Henrietta. I didn't know you knew them, Emma?'

'Oh yes,' said Emma. 'Racing, you know.'

'And Prince Faisal and Brigetta. I don't know her, but he was at my prep school for a short time.'

'Again, racing,' said Emma, 'through Paddy, who trains for him.'

'Oh, yes,' replied John, 'and is Ursula de Vere bringing that strange black chauffeur chap? We'd better see that there is some supper for him.'

Despite the dreadful possibility of Sabhu putting in an appearance, Emma sighed with relief. John's reactions did not appear to indicate that he suspected that any of the guests were involved with her, and she hadn't seen some of her old friends, like Mark and Isabella, for ages. She went over to greet them. Mark slid his hands around her back, and very nearly cupped her breasts with them as he kissed her. Isabella kissed her on the lips. 'Darling, she said, 'you look marvellous.'

Ursula looked across at Emma. She was wearing a deep maroon trouser suit with a ruffled shirt. She saw Isabella's kiss, and made her way over to be introduced. Emma could not resist introducing her to Henry at the same time, and laughed to herself as she saw Ursula's lips purse with distaste, and the way in which she ignored his proffered hand. Henry's hand slid down on to Emma's bottom as he drew her to him. 'Find time to dance with me,' he whispered in her ear. 'I haven't finished with you yet.'

Paddy had brought along a very attractive woman for whom he had previously trained racehorses, and with whom he had also slept. 'My sweet tooth is missing its honeypot,' he said quietly. 'I badly need some on my tongue to take away the taste of salt.' He glanced at his companion.

Prince Faisal was wearing a beautiful gold-embroidered black cloak over his immaculately ironed white robe and headdress. Brigetta arrived separately in the care of the Prince's two white eunuch pageboys and was dressed, or rather hidden, in a chador and an all-embracing black shroud, just as Emma had had to wear in public. However, the Prince authorised them to take her upstairs and, moments later, they escorted down a ravishing creature, demurely dressed in a loose high-necked dress, a little like a caftan, which was embroidered with tiny pearls and bugle beads.

The pageboys never left her side as, obediently, she followed the Prince around, her eyes dutifully lowered, as he strolled around the room greeting old friends. He made no attempt to introduce the silent Brigetta and when, rather dashingly, Henry had tried to speak to her, the pageboys had told him curtly that she did not like to speak English.

The Prince had bent over to kiss Emma's hand and he smiled as he saw she was wearing the collar of pearls with the diamond clasp which he had given her as a gift when she had agreed formally to becoming his Mistress all those months ago.

'I wish to have a private word with you. Please grant me the time,' he said.

'Oh course, Your Highness,' Emma had smiled.

Emma had then embraced Brigetta. They turned away so that their kiss was unobtrusive. 'I'll always love you, darling,' whispered Emma, so that the pageboys did not hear. 'Me too,' murmured the beautiful girl eagerly.

'Be happy,' added Emma.

'Oh, yes, I adore him,' murmured Brigetta, glancing

nervously at the two pageboys, 'and I have been taught ways to keep him needful of me.'

'Well, don't get sent back to the harem for any more discipline or training,' laughed Emma.

'Oh no,' whispered Brigetta, with a scared look.

After dinner, the music started upon a romantic theme, and the couples drifted into the now darkened hall to dance.

'Come on, darling,' said Paddy to Emma. 'Let's be having a wee turn.'

They circled the dance floor once, Emma's cheek against his, and her body aware of his arousal. 'Oh, it's only a torch in my pocket,' he said, as she giggled and gave a wriggle against it, 'to light up the dark passages.'

Paddy had manoeuvred her up to a door, and he deftly opened it and waltzed them both through. It was dark, but he knew the way to the back staircase.

'Get your dress up,' he ordered, 'and lie backwards up the stairs.'

As she arched her body, her dress rustling up around her waist, she felt Paddy's tongue licking up her inside knee, then higher up her thigh. Then a tingle went through her body as he reached the gold rings and ran his tongue up and down them. Her beauty lips opened like petals and she felt her honey flow, and then Paddy began licking and sucking her beauty bud, all the time making greedy noises. His long tongue snaked deep into her. It was so sexy and blatantly lustful, and then, 'Oh my goodness,' she cried, as her orgasm contracted her body, and the ecstatic flow of release shuddered through it.

Paddy took away his lips and tongue and kissed her deeply on the mouth. 'Taste yourself, my darling, isn't it just like honey?'

Emma felt he was the best friend she had in the world, one who had known her since childhood. She reached down to give him his final pleasure.

They returned to the dancefloor, lightly touching and smiling at each other.

'Did you two get lost?' asked Mark as they passed him, dancing with Isabella, on their way back to the drawing room.

'Nearly, darling,' replied a straight-faced Emma, 'but luckily Paddy had his torch with him.'

John was looking serious and discussing something with Henry. 'Emma, I've got some calls to make. If anyone leaves before I come back, say goodbye for me.'

'What's all that about?' Emma asked Henry, as John strode from the room.

'You'll know soon enough,' said Henry in his blunt dismissive way.

Emma stayed silent, thinking that if she took him somewhere alone and pleased him in a sufficiently humble way, she might learn just what was hanging over her, and so be prepared for the worst, before John broke the news.

'Master,' she said, and saw him smile, 'I have something to show you. Do come with me!'

Henrietta was dancing, so the coast was clear as they left, but Ursula had noticed them. A deep frown creased her forehead, her lips tightened, and a plan formed in her angry mind.

Emma led the way to the study, and switched off two of the lights. As she leant over John's desk to reach a third lamp, she felt her dress being lifted, and before she could reach a fourth one, Henry had got her loose French knickers down around her knees.

'Shut up, little slave,' he ordered, and with one hand pressed the small of her back so that she was bent over the desk, with her legs being forced apart by his knee. He used his other hand to unzip his dinner-suit trousers, and then pressed his manhood against her rear orifice.

Oh, damn Henry and – as he called it – his little predilection, thought Emma. Anger was about to make her kick out backwards, when she remembered about the information she wanted. Henry used both hands to part her buttocks, and then thrust into her. Henry pushed hard, and went as far into her as his large manhood could go.

He slapped a buttock hard. 'Take that, Your Ladyship! You're nothing but a tart. A tart for my pleasure!'

He was extremely strong and took his time, but he knew Emma well enough to be aware that she had relaxed and was now responding to his rhythm.

'Slaves aren't allowed to enjoy themselves,' he growled, and thrust harder and harder until he felt he had passed the moment of no return. He let the spontaneous ejaculation spend itself in a glorious relief. Oh, how he had needed to do that! Oh, how he gloried in his power over Emma.

He did not care about whatever it was she had wanted to show him. He just knew that this would be the last time he mastered her, and he wanted to savour every moment.

'Clean me,' he ordered. The compliant Emma obliged, despite her disgust, and then gently put his spent manhood back into his trousers and zipped them up.

'Please, Master, may I ask you something . . . ?' She stopped in horror. Standing in the doorway was Ursula, with Francesca looking over her shoulder. They were both puce with rage.

Henry turned, having seen Emma's transfixed gaze.

'Oh, so it's you two bloody dykes!' he scoffed. Come for your turn, have you? Got your dildos then?' His laugh was hollow and, without a backward look at Emma, he pushed his way past the two women.

Ursula let fly a torrent of abuse. She said how disgusting Emma was, how disloyal! Didn't she appreciate how much Ursula had loved and spoilt her? Didn't she appreciate that everything had always been for her pleasure and delight?

Emma found herself being overcome with remorse. She knew that Ursula loathed men, and that she must have hated meeting Henry. No wonder she was furious. Emma had never seen her so upset. But there must not be a scene at the party.

'Darling Mistress,' she said, trying her best to sound sincere. 'I really hated it and I did try to stop him. I really did. It was awful. He defiled me. But I just wanted him to go away as quickly as possible. You know as well as I do, Madam, that the only real pleasure I've ever had has been when I've been serving you. Please, please tell me what I can do to make you forgive me. Please!'

She burst into tears.

Listening to her Ursula had calmed down, and she now exchanged a glance with Francesca.

Francesca had been totally mortified to see the beautiful Brigetta glancing adoringly up at the Prince who clearly enjoyed having her at his beck and call. Francesca had sold the girl, at a great profit, to the Prince, on the understanding that she was going to be kept locked up out of sight in his harem. And now here she was back in circulation and probably telling the whole world about her former Mistress' penchant for keeping pretty girls dressed up as babies and in a playpen. Oh, how humiliating!

So both women had suffered the mortification of seeing, with a man, a girl whom they had once regarded as their own private property. A primeval urge to dominate Emma surged through them both.

'You will go to your bedroom, Emma. Now! And you will wait for us there. Go on, go!'

As Emma passed the drawing room, she saw Henry with his arm around his wife. There was no sign of John. Nervously, she made her way up the staircase, quickly taking and drinking a glass of champagne. What now? she wondered. Her bottom still felt sore from Henry's manhood – and from the hard smack he had given her.

Reaching her room, she noticed that her dress was wet – stained with Henry's excesses. Quickly she stepped out of it, rubbed the wet patch with a damp flannel, and laid it over the radiator in the bathroom.

Then, on an impulse, she slipped into her harem clothes, looping closed the tight bolero but taking care to leave her nipples showing over the top. Then she reddened them with lipstick and then, with a little giggle, drew the lipstick inside the cutaway in the front of the gauze trousers and up and down the inside surfaces of her beauty lips. She felt herself respond, and the feeling grew as she anticipated the imminent arrival of the angry Ursula and Francesca.

* * *

A voice was calling up the stairs.

'Emma! Emma! Are you there? Prince Faisal wishes to say goodbye.'

'I'm in my boudoir,' Emma called down. 'Please tell him where to come to.'

She slipped next door, into her own dressing room. She had adapted it as a secret room, in which she could play with herself and fantasise.

She placed the mask and the veil, which the Prince's pageboys had so often made her wear, over her face. Suddenly the Prince walked in. He was alone.

He looked very suave in his beautiful gold-threaded black cloak. He looked at the seductive girl in front of him. Loose tendrils of blonde hair had strayed from her chignon. His fabulous gift of the pearl and diamond necklace gleamed around her neck.

Emma knelt in front of him and bowed her forehead to touch his shoes. 'Goodbye, my Lord and Master,' she said, and straightened up, still on her knees. He took her wrist and clasped a beautiful matching pearl and diamond bracelet around it. Emma looked down at it open-mouthed.

'Your reward for finding Brigetta for me,' he said, 'and tell me, did you find the key?'

Emma blanched. 'Please don't be cross because I didn't tell you! And I hope you weren't too angry with the pageboys, either.'

The Prince laughed. His hands were by his side and, just by raising the hem of his robes an inch or two, he made his wishes clear.

Emma had adored this man, had worshipped him and had feared him. She would do anything to please him. Obediently, she raised the embroidered hem of his cloak and then, under that, the stiff starched hem of his white robe – and disappeared under them.

With her hands cupped around his huge testicles, she licked under them, smelling his pungent odour and feeling his erect manhood pulse straight out at her eager mouth. She ran her tongue up and down the side and licked the dew from its tip. Then she put her lips on either side of it, and took him deep into her throat, rocking back and forth, rubbing the tip against the roof of her mouth and licking the sensitive underside.

Her lips tightened around him, and she worked hard to stimulate him to a climax. Her fingers stroked his testicles and then, further down, a questing finger slipped into him and moved with the same timing as her mouth.

There was a discreet knock on the door. 'Your Highness,' called out a pageboy. 'Your car is here, Sir.'

The Prince drew Emma out from under his robes. Other pleasures awaited him. He took each of Emma's nipples between a thumb and forefinger, and pulled her slowly to her feet by them. Then he gave her one final charming smile, kissed her forehead and went downstairs.

Emma admired her bracelet and then went back into her bedroom to be greeted by the stern faces of Ursula and Francesca.

She gasped as she saw, standing behind them, an equally grim-faced Sabhu, who was dressed in his chauffeur's uniform, with its long black leather boots and peaked cap. The boots had straps at the top. But it wasn't the boots which had made her gasp; it was the long thin cane he was holding menacingly across his chest, his powerful hands flexing it so that it was bent almost into a half circle.

But if Emma had been taken aback by the sudden appearance of Sabhu, so too were Ursula and Francesca taken aback by the sight of the houri who had just walked through the door. They had seen Emma's dress drying over the radiator. However, her transparent silk harem trousers, with the shiny, lipsticked beauty lips showing through the cutaway as she walked, and the tight bolero with the outthrust breasts and painted nipples, were beyond their imagination for her change of dress.

Their expressions turned from anger to greedy lust as they looked, speechless, at the apparition that was coming towards them.

'Twelve strokes for gross impertinence . . .' Ursula's

voice tailed off. Her heart was no longer in it. Now, she couldn't possibly wait until Sabhu had finished thrashing the girl. He always took such a long time!

'Yes, gross impertinence,' echoed Francesca. But her voice was hesitant too, as she remembered this same delightful little body crawling helplessly in the playpen.

'Thank you, Sabhu, that will be all,' said Ursula in an unsteady voice. 'Just leave the cane on the bed.'

As Sabhu went out through the door, they both fell on Emma, fingering her nipples, unfastening her bolero and ripping her trousers down. A total orgy ensued, and Emma, her eyes never far from the cane, was sensually excited by the frenzy of these two now half-naked women. Rage had heightened their senses and they were passionately aroused. They kissed both each other and Emma, sucked her nipples and thrust their tongues into all her orifices.

Ursula rolled over and picked up the cane, using it on the front of Emma's thighs to make her pleasure Francesca, who was sitting on her face.

Moments later it was Francesca's turn to use the cane, this time on Emma's backside, as she made Emma lick the kneeling Ursula from behind. Then she thrust Emma aside and took her place.

Emma slid off the bed. Both women's eyes were closed in bliss. She crept into the bathroom. The noise of lust continued as she quietly closed, and locked, the connecting door.

It took her some moments to tidy her hair, to dress herself again in the rustling blue wild silk and to make her face look as immaculate and beautiful as it had been at the start of the evening.

There came a cry of, 'Emma, where have you gone?' from the bedroom and then there was a furious tugging at the bathroom door. Emma ignored this and, leaving the bathroom by the other door, made her way on to the landing, down the stairs and into the darkened hall.

Many guests were still dancing, in fact, no one seemed to have left. Even the Prince and Brigetta were still in the drawing room, the former in deep conversation with John, whilst the latter stood dutifully, and silently, behind him.

Emma walked to her husband's side, and he smiled as he took her hand and kissed it. 'Darling,' he said, 'I think we must break up the party. I'll ask everyone to come in here, and then you'll have the answer to my mystery.' He left, to turn on the hall lights and to muster the guests. Then he stood in front of the fireplace and looked at Emma who crossed the room to his side.

'Thank you all for coming and making it such a marvellous evening,' he began. 'Some of you know that my cousin has been very ill. He was a bachelor and a recluse, living in the south of France. Recently, I was told that he had died, and that I am his sole heir. There has been a great deal to organise, which is why I have been so long on the telephone tonight. There is a title and I would like to present my darling wife, Emma, who is now the Countess of Rossrae.'

Astonished, Emma was struck dumb. What should she say? To her relief, John turned to her. 'Goodbyes are now in order, darling,' he said.

Emma knew that there was a hidden meaning to his words. Oh yes, she had learnt her lesson. How nearly, she believed, she had lost him. She now longed for the guests to hurry their departures so that they could go to bed and she could relax in her husband's arms.

But a sudden thought plunged her into insecurity again. 'How the hell do I explain those bloody rings to him?'

NEXUS NEW BOOKS

To be published in November 2005

PUNISHED IN PINK
Yolanda Celbridge

Sultry ebony beauty Nipringa, and innocent blonde Candi Crupper, are both English girls living in Brazil, and studying at Dr Rodd's Academy, with its traditional English regime of bare-bottom caning. They escape to Rio for romantic adventure, but find the boys there just as enthusiastic about spanking them. Fleeing to the comfort of a seaside villa in the far north, they find themselves in thrall to the whip-wielding master, who enslaves them on his tulipwood plantation. Groaning naked under the lash, they discover who Dr Rodd really is.

£6.99   ISBN 0-352-34003-7

SILKEN SERVITUDE
Christina Shelly

Pretty she-male Shelly has had her secret dreams of domination and feminisation fulfilled by Aunt Jane. Yet her willing slavery has taken a new and even more kinky turn with her induction into the Bigger Picture, a secret society of female dominants dedicated to the worldwide subjugation of the male. In this intensely erotic and exciting sequel to the Company of Slaves, we discover a plot to turn the entire male sex into helpless sissy slaves and follow Shelly's final journey into a realm of total silken servitude. This wicked, highly erotic tale is a must for lovers of female domination and forced feminisation.

£6.99   ISBN 0-352-34004-5

RITES OF OBEDIENCE
Lindsay Gordon

Lindsay Gordon's classic debut is finally available again. Featuring the most intense erotica at Whitehead Academy: an adult school responsible for producing an unusually high number of successful corporate executives. Cub reporter, Penny Chambers, is sent to investigate. Once there, it's not long before the strange syllabus, lascivious students and stern staff awaken a dark sexuality she has always denied herself. A glamorous dean, a haughty Prussian doctor and the peerless Celeste twins all help her to explore new realms of sensation. Like every other student, Penny's education consists of a wide variety of specialist erotic training – in both submission and domination – under a strict regime of discipline. Will Penny expose the bizarre institute, or will she learn to accept the pleasure of fulfilling her most perverse fantasies?

£6.99   ISBN 0-352-34005-3

If you would like more information about Nexus titles, please visit our website at www.nexus-books.co.uk, or send a stamped addressed envelope to:
  Nexus, Thames Wharf Studios,
  Rainville Road, London W6 9HA